PENGUIN

Some Girls Will

Denise Sewell was born in Cavan in 1964. She now lives in County Monaghan with her husband and two children.

To Donnacha
Best wishes
Denise Sewell
7. 3. '06

Some Girls Will

DENISE SEWELL

PENGUIN
IRELAND

PENGUIN IRELAND

Published by the Penguin Group
Penguin Ireland, 25 St Stephen's Green, Dublin 2, Ireland
(a division of Penguin Books Ltd)
Penguin Books Ltd, 80 Strand, London WC2R ORL, England
Penguin Group (USA) Inc., 375 Hudson Street, New York, New York 10014, USA
Penguin Group (Australia), 250 Camberwell Road,
Camberwell, Victoria 3124, Australia (a division of Pearson Australia Group Pty Ltd)
Penguin Group (Canada), 90 Eglinton Avenue East, Suite 700, Toronto, Ontario, Canada M4P 2Y3
(a division of Pearson Penguin Canada Inc.)
Penguin Books India Pvt Ltd, 11 Community Centre,
Panchsheel Park, New Delhi – 110 017, India
Penguin Group (NZ), cnr Airborne and Rosedale Roads, Albany,
Auckland 1310, New Zealand (a division of Pearson New Zealand Ltd)
Penguin Books (South Africa) (Pty) Ltd, 24 Sturdee Avenue,
Rosebank, Johannesburg 2196, South Africa

Penguin Books Ltd, Registered Offices: 80 Strand, London WC2R ORL, England

www.penguin.com

First published 2006
1

'Some Girls (Won't)'
Composed by Michael Chapman/Nicky Chinn. Published by Chinnicap Music/
BMG Music Publishing Ltd. Used by permission. All rights resreved.

Set in 13.5/16 pt Monotype Garamond
Typeset by Rowland Phototypesetting Ltd, Bury St Edmunds, Suffolk
Printed in Great Britain by Clays Ltd, St Ives plc

A CIP catalogue record for this book is available from the British Library

ISBN-13: 978-1-844-88037-9
ISBN-10: 1-844-88037-7

To my children, Kevin and Olivia
With love, all the way up to the moon and back

Marcella

'Ma, watch it, will you? Your fag ash fell into the sink.'

'Divil the bit of harm it'll do.'

'Ah, Ma, for feck's sake!'

'What?'

'Ugh! That's what.'

'Just leave me alone, will ya, and dry the bloody dishes.'

'I'm just saying—'

'Well don't.' She held the cigarette between two wet fingers, took a final drag and dunked it into an unwashed mug. 'Is that good enough for ya, oul pernickety drawers?'

'Gawd! There's no need to get so thick about it.'

'Ah, will you shut your gob, Marcella?' she said, pulling the left sleeve of her jumper back up to her elbow. 'You're doing my head in.' As soon as she lowered her arm, the sleeve slid back down again.

'Gee-zus, sorry I spoke.'

Her face flushed, her lips tightened and the mug in her hand landed on the draining board with a clank.

I dried it, saying nothing even when I felt sugar still caked around the inside.

We worked away in silence, broken only by the clatter of greasy dishes.

Outside, the sky darkened and rain started pelting the windowpane over the sink.

'God, look at that; it'd put years on ya.'

'Mmm.' I didn't look up.

'Och, I'm sorry for cutting the socks off ya, love, but it's not been one of my better days.'

'Don't worry about it, Ma. Forget it.'

'So how was school?'

'All right.'

'It'll not be long till the holidays now.'

'Three weeks.' I rooted in the drawer underneath the draining board for a clean tea towel but couldn't find one. 'Oh, by the way, before I forget, I need four pounds for the school tour.'

'Where are youse going?'

'Dublin. The art gallery and Kilmainham bloody jail.'

She sniggered. 'Lovely. Well, you'd better ask your da for the money on Thursday, after he collects his dole.'

'But we have to have the money in tomorrow, Ma.'

'And where in the name of God do you think I'd get four pounds of a Monday? Can you not put them off for a couple of days? Say you forgot to bring it in?'

'It's Mr Dermody, Ma; he'll eat the arse off me. We were warned to have it in tomorrow.'

'Too bloody bad then. Forget about it. Stay at home.'

'It's not fucking fair,' I muttered, feeling both angry with and sorry for my mother.

'The sooner you finish up there and start work down the factory, the better.'

'The factory! Forget it. No way.'

'Bernie says they're taking on a lock of new ones in June and she has your name down.'

'You mean a summer job?'

'No, not a summer job, Marcella. A full-time job.'

'But I want to stay at school.'

'What would you be doing that for?' She emptied the slug-grey water down the plughole.

'An education, Ma, that's what.'

'But sure, look at that Carolan lassie down the road. Three years she spent in that tech and still ended up down the factory. Anyway, didn't you say the other day you weren't going back to the tech next year?'

'I'm not leaving to go to work in some dead-end factory job. I'm changing school and going to Loreto.' My mind was made up and there was nothing she could do about it.

'Loreto! Loreto, she says. Jesus, Mary and Joseph, dawther, are you mad? A Buckley at Loreto!'

She laughed so hard, I wanted to thump her, but it was the first time I'd seen her laugh in ages, so I didn't.

'Well, I'm glad *you* think it's funny.'

'You know what, Marcella, but you're some tulip. Loreto, ah Jaysus now, go way outa that,' she said, wiping her tears with the back of her shabby sleeve.

'Ma, I want to do the Leaving, get a decent job, be a teacher maybe. I'm not ending up in the crummy old factory waiting for some old gobshite to come along and marry me. I'd rather jump off the nearest cliff, thank you very much.'

3

'Oh I see, so it's good enough for Bernie and Josie, but it's not good enough for you, is that it?' Chuckling and coughing, she opened her packet of cigarettes, sat down at the table and lit up.

I took a long hard look at her – my mother – her tired eyes, her limp hair, her skinny bones lost inside my father's old jumper, her saggy tits halfway down to her belly button. She was resigned to her aimless little life of nothingness, stuck in our poky house on Fatima Hill, waking up every morning next to the same grumpy ugly face, staring at the same wallpaper for years on end, living one day just like the next, scrimping and saving and getting nowhere. There had to be a better way. I wanted more out of life, out of love, out of me.

'You know your da won't hear of you staying on at school when there's a perfectly good job up for grabs.'

Stacking the last of the plates in the cupboard, I decided not to argue with her any more. I knew that it wasn't up to her. Da had the final say. I had my work cut out for me. First, I'd have to get him in a good mood.

I was still awake that night when Bernie got into the bed beside me, her feet like two blocks of ice. She'd always try to warm them up on my nice cosy legs, and I'd always let her because I knew how awful it was to feel so cold. This time she turned her back to me and never said a word. I closed my eyes and started fantasizing about being in Loreto, visualizing myself in the school uniform, being involved in the debating

4

team or maybe taking part in the school musical, yes . . .

Then I heard a snivel.

'Are you OK, Bernie?'

'Yeah,' she sobbed.

'Oh, don't tell me that bastard Noel hit you again. I told you to dump the—'

'No, no, he didn't.'

'Well, what's up then?'

She turned to me and tugged at the sheet, using it to wipe her eyes.

'Come on, Bernie, tell me. You know I'll not say anything.'

'I'm pregnant, Marcella. I'm fucking pregnant.'

'Oh shite.'

Burying her face in the pillow, she cried some more.

'Ssh . . . ssh,' I whispered, trying to comfort her and conceal my own panic at the same time. Although Bernie was three years older than me, she was physically much smaller and always referred to as 'the scrawny wee Buckley one'.

'He'll kill me, Marcella, he'll bloody kill me.'

'Who, Noel? The creep.'

'No, Da. He'll go mental.'

'And what about Noel?'

'He says he wants to marry me.'

'You didn't say yes, did you?'

'What choice do I have now?'

'Oh, don't marry him, Bernie. He's a bollocks. He'll hit you again, you know he will. And he doesn't even have a job.'

'It's *his* baby too.'

'It'll be worse than being married to Da. Even *he* never hits Ma.'

'He swore it'd not happen again; he promised.'

'Do you love him?'

'I had sex with him, didn't I? Loads of times.'

'But do you really love him?'

'I think so. Sure, who else is going to have me now with me up the bloody duff?'

'Get rid of it. Have an abortion.'

'Jesus Christ, don't be disgusting. I'm not a bloody murderer.'

'Ssh . . . ssh. Here's Da coming up the stairs. We'd better shut up.'

Bernie turned towards the window. I lay on my back, stared at the ceiling and let the news sink in. I heard the clock tick, the toilet flush, Da's heavy footsteps on the landing, his bedroom door close, his gruff voice, a bit of a rumble, a creak here, a groan there. I hated it. Then the headboard, knock, knock, knocking on the wall behind me and Da, grunting like a pig. I wanted to puke, scream out, 'Fuck off and leave Ma alone.'

'Jesus, that must be every night this week,' Bernie whispered. 'Randy oul sod.'

'That's what you'll have to look forward to if you marry yon waste of fucking space.'

'Ah, stop.'

'You should have said that to Noel, instead of allowing him to land you in this bloody mess.'

*

6

I sat at the kitchen table the following morning, struggling to swallow a piece of toast. Ma was turning rashers on the grill, a fag dangling from her thin lips. She pulled a few crumpled pound notes from her pocket and put them down in front of me.

'There you go,' she said. 'Bernie left that for you before she went to work. Said you could pay her back on Thursday when you get it off your da.'

Poor Bernie, I thought, her life's up the frigging Swanee and she's still looking out for me.

'Are you not going to say anything?'

'Yeah, thanks. She's very good.'

'She's a big softy is our Bernie.'

I kept the money tucked securely in my jeans' pocket all day wondering what I should do. Bernie was going to need every penny she earned for her baby, and Da might not even give me the money.

I was still mulling it over when I heard Mr Dermody say, 'Marcella, I asked if you had your money in for the tour.'

'Oh, no. Sorry sir, I can't go.'

I practically ran home from school that day, so I could catch Bernie before she decided to tell Ma and Da the big news. If Da was going to go mental, I wanted to be there to stand up for her. She was stuffing something into the bin in the yard as I turned through the side gate.

'Bernie, I need to talk to you.'

'What?'

'Feel like a walk?'

'Yeah, OK. Hang on till I run a brush through my hair.'

It was hot out, so I followed her inside to take off my cardigan. She ran upstairs to the bathroom. Da was lying stretched out on the couch, watching the racing on TV, the paper in his hand and an ashtray resting on his big pot belly.

'Well,' he said as I sat down on the armchair to wait for Bernie.

'Well.'

'Stick the kettle on for me. I'm parched.'

It was on the tip of my tongue to tell him where I'd like to stick the kettle, but I thought it best to keep him sweet for Bernie's sake.

'Any biscuits?' he asked, as I put the mug of tea down on the floor beside him.

'You scoffed the last of them with the tea I made you an hour ago, Da,' Bernie said, coming back into the room. 'Come on, Marcella, let's go.'

As we headed down the hill, elderly neighbours we'd hardly seen sight of for months were standing in their doorways or sitting on their front steps soaking up the sun and watching the youngsters playing hopscotch and football.

'That's your weather now, lassies,' Mrs Duffy said, leaning on her stick and struggling to hold up her wilting head to get a proper look at us.

We walked through the town, past the cathedral and out along Wesley Road, passing all the posh houses and inhaling the smell of the freshly mown lawns.

'I'd love a wee garden, would you?' Bernie said.

'No,' I told her, 'I'd love a big one.'

'So when do you think I should tell Ma and Da?'

'As soon as we get back.'

'He'll blow his top.'

'Fuck him. Don't take any crap from him, Bernie.'

'You know what he's like.'

'Yes I do, so I think you should just drop the bomb-shell and walk out the back door. We'll go to Josie's.'

'Yeah, you're right. Sure, she had to put up with it when it happened to her.'

'Exactly, so we'll go there. She's bound to be on your side.'

'We'll be leaving Ma to put up with him, then.'

'I know, but she'll be OK. She's survived the crabby old sod so far, hasn't she?'

Before we knew it, we were a mile out of the town and at the entrance gates to Loreto College. I stood there looking up the long tree-lined avenue leading to the convent school.

'Bernie,' I said, 'that's where I want to go.'

'You want to walk up there?'

'No, I want to go to school there, do the Leaving, maybe even go to college. I fancy being a teacher.'

She gave me a funny look.

'What's the face for?'

'God, you're serious, Marcella, aren't you?'

'Yeah. What's wrong with that?'

'Nothing, it's just—'

'Just what?'

'Well, have you ever heard tell of anyone from Fatima Hill going to Loreto?'

'So? There's a first time for everything.'

'They'd give you fierce stick about it.'

'Who would?'

'All of them – the neighbours, your friends, Da.'

'Fuck the lot of them. See if I care. Shower of morons.'

'God, you have some guts. I'd not have the nerve to do the like of that, not that I'd want to. But if that's what you want, go for it, girl.'

'When that baby of yours comes into this world, it'll have an aunt at Loreto College. What do you think of that?'

'I think you're off your rocker, but, sure, I'm still crazy about you, you mad wee bitch.'

'I'm away down for a pint.'

'Hang on a second, Da,' I said. 'Bernie and myself have something to tell you and Ma.'

'So gwan, tell us then, but hurry up.'

'Right. You and Ma, you're going to be grandparents again.'

There was a deadly silence as he looked from me to Bernie and back to me.

'You!' he shouted at me. 'You stupid little tramp. You don't even have a boyfriend. Whose is it?'

'Jesus Christ, Marcella.' Ma stared at me in disbelief.

'Not Marcella, Da. It's me.' Bernie's voice quivered.

'There'll be no bastards living under my roof,' he

snapped at her with such venom I wanted to lift the bread knife and stick it in him.

'Right. You'll have to get married,' my mother piped up. 'You've made your bed now, dawther—'

'Come on, Bernie, we're out of here,' I said, pulling her by the arm and leading her out the back door.

'There's only one bastard in this house, Da, and you're it,' I yelled at him as he followed us out into the yard shouting, 'Get out to fuck, the pair of you.'

There were neighbours out in their backyards and more passing by on the footpath. There go that Buckley lot again, I imagined them saying, as we ran off towards Josie's.

We spent the night there, drinking tea. Josie told Bernie to have a fag to calm her nerves. I told Josie it wasn't cigarettes she needed, it was food; she'd hardly eaten a thing all day. But she didn't eat, she smoked. With it only being a one-bedroomed mobile, it was a tight squeeze for myself, Bernie, Josie, PJ and the two kids. It wouldn't have been fair on Josie's family to stay any more than one night, so it was inevitable that Bernie and myself would have to head back home again the following day to face the music.

'I can't believe you said that to Da,' Josie said as she threw me a sleeping bag.

'Yeah,' Bernie said, 'she's probably in even more trouble than I am.'

I slept better that night, stretched across the floor in Josie's sleeping bag, than I had in a long time. It was good being away from home – calmer, happier. I woke when I heard Josie's husband PJ get up for work. With one eye open, I watched him make his breakfast. He wasn't what you would call irresistible, sitting there chewing his toast with his mouth wide open, slurping his tea, and a head on him like an upturned mop. But he was a gentle sort of man, so all in all, it could have been argued that, for a Buckley, Josie hadn't done too badly for herself.

As soon as he left, I got up and made breakfast for everyone. Bernie ate all her scrambled egg and I was happy to see her off to work on a full stomach. I didn't feel in the mood for heading home for my school bag in case I ran into Da, so I decided to take the day off. Besides, there was something I had to do. After walking my nephew, little Jimmy, to school, I asked Josie if I could borrow PJ's bike.

'Of course you can. That's if you can ride it; it's a big heavy brute of a thing.'

I wavered a bit at the start, finding it hard to balance, but I soon got the hang of it and started out on the road towards Loreto. There was a strong wind blowing in my face, trying to slow me down, push me back. Lifting my backside off the seat, I pedalled with all my strength, gasping, panting and cursing the blasted wind. I could see the college in the distance, up on the hill surrounded by acres of green. I wanted to be surrounded by that green, that tranquillity, on top of that hill looking down.

I parked the bike in the bicycle shed. It stood out from all the others like a big ignorant heap of junk. It was half ten when I entered the main door. I could hear short, quick, light, echoing footsteps coming along the corridor, the sound of a busy little woman, a woman with a purpose.

'Can I help you, dear?' she asked, coming around the corner.

'Eh, yes, Sister. Could you tell me where I'd find the principal's office?'

'I am the principal – Sister Goretti – how may I help you?'

She had a round healthy-looking face and her smile exposed unusually white teeth. She could have been in an ad for Macleans.

'Actually, I came to enrol for September. I've been at the tech for the past two years and I'm due to go into the third year now.'

'Right, mmm.' The smile faded and she looked me up and down. 'I must admit we don't get too many tech girls coming here, but if you'll follow me to my office I'll take all your details and see what I can do.'

I trailed a step behind so she wouldn't see my nervous excitement.

'Why have you decided to change school at this stage of your education?' she asked as she sat down at her desk and gestured for me to take a seat.

I couldn't tell her that it had always been assumed a Buckley wouldn't dare go to Loreto, so I'd never really had any choice in the matter until now, when I had decided to take control of my own life. That would be too long-winded and complicated.

'I'd like to be a teacher, Sister, and, from what I hear, I'd have a better chance of getting the points I need at this school.'

'A teacher, mmm, I see. Very good.' She opened a drawer at the side of her desk. 'Just fill out this form here. I'm very sorry, I didn't get your name.'

'Marcella, Sister Marcella Buckley.'

'From where, Marcella?'

'Fatmaill,' I mumbled and coughed into my hand.

'Pardon? I didn't quite get that.'

'Fatima Hill, Sister.' Feck it, she'd read it on my enrolment form anyhow.

She nodded slowly, as though she was genuflecting at the altar, and then smiled again. God, those teeth looked freaky!

'And your parents, Marcella, do they think this is the best move for you?'

'Absolutely, Sister,' I lied, filling in my date of birth and handing her back the form.

'Very well then,' she said, placing it on the desk and interlocking her fingers as if she was about to pray. 'Provided we get a good reference from your current school's principal, Mister . . . ?'

'Dermody.'

'Dermody, you can certainly start here in September. You'll be very welcome.'

'Will I be able to do honours subjects, Sister?'

'If you get the results in your summer exams, certainly.'

'Oh, that's fantastic.' I beamed across at her, wishing I could reach over and give her a great big hug.

'You'll receive notification in the post, along with your book list and uniform requirements.'

'OK, Sister.'

'And Marcella, there are grants available towards these expenses if you need them. I'll pop that form in the envelope too.'

'Thank you very much.'

Wow, I thought, I've done it! No stopping me now. I was on my way.

'We'll see you in September. It's refreshing to meet an ambitious young lady like yourself. Teaching is a very satisfying career. With a bit of hard work, anything is possible.'

That was one of the nicest things anyone had ever said to me. I didn't tell her. I didn't want to sound pathetic.

As I made my way down the corridor, the bell rang and droves of girls in their maroon uniforms emerged from different classrooms, chatting and laughing. The first person I recognized was Leona O'Brien, who had been in my class in primary school. Her family was loaded, lived in a huge house on the outskirts of town. Southfork, my lot called it. She stared at me in disbelief, then quickly turned away, just like she had when I'd ended up sitting next to her at midnight Mass one Christmas Eve. That night she had been all dressed up in a red fur-trimmed coat with matching hat and hand muffs, like Santa's long-lost daughter. It was good to see her in her plain uniform, dressed just like the rest

– no fur, no trimmings, no standing out from the crowd.

Later that evening while we were eating our tea at Josie's, I told the girls where I'd been that morning. The pair of them burst out laughing.

'Hey Bernie, can you imagine the cut of her parading down Fatima Hill in her Loreto uniform?'

'Rather you than me, Marcella. Most people can't wait to leave school and here you are fighting to stay on.'

'But, sure, she never took the easy way out, our Marcella,' Josie said.

'Youse may be happy with your lot, stuck in this one-horse town for the rest of your lives, but I'm not. All right?'

'Hey, Marcella,' Josie said in a droll, John Wayne accent, 'this town just ain't big enough for the two of us.'

I said no more. Pissed off, I was, at the pair of them, in knots laughing at me at what Josie'd call my uppity ideas. The bitch.

'Don't mind Da,' Josie told Bernie just before we headed back home. 'He's all gob and no trousers. Things will be back to normal in no time. It's not you who should be worried, it's Marcella having to tell him she's going to the snobs' school.'

Da huffed and puffed and stomped about the house for a few days, with a face on him like a constipated bear.

Ma pussyfooted around him, handing him tea, fags, big thick bacon sandwiches and bottles of stout.

'It's hard on a man,' she said, as we were clearing the table after tea one evening, 'to hold his head up high when the likes of this happens.'

I was bulling. 'He could hold his head up high if he got up off his fat arse and found himself a job instead of blaming poor Bernie for his misery.'

'Your father's no layabout. He's worked at several different jobs over the years, as you well know, madam.'

'Yeah, and he would still be working if he hadn't threatened to rip the head off every boss who's dared to cross his path.'

'He's just not the type of man who can take orders.'

'You don't say.'

'I don't know why you're having a go at him, Marcella,' she said, slamming the cupboard door. It swung open again. 'You have a nasty little temper your-self, and it wasn't off the grass you licked it.' She flung the door shut again, this time knocking it off its hinges. 'Now see what you've made me do!'

The school year ended and I took up my job at the factory, still waiting for an opportunity to break the news to my da that it wasn't going to be permanent. Bernie was trying to organize her wedding for August and asked me to be her bridesmaid. I caught her crying again one night in bed and was worried Noel might have been up to his old tricks and had hit her again. But she denied it, saying they'd just had a row. I put my arm around her and stroked her tiny protruding bump until she fell asleep.

Teresa, my aunt, arrived one evening to let my mother try on a couple of her dresses for the wedding. Teresa was thirty-one, ten years younger than my ma and the only one of her sisters who wasn't married, although she did have a twelve-year-old son called Clint, named after the object of her desire. When my da came home from the pub that night, she was still in the kitchen chatting with my ma. This was the only occasion that Loreto was mentioned at all over the whole summer. My ma decided to give the pair of them a good laugh and tell them I had my nose up to go there. I could hear them all laughing from my bedroom.

'It's your fault, woman, for giving her such a fancy name. Marcella, indeed! From the day she was born, she always thought she was something special, a cut above the rest of us,' my da said.

My blood was boiling. I felt like shouting down the stairs that everyone on the planet was a cut above him, the bloody eejit.

'Well,' Ma said, 'she's got it into her head that she's going to Loreto and, if I know her, she'll have us puked till she gets her way.'

'Like father like daughter,' Teresa said.

'The nuns, bejaysus! Wouldn't you think she'd have had her fill of them in yon primary school down the town? And them creeping around the corridors with their pasty oul faces poking out of the TV sets on their heads.'

'Hey, maybe she wants to be a nun herself. Can't you just imagine it – Sister Marcella Buckley?' Teresa started them all off laughing again.

'Loreto! Over my dead body.' That was the last thing I heard my da say about it until the day of the wedding.

A happy drunk, singing his way up the hill, woke me up very early on the morning of Bernie's wedding, early in August. Everyone else was out cold after a hard night. This was it, my last morning waking up with Bernie lying next to me. I was going to miss her so much. We had spent all our lives together, two little girls, chasing little girls' dreams of pretty dresses and heroes and happily ever afters. She was sleeping peacefully, her jet-black hair still tied back in a ponytail. She looked so young, so girlish, for her eighteen years. I couldn't see the wife or the mother. I couldn't see the happily ever after either.

The postman handed me two letters when I went to the front door to bring in the milk – one an electricity bill, the other, I guessed, was my school report.

It was addressed to my parents of course, which was ridiculous really because Ma couldn't read it and Da wouldn't want to. Once or twice, in the past, he had opened the envelope, but then realizing what it contained had handed it to me unread without as much as a how did you do?

'What are you looking so happy about?' he asked as he stumbled down the stairs gasping for a drink.

'Two As, two Bs and five Cs.'

'What?'

'Two As, two Bs and five Cs,' I said again, grinning from ear to ear, knowing full well that I wasn't making any sense to him.

'What are you raving about?'

'Dunno, Da. Maybe I'm losing the plot.'

He muttered something on his way back up the stairs, but I wasn't listening. I was much too excited because, in fact, I wasn't losing the plot at all. The plot was working out just right. These were good enough results to get me into the honours class. There was only one more hurdle to cross, and it had just fallen back into bed with a sore head.

I spent twenty minutes outside the church door feeling and sounding like the tricolour at full mast with my green dress and red hair flapping in the wind. The best man, Johnny, was pacing up and down in front of me, checking his watch every couple of minutes.

'Fucking women, never in time for nothing,' he said, raising his bleary eyes to the sky.

'Maybe you should have taken some more time yourself and given that shirt a bit of an ironing. What did you do? Sleep in it?'

He looked at me, then at his shirt. He tried to smooth it out with his hands. I started to snigger. I couldn't help it, the big goballoon. He grunted and began buttoning up the jacket.

'Is that any better?' he asked.

'A bit,' I told him. 'But you'd better wipe that dandruff off your jacket quickly, 'cos here's my da and Bernie coming now.'

The taxi driver opened the car door. Da emerged looking awkward in his suit. It made him walk funny. His legs were slightly apart, like he'd pissed himself, and his shoulders were jerking as if he was trying to shrug something off them. Bernie followed him, looking like an angel that had fallen off a Christmas tree, too gentle and pure for the slimeball who was waiting for her at the end of the aisle.

Come on, Jesus, I thought, it's time for a miracle. If there was ever a girl in need of divine intervention . . .

The organ started to play. She was on her way.

No miracle.

The reception was back at Dinny's pub. My cousin Joey had set up a bit of a disco in the corner for anyone who would be fit for a dance.

'You look nice with some make-up, Marcella,' my ma said, smiling at me. 'Why don't you get out and have a bit of a dance for yourself like the rest of the young lassies there?'

A few of my cousins were out dancing round their handbags to Racey.

> *Some girls will, ooh ooh ooh ooh,*
> *Some girls won't, ooh ooh ooh . . .*

'Ah, I will later, Ma,' I said.

'You know, you should have a few drinks, Marcella, loosen up a bit. You're far too sensible,' Teresa said, lighting another cigarette.

'I don't like the stuff.'

'Are you sure she's a Buckley, Mary? You weren't having it off with the milkman, were you?'

They all thought Teresa was hilarious. They were sitting round the table, their heads thrown back, gobs wide open, cackling like a bunch of morons.

Clint asked me to take him out for a dance, probably feeling as eager to escape as I was. He stood opposite me and started head-banging to Status Quo's, 'Rockin' All Over the World'. I felt like a clumsy clot in my maxi-dress. What I wouldn't have done for a pair of jeans.

As soon as the song was over, Ricky, Noel's younger brother, came clickety-clacking across the hall in his black studded loafers, whiter-than-white socks, ankle-length black trousers and the sleeves of his black jacket rolled up to the elbows. Oh, and his Shakin' Stevens' hairstyle.

'Wanna dance, Marcella?'

'I'm dancing with Clint.'

'It's OK,' Clint said, shying away before I could stop him.

And there was Ricky dancing away in front of me like Shaky himself, his arms going like billy-o, his legs flapping like the wings of an eagle.

Just the sight of him was making me dizzy.

'You're lookin' shockin' well today,' he said, wrapping his arms tightly around my waist just as the record ended and a slow one began.

'Oh, thanks,' I said.

'Your man doesn't do a bad job as a DJ.'

'No, I suppose not.'

'I love this song,' he said, singing along with the Bellamy Brothers to, 'If I Said You Had a Beautiful Body (Would You Hold It Against Me)'.

His hand started roaming smoothly up and down my back. With each downward stroke it moved closer to my buttocks, and I was beginning to feel uncomfortable. Then came a sudden tight squeeze and a wet tongue in my ear.

'Get lost, you dirty little fecker,' I shouted, pushing him away.

'What's wrong with you? You're a Buckley, aren't you? All the Buckley girls are up for it.'

'Would you like to say that in front of my da? Well, would you?'

'Hey, what's going on here?' Josie asked.

'Ask your lezzie sister. She's weird, she is.'

'Piss off, you little prick,' Josie told him, before dragging me over to a quiet corner to sit down.

'Are you all right?'

'Yeah, of course I am. It would take a lot more than the likes of him to upset me.'

'Listen, love, what he said – it's not true, is it?'

'What? Me a lezzie? No way. Why would you think that?'

'You're nearly sixteen, and you've never had a boy-friend, have you?'

'No, but it's not that I wouldn't want one.'

'You've had offers, haven't you?'

'Yeah.'

'So?'

'I don't want any of the fellas who fancy me. And the ones I want, well, they wouldn't be interested in the likes of me.'

There was a break from the dancing for tea, sand-wiches and cocktail sausages. Da was full to the gills at this stage and decided to entertain everyone with his rebel songs. Drunk and all as he was, he could still sing. Following a big round of applause after 'The Green Fields of France', he started into 'Men Behind the Wire'. He loved rebel songs with as much passion as he hated the English. He said they treated the Irish like second-class citizens, always trying to keep us down, oppress us. I wondered who these ogreish, English people were; I hadn't met any of them. And if he felt so angry with them, why was he treating me the very same way? He was my Englishman, the thorn in my side, the heavy hand always there to put me down.

By the time the disco music started again, the party was in full swing and the air was heavy with smoke, booze and sweat. I'd hardly seen Bernie all evening. Every time I went to talk to her, she was surrounded by half a dozen relatives. As I made my way out to the loo, the hokey-cokey was starting and everyone was on the floor. I was glad to escape.

I had to pull up the hem of my maxi-dress to avoid the muckiness of the toilet floor. I tiptoed to the nearest cubicle, went in and tried to shut the door, but the lock was banjaxed, so I left it slightly gaping. I had just finished relieving myself when the main toilet door swung open.

'Come on, come on, there's no one here. Quick!'

It was Teresa.

'Get in there and I'll hokey-pokey ya,' I heard my da say. My heart started to race. I didn't move or make a sound. I couldn't. I thought they were going to land on top of me, but they didn't. I heard their hurried foot-steps and another cubicle door slam shut. I couldn't believe what was happening. They were at it. I could hear them – panting, unzipping, moaning, slobbering all over each other.

'Give it to me. Go on, give me to me,' Teresa gasped as the partition began to shake furiously. The dirty bitch. I couldn't stand it. I wanted out. I stood up and was about to make a dash for the door when I heard it – that old familiar grunt, the one I'd heard so often penetrate the thin wall of my parents' bedroom even with the pillow over my ears.

The dirty sod, the rotten pig! I hated him. And her. I tried to move, but I felt sick and clammy. I sat back down on the loo and put my head in my hands.

'I'll have a look out and see if it's all clear,' Teresa said, unlocking the door. I heard her scuttle past my cubicle. 'Come on, quickly,' she said, giggling.

As soon as I heard him move, I flung the door open

and barged past the pair of them. Teresa, slobbering a pathetic apology, tried to grab me by the elbow, but I shrugged her off roughly and bolted out of the main toilet door. Da followed me.

'Marcella, get back here,' he shouted, but I kept going, pushing through the crowd and out the front door into the evening sun.

My head was spinning. I had to get away to think. I couldn't go too far decked out in my green maxi-dress, so I turned down the alleyway at the side of the pub and into the car park. I sat on the bonnet of someone's car and wondered what I should do. I wanted to tell Ma. She had the right to know, and that pair of deceitful bastards didn't deserve to get away with it. But would Ma want to know? I doubted it. And would it do any good? Would she leave him? I cherished the thought. But God, no, I couldn't see that happening. She wouldn't have the strength for it. My mother, I reckoned, thought she couldn't survive without my father. He would have told her so. And then there was Clint; he'd be devastated too. It was hard enough on him having a drunk for a mother, but a whore as well! No. I didn't want to hurt him or Ma. I swore I'd never speak a civil word to Teresa again. As for Da, he'd have to pay. There was only one thing to do.

By the time I got back, Ma, Da, Teresa, Clint, Josie, Bernie and PJ were all sitting at the one table. Da had his grubby hand on my ma's knee.

'Marcella, come over here,' Bernie said. 'I've hardly seen you all day. Where've you been?'

26

'Oh, just out for a walk, thinking.'

'You do too much thinking, lassie,' my ma said.

'Thinking about what?' Josie said.

'About Da.'

He glared at me threateningly.

'What about him?' Josie asked.

'Well, sometimes he surprises me, he really does.'

Teresa got up and shuffled nervously past Clint, PJ and Bernie, pretending to be going to the bar.

'Hang on there, Teresa,' I shouted after her, 'do you not want to hear the news?'

She didn't answer, just scuttled off in her high heels, nearly twisting her ankle in the process.

'Go on for God's sake, tell us,' Josie said.

'Marcella,' Da said, starting to loosen his tie.

'What, Da? They're all dying to know. Well, Da says I can stay on at school and go to Loreto. He's even going to help me buy a new bike, isn't that right, Da?'

'It is,' he muttered.

'Good girl yourself,' Bernie said. 'I don't know how you talked him round, but God, that's great.'

'Be Jaypers, I can't believe that! I've been married to the man for twenty-odd years and I've never once known him to change his mind.'

'Well, Ma,' I said with a satisfied grin, 'there's a first time for everything.'

It felt really weird getting into my uniform that first morning. Apart from the day of Bernie's wedding, I'd spent the past three years in denims. Exposing my white freckly legs to the world was bad enough, but when I got as far as the bathroom mirror there was a real surprise in store for me in the form of an extra-large shiny red pimple on the end of my nose.

'Lovely,' I shouted, 'just fucking lovely.'

'What's wrong with you?' Ma asked as she came through the bathroom door in her dressing gown.

'I grew a third nipple overnight, on the tip of my fucking nose.'

She started laughing and spluttering, pushing me out of the way to get to the loo.

'Jesus, will you shut up before I wet myself.'

'It's not a bloody laughing matter,' I told her, placing my two thumbs on either side of the monstrosity and squeezing until I couldn't stand the pain.

Without much success on the zit-zapping front, I went downstairs a few minutes later, feeling a little less than enthusiastic. Da was standing facing the fire, having a smoke, the hairs on his back creeping out through the holes of his string vest. He didn't turn to speak to me, so I went on out to the kitchen and poured myself a bowl of cornflakes.

'Imagine, Jimmy,' Ma said, handing him his mug of tea, 'Loreto. One of our lassies at Loreto. Would you credit it?'

'Arragh, she's a fucking eejit trying to hobnob it out there with that lot.'

'I'm as much entitled to go to that school as anyone else!'

'You were the one to let her go, Jimmy,' Ma piped up.

'That's right, Da,' I said, standing in the doorway between the two rooms. 'It's a bit late complaining now.'

I could sense his agitation from the way he was stomping out the fag butt in the ashtray.

'So why did you agree to her going anyways? I could never figure that one out.'

'Good question, Ma,' I said, staring into his face.

'I don't fucking know. Maybe I should reconsider.' He held my stare.

'Maybe you should, Da. After all, you can make some very foolish decisions while under the influence, and I wouldn't want you to think I had taken advantage of you just because you were pissed.'

'That's enough of your lip now, madam,' Ma butted in.

'I gave you my word and I'm a man of my word, but don't push it, Marcella,' Da said, pointing at me. I could see he'd reached the end of his tether.

Ma shoved me back into the kitchen and closed the door between me and Da.

'Don't pass any remarks on her, love,' she told him. 'She's probably feeling a bit nervous about her first day.'

'Aye, I know. Give us a smoke, will ya? I'm out of them.'

'Here.'

'Where the blazes does that one get her notions?' He sounded more baffled now than angry. 'I mean, who the hell would want to go to an oul poncy school like Loreto? They'll be looking down their snooty noses at her.'

'That'll not bother her. She's made of tough stuff that lassie.'

29

'She'd want to be.'

'They'll not get the better of our Marcella, you mark my words. She's a Buckley through and through.'

'So you keep telling me.'

'Aye, and I'm right.'

I heard a little squelchy sound and wondered who had kissed whom.

I left the house through the back door, not bothering to say goodbye.

'Hey, Marcella,' Ricky Doyle roared at me as I rode down the hill, 'your nose matches your uniform.'

Right, you bollocks, I thought, here goes. I swerved the bike up on the footpath, nearly taking the legs out from under him.

'You fucking lunatic,' I heard him shout as I sped on, feeling a little flutter of satisfaction.

At the bicycle shed, a couple of girls were putting locks on their bikes. My second-hand bargain bike didn't have a lock. 'You're far better off having one nobody would be bothered stealing,' Ma had told me the evening Da had landed home with it.

'Never seen her before,' I heard one of the girls say as I was throwing my bag over my shoulder.

'Must be a first year. God, but she's fierce big for her age, isn't she?'

'I'm not a first year,' I told them, refusing to be left out of the conversation.

'But you're new?'

'Yeah.'

'What year?'

'Third.'

'Oh, same as us. I'm Gabby. This is Mary B, as in Bridget.'

'Hi,' Mary B said.

'Hiya.'

'You see there are four Marys in our class,' Gabby went on, 'so to distinguish one from the other, we use the initial of their middle name.'

'Oh right. Good idea.'

'Mary B,' she pointed at her friend, 'Mary C, as in Catherine, Mary E, as in Elizabeth and Mary F, as in Frances.'

She was friendly. I liked her.

'Now don't go asking me what happened to Mary D. We've already decided: the D stands for disappeared.'

We were walking towards the main doors now and already, apart from my discovery of a streak of black oil on my white socks, things were looking up.

There was a big sack of laundry sitting on the back step when I arrived home. Dragging it in through the door, I saw Ma asleep in the armchair and the fire almost out. I wondered what made her so tired all the time.

'Ma, Ma,' I said, nudging her. 'I'm home.'

'Oh, right, right. God, what time is it?'

'Quarter to five. I found the laundry sitting outside the back door. Good job it didn't rain.'

'Ah, yeah. Aggie said Charlie'd drop it off for me at one o'clock. Save me hawking it up the hill.'

Aggie was Ma's best friend; she worked in the laundromat.

'You're not asleep since before one, are you?'

'Must have nodded off when I came home from Bernie's. How did you get on with the nuns anyways?'

'They're mostly lay people, Ma. I've only got one nun teaching me and that's for religion. Is there any dinner? I'm starving.'

'There's a bag of spuds out there. Why don't you throw on a few chips for yourself.'

'Ah shite. I hate peeling spuds.'

'OK, OK, just take that lot upstairs,' she said, nodding towards the laundry bag, 'and I'll make a start on the dinner.' She dragged herself out of the chair with a major effort.

Emptying the bag of laundry onto the bed, the first thing that struck me was a couple of beautiful white cotton sheets – sheets Ma could never have afforded. Looking a little closer, I saw Riverdale Hotel tags sewn onto each of them. As I was gathering them up to put them back in the bag, thinking it was some kind of mix up, I found a note: 'Not to worry, Mary. They'll not be missed. Aggie.'

Ma went into fits of laughter when I showed her the sheets and read her the note.

'Well, fair play to the bould Aggie, she's some character.'

'Ma, that's stealing for God's sake.'

'Ah, will you lighten up, love? Sure, as the note says, they'll not be missed. When she saw the state of me sheets this morning, she said it was about time I replaced them.'

'Ma!'

'I suppose I didn't do too badly getting twenty-odd years out of the last lot. They were a wedding present, you know.'

'I'm taking them back, Ma.'

'Indeed and you're not. Aggie's no fool. She'd not have slipped them in if she thought they'd be missed.'

'In that case, pass me the fucking scissors quick till I cut those tags off and get rid of the evidence.'

I called in to see Bernie at her flat the following evening after school.

'What are you doing here?' she asked, opening the door with a sweeping brush in her hand.

'What do you mean?' I walked past her into the kitchenette. 'Can I not call to see you now?'

'No, you're OK. Just wasn't expecting you, that's all.' She carried on with her sweeping.

'Here, I'll finish that for you. You sit down.' I took the brush from her. 'You have the place spotless.'

'He's fierce fussy,' she whispered, nodding towards the door that led to a small living room.

'Him fussy! Since when?'

'Shut up, will you? He'll hear you.'

'Where's the bin?' I asked, shovelling up the little bit of dirt I'd gathered.

'He has it in there. He was cutting his toenails.'

I opened the door.

Noel had his arse parked on the armchair and his bare feet up on the coffee table watching TV. He took one look at me and sneered.

'What are you smirking about?' I glared at him.

'Usually there's nothing more sexy than a girl in a school uniform but not in your case, sweetheart. You look more like someone's granny.'

'Drop dead.'

'He's only slagging you,' Bernie piped up in his defence, 'aren't you, Noel?'

'I'm just telling her straight. She'd look a lot better if she hitched that skirt up a foot or two,' he said, laughing.

'The only thing that'll be going up a foot or two is my boot up your arse,' I snapped.

'Will you stop, the pair of youse! I don't want no arguing, not today, I'm tired.' Bernie was upset by the whole thing.

'Tell that to your drippy sister,' Noel said, leaping up from the armchair, roughly brushing past Bernie and heading out the door.

'What the hell is wrong with him?'

'He was only messing with you, Marcella. Why did you have to go winding him up like that?'

'I wasn't. He started it.'

'Ah, look it, just drop it will you? Don't forget it's me that ends up with the husband in a bad mood.'

'Don't tell me he's hitting you again.'

'No.'

'Are you sure, Bernie?'

'Yeah.'

''Cos I didn't like the way he pushed past you just now. It was very threatening.'

'He's not beating me, Marcella. Now shut up.'

I was beginning to feel sorry I'd called at all, but I'd really wanted to tell her all about Loreto. Now I didn't think she'd be interested.

'Do you want coffee?'

'No. Tea, please.'

'I have no tea bags. Noel only drinks coffee.'

'And what about you? You drink tea, don't you?'

I could see she wasn't in the mood for any hassle. She was distracted.

'Coffee's fine,' I told her.

'You haven't any money on you, have you?' she asked me as she filled the kettle. 'I'm bursting for a fag.'

'I've fifteen pence.' I rooted it out of my uniform pocket. 'That's hardly much use to you.'

'Ah, good woman. Tip across there to Barry's, they sell them in singles for twelve pence each.'

'So you've no money of your own, then?' I asked her, heading towards the door.

'Och, it's just that Noel doesn't like me smoking while I'm pregnant. He's only thinking about the baby.'

Likely fucking story, I thought as I ran down the stairs. I wasn't too gone on the idea of her smoking myself, but I could see how badly she wanted a fag and I was glad she had the guts to defy him. The bully. Thinking about the baby, my arse!

*

Ma, having been in rough form herself all week, was all agitated on Friday morning. Her hands were trembling as she tried to light her cigarette.

'Are you all right there, Ma?'

'I'm just not feeling the best.'

'Are you sick?'

'No, no, it's not that. Don't worry about it. I'll be all right.'

'But you're shaking.'

'I'm just cold.'

'What's keeping you with the tay?' The roar came tumbling down the stairs.

'It's on the way,' she shouted back, fumbling around in the cupboard.

'Why do you let him speak to you like that? You're not his slave, you know. Bloody ignoramus.'

'Don't speak about your da like that, Marcella. He's a good man.'

'Why? 'Cos he doesn't batter you like your da did, you think you should be grateful?'

'I am grateful, Marcella, and you would be too if you'd known the life I had growing up.'

'Just because he's not Granda Reilly doesn't make a saint out of him. Now give me that tea and I'll bring it up to him. You sit down and have your own.'

'I haven't seen sight nor sign of Bernie since Monday. Do you think she's all right?' she asked me when I came back down the stairs.

'Yeah, why wouldn't she be?' I said, wondering what was on her mind.

'Maybe you'd drop in on her after school.'

'No. Fuckface will be there. I'll wait till morning. He'll be working till one.'

'Fair enough.'

My first week in Loreto was over and it had gone well. I was happy there. Now that Bernie had left home, I had the peace and quiet of my own bedroom for getting my homework done. I could tell I was nowhere near the top of the class, as I had been in the tech, but I was going to do my damndest to get there. I hadn't had the misfortune of running into Leona O'Brien either, since luckily she was away in France on holiday and wouldn't be back until the following Monday. But I couldn't help thinking about Bernie. By rights, if she hadn't come from Fatima Hill she could have been in Loreto with me, a fifth year, with friends and a future, not stuck indoors with a baby in her belly and a brute in her bed.

The house was empty and cold when I got home on Friday evening. There was no sign of a fire having been lit all day.

'Ma! Da!' I shouted up the stairs, but there was no reply. The only sound was the rumbling in my stomach and the chattering of my teeth. I put on a pot of soup and started clearing ashes from the grate. Then I heard the side gate close.

'Jaysus, don't tell me she's not out of the bed yet?' Da said to me, sounding disgusted.

'I don't think she's in bed.'

'She is surely. Went straight up after the dinner.'

I tipped up the stairs and put my head around Ma's bedroom door. She was there all right, out for the count, not a sound out of her. Except for the rise and fall of her chest, I'd have sworn she was dead. The thought sent a shiver through me. I decided to leave her be. She looked peaceful; maybe she needed the rest.

'Where's Ma?' Josie asked, arriving just after seven. 'I need to talk to her.'

'Sleeping all day it seems.'

'Them sausages were like rubber,' Da said, coming into the kitchen and banging his plate down on the table. 'Do they not teach youse how to cook in the snobs' school?' He went back to the living room and turned on the telly.

'That's the ungrateful—'

'Never mind him,' Josie said, dragging me out into the hall and up the stairs. 'I need to talk to you and Ma. It's important. It's about our Bernie.'

'What?'

We were in Ma's room now; Josie sat on the edge of the bed.

'Wake up, Ma,' she said, tapping my mother's shoulder.

I noticed a bag from Dillon's chemist sitting on her bedside table.

'What's wrong? What time is it? Jesus it's dark. Your da hasn't had his dinner yet. He'll be—'

'Shut up, Ma, and listen,' Josie said. 'Da's all right; he's fed and watered. It's Bernie we have to worry about.'

Before she opened her mouth again, I knew what she was going to say.

'Noel's hammering her, Ma. I called to see her today. She's a big bruise on her face, just underneath her eye.'

'Bastard,' I said, feeling my face begin to burn with anger.

'And what did she say about it?' Ma asked.

'She claims to have slipped on the bathroom floor and hit her face on the sink on the way down.'

'Maybe that's all it was,' Ma said, sitting up.

'Bullshit!' Josie said. 'I don't believe her. She'd not have been trying to cover it up with make-up if it had been an accident. That bloody Noel boy, I always thought he had a mean-looking head on him.'

'But sure he's never done the like of that before. I know he's got a bit of a temper but—'

'He did, Ma,' I blurted out. 'He hit her at least once before, and I'm sorry I didn't tell youse but—'

'Oh, the poor lassie.' Ma started to cry.

'Never mind poor lassie, we'll have to tell Da,' Josie said.

'He doesn't know nothing yet?'

'Not a hate.'

I was glad Josie was there; she was strong and always knew the best thing to do.

'Sorry, Josie,' I said, on our way downstairs. 'I should have told you before.'

'It's not your fault, Marcella,' she said. But the guilt lingered.

With a bottle of stout in one hand and a cigarette in

the other, Da didn't look like he'd take too kindly to being disturbed, especially not in the middle of watching Benny Hill. Ma came in after us.

'Jimmy,' she said, 'myself and the girls, we need to talk to you but you have to promise not to lose the rag.'

'Ah, Christ, don't tell me this one's up the spout now,' he said, nodding towards me.

'My name is Marcella, you blockhead, not "this one", and no, I certainly am not up the spout, thank you very much.'

'Noel's hitting our Bernie,' Josie announced, 'and we've got to put a stop to it.'

'None of my business.'

'None of your business!' Josie shouted. 'Da, this is your daughter we're talking about.'

'She should have been more fucking careful about who she was screwing around with.'

'Don't forget, there's a wee babby to think about here,' Ma said gingerly, probably trying to hit a soft spot.

The only spot I wanted to hit was the bald patch on top of his head – with the poker. Heartless bastard, sitting there unmoved. I'll move you, you ignorant git, I thought, if it's the last thing I do.

'Oh I see,' I said, 'so it's all right for you to go sneaking around in the middle of the night plastering "Wanted for Murder, Maggie Thatcher" posters all over town to support a bunch of fools willing to starve themselves to death, but when it comes to your own family—'

'Marcella, put a sock in it!' Ma roared.

'By Jaysus, I'm utterly ashamed – a daughter of mine referring to those fine brave freedom-fighters as a bunch—'

'Will youse shut to fuck up!' Josie shouted. 'This is about our Bernie and what's best for her and the baby. And Da, I'm not codding you, if you don't do something about it, I'll go down there right now and knock some sense into the wee fuck myself.'

'Right. Youse want me to sort him out, do youse?' Da said, hopping up out of his chair, 'I'll – I'll – I'll—'

'You'll take it easy now, Jimmy; maybe have a few words with him. He'd not chance crossing you again,' Ma pleaded with him, knowing full well how dangerous Da could be when he was all fired up. But she was wasting her time. He was bulling out the back door like a flaming lunatic. He kicked the bin out of the way, sending it clattering across the yard.

'Go after him, Josie, or he'll bloody well kill him.'

'I'll run down and bring Bernie up home,' I piped up, hoping to be of some help.

'Shut up, you,' Ma told me. 'You didn't help, winding him up like that about the hunger strikers.'

We were all at the gate now, looking down the hill after him.

'Come on,' Josie said, 'we'll all go down, just in case things get out of hand.'

'The only reason I mentioned the hunger strikers was to get him going, Ma,' I explained as I ran alongside her.

'You crafty wee bitch.' Josie laughed.

People stopped and stared as first Da passed them like a bat out of hell, followed by us running after him, Ma still in her slippers.

'Nosy bloody parkers,' I said.

'We must look like the end of the *Benny Hill Show* where he gets chased down the street by three mad horny women,' Josie said, making us all laugh.

Bernie's flat was above the Harp on Main Street and the doorbell was just next to the pub door. By the time we caught up with Da, he had his finger pressed on the bell and was roaring at the top of his voice, 'Get down here, Doyle, you little runt, or I'll kick this fucking door in! Come on, you bastard. I know you're up there.'

'Calm down there, Jimmy,' Ma said coaxingly, but he didn't seem to see her, never mind hear her.

Half a dozen customers came from the bar to see who was causing all the commotion, including Teresa, who was looking the worse for wear.

'Will someone tell me whah the fuck is goin' on here?' The words just slithered out of her as she staggered towards Ma.

'Jimmy? What are you at there?' Mick the publican said, raising his voice above all the rest.

'Stay out of it, Mick. This is family business.' Da gave the door a couple of kicks.

Bernie opened the door and stood there, dumbfounded, in a pair of old jeans and a baggy jumper that made her look like she was shrinking, not blooming.

'Where is he? Let me in. I know he's been knocking you about.'

'That's the wee prick,' Teresa piped up from behind us, 'and him sittin' in there havin' 'is pint. You'd think buther wouldn't melt in 'is mouth.'

'I don't want any trouble now, Jimmy,' Mick tried to warn Da as he burst through the bar door.

'Ma, stop him, will you?' Bernie pleaded, but it was too late. Wild horses couldn't have stopped Da at that stage.

'Stop shaking, Ma,' I said, putting my arms around her. I knew she hated violence. It frightened her, reminding her too much of the past, so she'd told me once, but this was one time when I felt Da was doing the right thing. He was justified and I told her so.

Da was back out on the street in no time, pulling Noel by the scruff of the neck.

'Let's see what you're made of now, hard man,' he was roaring at him.

'I didn't touch her, I swear, Jimmy, on me mother's li—'

Da didn't let him finish. He head-butted Noel straight on the nose before a couple of men dragged him off him. There was a scuffle as Da tried to get at him again, but the men held him while Noel, whimpering, struggled back into the bar with his nose dripping blood all over the place.

'You've made your point now, Jimmy. Don't make matters any worse or we'll have the Guards round,' Mick told him firmly but respectfully.

'Come on, Bernie,' I said, taking her by the arm, 'I'll help you pack some stuff. You're coming home with us.'

She followed me, saying nothing, still in a state of shock.

'You're safe now, Bernie,' I tried to comfort her as we threw a few of her bits and pieces into a bag. 'Don't cry. None of this is your fault.'

'It's not all his fault either, you know. He's really been doing his best recently.'

'Bernie!'

'You don't know the whole story about his past and all the problems he's had.'

''That's no fucking excuse.'

She stood looking out the window, biting her nails.

'Come on,' I handed her one of the bags, 'let's get out of here.'

We left the flat and joined Ma, Teresa and Josie, who were still hanging around outside the pub among the lingering crowd.

'Come on,' Teresa said to Ma, 'we'll all go back to your house.'

Josie came over, gave Bernie a hug and linked her down the street. A couple of men were clapping Da's back and offering to buy him a drink down at the Horse and Jockey. He didn't refuse.

'Where's your Clint?' Ma asked Teresa as we were about to leave.

'Oh, sweet Jesus,' she exploded, laughing. 'I left the wee bastard playing space invaders in the pub with a bottle of Coke.'

'You stupid bitch,' I snapped at her and turned on my heel to go and get him.

Noel was sitting at the bar, his nose buried in a wad of blood-stained bog roll. There was no sign of Clint.

'If you're looking for Teresa's lad, he's in the back,' Mick shouted over the bar. When I found Clint, leaning against the juke box watching a couple of men playing pool, I could see the sadness written all over his face.

'Are you OK, Clint?'

'Yeah, just waiting to take my mam home. She's drunk again.'

'She's with my ma. They're on their way up to our house. Come on.'

'Look,' he said as we were passing the space-invader machine. 'I got the high score – fourteen thousand, three hundred and fifty.'

'Yeah, that's great,' I said, nudging him in the direction of the main door.

Outside, I put my arm round him and we quickly caught up with the others. Teresa was now leaning on Ma to stop herself from staggering.

'I'm a good bloody mother I am, no matter what any of them say,' she was slobbering.

I wasn't sure if Clint had heard her.

'He means everything to me, that boy.'

'I know, I know,' Ma said.

'It's all his fault, you know, Mary.'

'Whose fault?'

'That evil fucking father of ours.'

'I know, love, I know.'

'She always says that when she's drunk,' Clint said, looking at the ground.

Despite myself, I had a little flurry of pity for the aunt I'd come to hate.

Teresa

'Keep the bloody noise down, will you?' I wasn't sure who I was calling out to. 'My head's splitting.'

My voice was weak and croaky, my throat parched and my lips sticky. It was only when I opened my eyes and saw Clint lying with his back to me on two armchairs, pushed together, that I realized where I was.

'Feck off, Teresa, you dozy bitch,' Marcella shouted from the kitchen, banging a couple more pots around. I'd swear she was doing it on purpose.

'How about a nice big fry-up with a runny egg?' she hissed at me, sticking her head around the door.

'Get lost, you little bitch,' I muttered to myself. I was in no state to retaliate.

It was as though there was a little cobbler inside my head, tap, tap, tapping away, the wee bastard. It must have been those Harvey Wall Bangers that had done it, some cocktail the young barman had come across on his holiday in the Isle of Man. He'd had half the pub on them in the end. Gorgeous they were too but, fuck me, never again. I wanted to go back to sleep, but I was bursting for a wee. It was only when I stretched my leg out, to put one foot on the floor, that I realized my knickers were down at my ankles. Oh Jesus, no, I thought. I couldn't have, could I? I did, didn't I? Had it off with Jimmy last night, right here on this couch. Shite! I could remember him on top of me, whispering that Clint was asleep. I had been half asleep myself; it was all a bit of a blur. My heart started thumping. I didn't want to be here, at the scene of the crime. I wanted to run, hide, disappear. Oh God above, I begged him, whatever else, please don't let Clint have been awake and aware of what was going on. If he'd grant me that one wish, I'd stay away from Jimmy; I'd not do it again.

It had been bad enough Marcella finding out about Jimmy and me on the day of Bernie's wedding. A week of pure torture I had gone through after that, waiting for the shit to hit the fan, but she'd not said a word to anyone or, by God, I'd have known all about it. She obviously hadn't heard us at it in the wee hours of the morning, seeing I was still alive to feel the guilt. And Mary, she'd gone straight to bed after a cup of tea and a couple of her sleepers. She wouldn't have known a thing, for sure.

I'd have to move, or else there'd be an accident. I stumbled to my feet, my head throbbing. Of course the bathroom door was locked when I got there, just so I'd suffer a little longer. I wanted to kick it, but my legs were firmly crossed, which was the way they should have been when Jimmy came sneaking in under my blanket.

'Morning, Teresa. The head's not the best this morning, is it?' Bernie asked as she came out of the bathroom. I didn't answer, just dashed past her to relieve myself. I didn't even shut the door.

'I'm getting up now if you want a couple of hours kip in our bed,' Bernie said.

48

'Yeah, great. Thanks, pet.'

I could hear the snores of himself as I tiptoed across the landing to the girls' room. Bernie came up with a couple of aspirins and a glass of water.

'You're a good lassie, and you deserve a lot better than that Noel fella.' I gulped the water down fast, feeling the cold liquid trickle into my stomach. Lovely.

I tried hard to sleep. I needed sleep, but the goings-on of the night before were coming back to me bit by bit. I had never set out to hurt Mary of all people, but Jimmy was a hard man to resist. Over the years men had come and gone, but Jimmy was always there, a constant man in my life, the only one who'd never left me. And through all that time the spark between us had never dwindled. He was a great man for the compliments too. I liked that. Things just weren't the same with him and Mary any more, so he said, but I could tell that myself by the way she had let herself go: her hair always matted and greasy, baggy clothes hanging off her like an old scarecrow, not a scrap of make-up. The way things were going, if it hadn't been me, it would have been someone else. I knew her nerves weren't the best, but it seemed as though she'd lost all interest. And sure, as Jimmy said, what she didn't know couldn't hurt her. No, it was just a bit of harmless fun – two people fulfilling each other's needs. That's what he said. I shut my eyes to say a prayer that Clint hadn't seen anything. Hail Mary, full of grace – Holy Mary . . .

*

49

'Mother of God, are you going to get out of the bed at all today?'

'Mary? What time is it?'

'Half one. I don't know how you slept through all the racket downstairs.'

'What racket?'

'That Noel boy banging on the back door looking for our Bernie.'

'The nerve of him.'

'He must have seen Jimmy going out. He'd not have the guts to face him.'

'What did youse do?'

'Marcella went out into the yard with a kettle in her hand, threatening to scald the balls off him if he came near the house again.'

'Well, fair fucks to her.' I laughed, admiring her guts and her tactics. 'No better woman.'

'Come on down for a drop of tay.'

'Right. You haven't a pair of tights I could borrow? I've a big bloody ladder in mine.'

'Here you are,' says she, arriving back into the room with two pairs of tights, one leg cut off each pair.

'What what am I supposed to do with them?'

'What's wrong with them? Haven't they got two perfectly good legs between them?' she said, holding them up for me to examine. 'Put on the both of them and you get two knicker bits for extra warmth.'

We were both in stitches when Marcella burst in to tell us to clear out; she had her studying to do.

'Oh, your studying,' I said, teasing her. 'It's not your

lessons like you used to do in the tech. It's *studying* now in Loreto, is it?'

'Just shut up and clear off,' she said, turning on her heel, 'and don't bother your arse making the bed. I'll be changing the sheets.'

With all the women in the house, they hadn't a scrap of make-up to lend me between them, and when I asked Marcella if I could use a bit of her Pond's, she said, 'Yeah, I suppose. That face needs all the help it can get.'

I wanted to flatten her, but she had me by the short and curlies after the wedding incident and she knew it.

Luckily Jimmy hadn't come back by the time I got downstairs.

'How's the head now, Teresa?' Bernie asked.

'Still a bit dicey, but not too bad. I hear your fella was around this morning.'

'Yeah, but they chased him; didn't even give him a chance to talk.'

'Sure, you didn't want to talk to him, did you?'

'Oh, I don't know. Suppose not.'

I could tell she wasn't convinced. It'd take a bit of persuasion to keep her away from him.

'Is Clint watching TV?'

'No. He said to collect him in the ball alley on your way home.'

After a quick cup I headed off, still a bit anxious in case Clint knew something about the night before. I could have done with a stiff drink to prepare myself for some very awkward questions or a possible showdown.

But I kept going, sluggishly, with a lot less gusto than my pounding heart. Without the bit of make-up I felt naked – all my flaws exposed for the world to see. I had a fag, but it didn't help; in fact, it made me feel even more edgy.

I could hear the noise from the ball alley now, the echo of the ball and lots of shouting and cheering. A handball match. That was all I needed – having to face the crowd looking like a dog's dinner. I couldn't wait to be home and get out of the clothes I'd slept in. Clint was sitting up on the bank with a couple of lassies about his own age, head stretched back, blowing smoke rings. Maybe he was trying to impress the girls. I'd never seen him smoke before. Making my way across to him, I got my stiletto stuck in the muck and stepped straight out of my shoe and into the wet mud.

'Well, fuck it!' I roared. All heads turned. Then came the chorus of wolf whistles from the men and dirty looks from a few of the women.

'Do you want a hand out of your stockings there, Teresa?' some fella shouted and they all laughed. I wanted to cry because Clint was on his way over to me, his head hung low, his ears burning with embarrassment. I could take a bit of a slagging myself, no problem, but I didn't want to humiliate my boy, show him up in any way. I loved my son, and yet I'd let him down so often: got drunk when I'd promised to stay sober, gone out when I'd promised to stay in. It's not that I meant to let him down; it was just that I found it easier to be out having a bit of a laugh and a few jars than to be home, sober, with the past, like the darkness of the night, creeping up on me.

'Come on, Mam, let's go,' he said, linking me away.

'Sorry, pet. I didn't mean to mortify you like that.'

'Yeah, yeah.'

'No, really, I didn't.'

'And what about last night?'

'What about it?' I asked, dreading what was coming next.

'In the pub, Mam, you were scuttered. Again.'

'It was just with all that was going on with Bernie—'

'Bullshit, Mam. You were drunk before you knew a thing about that.'

'Arragh, for God's sake, Clint, I don't need a lecture. I'm a young woman, entitled to have a bit of fun now and again.'

It wasn't what he wanted to hear, I knew that, but I didn't know what else to say and I needed him to shut up. I felt guilty enough as it was. The rest of the walk home was silent, apart from the odd big sigh out of him, letting me know that he still wasn't happy.

'And since when did you start smoking?' I asked him as I turned the key in the door.

'Just a couple of weeks ago.'

'They'll stunt your growth, you know.'

'So Marcella keeps warning me.'

'Trying to impress the girls, are you?'

'What girls?'

'The two you were with down the alley.'

'Those two? No way.'

'Right. So you don't fancy either of them, then?'

'No.'

'Ah, sure, you probably wouldn't tell me anyway.'

'There's lots of things I wouldn't tell you, Mam,' he said, not meaning to hurt me but hurting me all the same.

I spent the rest of the afternoon cleaning the house from top to bottom, except for Clint's room. He didn't like me rooting through his stuff. I needed to occupy myself. It kept my mind off things like Jimmy and Mary and the guilt I felt, or my poor mother, God rest her, and my father and all that carry-on over the years. Yes, it was best to keep busy. If I didn't, I might be tempted to have a drink.

Even with the vacuum cleaner on, I could hear the music blaring from Clint's room and him singing, 'Message in a Bottle'.

Although I was a big rock fan myself, I was beginning to get used to all the modern stuff: the Police, the Boomtown Rats, Duran Duran – they were some of his favourites. Music was the one thing we could always talk about. Mad into it, the pair of us.

'Are you heading out tonight, Mam?' he asked while we were having our tea.

It was Saturday night. I loved my Saturday night on the town – always a great night's crack in the Well.

'Well, are you?' he said and let out a big sigh as though expecting to be disappointed.

'Och, I'll not. I'll stay in.'

He smiled. God, he was the beautiful boy when he smiled – so, so handsome: a big wide smile, high cheekbones like David Bowie's and straight black hair. Many's the night while he slept in his bed, especially when he was younger, I'd study his face, searching for a clue, for a hint of who his father was. But it was like groping in the dark, I couldn't make a connection. I just didn't know whose he was. Of course, I never admitted that to anyone. They did enough bitching about me without giving them any more ammunition. And it wouldn't have been fair on Clint either. It had just been my way of life in London at the time – too many wild parties, drinks galore, hot-blooded men, handsome faces, ugly faces, blurred faces, no faces, just the feel of human flesh and a quick thrill.

'We'll have a few hands of cards,' Clint said.

'Right, but you run down to the shop and get me twenty Carroll's and some Coke and crisps for yourself while I have my bath. Deal?'

'Deal.'

Just as I slid myself down into the bath to wet my hair, I thought I heard a rap at the kitchen window, but with the water in my ears, I wasn't sure. I sat up. Nothing. Back down again. Rap, rap, rap. Back up.

'Teresa.' Rap, rap, rap. 'Teresa.'

It was Jimmy, the chancer. What the hell was he doing here? I was afraid someone might hear him shouting. Then I heard the snooping old bag from next door come out into her backyard. So I jumped out of the bath, wrapped a towel around myself, raced down the stairs and let him in.

'I'm having a bath, you bollocks. What do you want?'

'You, me little sexpot, you,' he said, pinching my bum as I walked away.

'Feck off, and don't you "sexpot" me. That carry-on last night, it shouldn't have happened, Jimmy. Jesus Christ, what were you thinking of?'

'You. I can't stop thinking about you.'

'We're going to have to put an end to it. It's far too risky.'

'Teresa, Teresa, what are you on about?'

'Will you listen, for fuck's sake?' I said trying to put my foot down, to be serious. He wasn't having any of it, standing there with a grin on him like a Cheshire cat.

'I didn't hear you complain last night,' he sneered. 'Come on, you loved every minute of it.'

He was right though. I had loved every minute of it. Not last night, I could barely remember it, but all the other times. It was great between us.

'Shut up,' I said, lighting a fag.

'Oh, playing hard to get now, are we? It doesn't suit you, hen,' he teased, trying to loosen my towel. 'Come on, I'm as horny as hell.'

'Will you fuck off! Clint will be back any minute. He's just gone out to the shop,' I said, pulling back and hanging on tight to my towel.

But he was getting to me. I knew if Clint hadn't been due back, we'd have done it there and then on the kitchen table, the floor, up against the wall – wild, hot, spontaneous, that's how it was between us, that's how I liked it: the rush, the excitement, the passion. Then I remembered the promise I'd made only that morning to Himself, about staying away from Jimmy if my prayer was answered.

'Well, what about later then?'

'I'm staying in.'

'On a Saturday night?'

'I promised Clint.'

'Promised him what?'

'That I'd stay in and play cards with him.'

'Sure, get Marcella down. She'll keep him company.'

'No.'

'Go on. She'll be glad to get out of that madhouse for a couple of hours.'

'No.'

'Come on, the drinks are on me. I got lucky on the nags today,' he said, pulling a wad of notes out of his pocket.

I knew Marcella would come down all right. She'd do anything for Clint. Mad about him she was: treated him like a younger brother. Even though there were times when I could have choked her, I liked the way she was with Clint.

'G and T, a wee vodka, a brandy? Whatever takes your fancy, it's yours.'

And if it was just a bit of company Clint wanted, he'd have as much crack with Marcella as he'd have with me. More. I was raring to go now. I was thirsty.

And Jimmy was flush. Feck it, I thought, if a girl can't go out and have a few drinks on a Saturday night . . .

'Wear that black leather mini-skirt, you look smashing in it,' he told me on his way out.

'I'll see you in the Harp in half an hour,' I said.

'Yeah, yeah.'

That's all Clint said when I told him Marcella was on her way over to stay with him.

'She never keeps her promises,' I heard him tell her while I was putting on my jacket in the hall. I felt a pang of guilt and stopped to reconsider. He was right: I didn't keep my promises, not to him, nor to Him. But there was a drink waiting for me at the bar, any number of them, so I postponed the guilt and kept on going.

Clint was still in a huff with me on the Tuesday morning.

'Here's your Rice Krispies,' I said.

'I'll get my own.'

'Sure they're poured now.'

'Have them yourself then.'

'I don't eat breakfast, you know that.'

'You should.'

'Clint.'

'What?'

'Don't do this.'

'Don't do what?'

'Not talk to me.'

'I am talking to you.'

'You know what I mean.'

'What *do* you mean?'

'Look, I'm sorry. Is that what you want me to say?'

'No.'

'Well, what then? What?'

'Work it out for yourself.'

We said no more. I drank my coffee and looked out the back window while he munched his way through his cereal, his head leaning on the palm of his hand. I stood staring out on the dullness of that autumn morning. Deep down I knew what he wanted. I just didn't know how to make those changes, how to find the courage.

I couldn't stop thinking about him all day at work. Teenagers, I told myself as I stuffed sheets into Mrs Pollock's washing machine. He was almost thirteen. That's all that was wrong – he was being a typical moody teenager. He just needed a bit of cheering up. I'd surprise him, buy him a Walkman. He'd mentioned that some lad in his class had got one and how it was really cool.

I went into town straight after work on Friday. Thirty pounds the bloody thing cost me, almost two days' wages. But it would be worth it to put a smile back on his face and have him talk to me again. I tried it out myself before he arrived home from school with one of my Rod Stewart tapes. It was only mighty. There I was boogieing around from room to room, Rod full-blast in my ears, singing just for me. Oh, the hunk! I adored the man: the husky voice, the spiked hair. Away in another world I was, imagining myself being picked out from a crowd of screaming fans and dragged onto the stage with him. Me and him, an item – cameras flashing, newspaper headlines. Rod and Teresa, Teresa and Rod? No, it just didn't have that ring to it. Rod and Tess, Tess and Rod? No. Rod and Therese, Therese and Rod? Better. Ah, fuck it, change my name altogether. Rod and Mandy. Rod and Kim. Rod and Pam, Pam and Rod. Rod in Pam. Oh, shut up, you big eejit, thirty-one years of age and still dreaming like a teenager.

'Now don't you go having another son, Teresa,' Marcella had warned me once. 'I can handle having a cousin called Clint Reilly, but Rod Reilly – I don't think so! Anyway,' she'd gone on, 'Clint Eastwood I could have myself, but that other gobshite with the hedgehog stuck to his head, a nose on him like Fatima Hill and a bum like two bananas, what a drip!'

'You'll do extra time in purgatory for saying that,' I'd told her.

Thrilled to bits Clint was about his Walkman. Worth every penny it was just to see his face. He gave me the biggest hug, as though he really loved me.

'You're the best, Mam,' he said, kissing my cheek.

With tears in my eyes, I thought of my ma. I imagined her up above, sitting by the fire, her favourite spot, smiling, no bruises, no black eyes. She was sprinkling a little heaven dust down on me, saying, 'There you are, lassie, a little taste of heaven.'

*

60

I took it easy on the booze for the next couple of weeks for Clint's sake. I had a couple of half-ones every night after he'd gone to bed. I needed that. At least it was something to look forward to at the end of the day. I managed to stay in too, except for a couple of nights at the bingo with Josie. But bingo wasn't for me. I'd rather have a night down the pub any time – at least there'd be a bit of crack. It was just more my scene than sitting with a bunch of old biddies ticking numbers off a card. A few drinks, a bit of company, it did me the world of good. I was more myself when I was drinking, more together, stronger.

I needed a break, a night out. Surely Clint could see how I had really been making an effort recently; he'd hardly begrudge me my bit of fun now and again. I was just thinking that one Thursday morning when Bernie came running round the side of my house shouting at me to open the back door.

I'd been sitting by the fire which I'd only just lit, treating myself to a drop of vodka in my tea.

'Will you settle the head, girl?' I said. 'What in the name of God is wrong with you?'

She was panting, trying to get her breath back and holding her little bump as if she was afraid her baby was going to drop out.

'Oh, Jesus, you're not in labour, lassie, are you?'

'No,' she gasped, 'it's Ma. She wants you, Teresa. She's been shouting for you this hour.'

'What's wrong with her?' I asked, knocking back the rest of my drink.

'I don't know. She just keeps crying and shaking; she's been a bloody wreck for the past few days.'

'Is your da not there?'

'No, he's been away fishing since early morning. Says we're a house of mad women. She just keeps asking for you.'

'Right so,' I said, pouring myself a neat vodka and downing it in one. What if Mary knew about Jimmy and me? I thought. She'd never speak to me again. I'd not be able to handle that, falling out with Mary. She was the only one of the family who'd stuck by me after all that hassle when my da died. The rest of them, the greedy feckers, resented me being left the few hundred pounds in his will. God knows, only that I was heading for England at the time, they could have had his stinking money. I wanted nothing off him. All I wanted was to bury him, forget him, wipe him out of my memory for good. But getting rid of the money had been a lot easier than getting rid of the memories.

'I'm bursting for a piss.'

'Go on so, Bernie, and I'll get my jacket.'

I didn't bother pouring the next one, just put the bottle to my mouth . . . glug, glug, glug, down the hatch.

'Any bother from your fella over the past few days?' I asked her on the way over to the house.

She said something about him sending his mother round to talk to her, but I was only half listening. My mind was racing, trying to predict the questions, prepare the answers. Are you and Jimmy at it? Well, are youse?

No, Mary, Jesus no. So our Marcella's making it up then, is she? That's it, I'd had it. If Marcella had spilt the beans, there was no bloody hope. You could accuse the girl of being many things but a liar she was not, and nobody knew that better than Mary herself.

'So what do you think I should do, Teresa?'

'About what, love?'

'Noel. Should I talk to him, give him a chance?'

'The only thing I'd give that fella is a size ten boot up the arsehole,' I told her as we went in through the side gate.

Hey, You up there, I prayed silently, I need your help. Again. One last request, please. If not for me, then for my Clint.

'You go on up to her, Teresa.'

'She's still in bed?'

'Yeah.'

I went in through the back kitchen and headed for the stairs. I got to the landing and took a deep breath.

'Teresa, love, is that you?' Her voice was weak and panicky, not angry or challenging.

'It's all right, Mary, I'm here,' I said as I opened the bedroom door. It was awful: the staleness of the air, the curtains drawn, only a ray of sunlight sneaking through to highlight all the dust, full ashtrays, half-drunk mugs of tea with fag butts floating in them. And there was Mary, the same beautiful sister I'd been flower girl for over twenty years earlier, drawn, un-washed and old, sitting on the bed, her knees drawn up

63

to her chest, her eyes wild and frightened. My heart sank.

'Mary, what's wrong, love?' My voice came out in a whisper. It had lost its strength.

'Sit down,' she said tapping the side of the bed. 'I need you to do me a favour.'

I sat down next to her and took her trembling hand in mine. It felt so cold.

'What is it, you poor crathur?'

'I'm out of my tablets. I need a script. That's all that's wrong with me, love – the oul nerves, you know.'

'So you want me to collect it for you?'

'Sort of. I need you to axe the doc for them for yourself. Tell him you've been feeling a bit under the weather lately.'

She was squeezing my hand now, as though she was pleading with me.

'He'll not give me another script for a fortnight,' she went on. 'I won't last another bloody day, never mind a fortnight.'

'You're hooked on them yokes, aren't you?'

'Please,' she said, reaching out and grabbing my shoulder tightly. 'Please.' The tears came streaming down her cheeks.

I couldn't bear to see her in that state.

'I can't eat, I can't sleep,' she gasped. 'My fucking head is spinning and if I don't—'

'Ssh, ssh, calm down.' I rooted through my pockets in search of a tissue to wipe her sticky, soaked face.

'You know what it's like to be craving for a fucking drink, don't you?'

What did she think I was, a bloody alco?

'It's all right, I'll do it. I'll go down straight away before the surgery closes for lunch.'

I lit a couple of fags and handed one to her. 'Try and relax. Have a bit of a rest for yourself and when I get back, you can get up and dressed.'

'Right. Whatever. Go on now. Don't be long.'

I pulled back the curtains and opened the window before I left, taking a handful of filthy mugs.

'Bernie, Jesus, she's losing it. She's in a fierce state and you should see the fucking cut of the room. I've seen cleaner pigsties. Would youse not clean the place up a bit between yourself and Marcella? And what about Josie? Does she know what's going on?'

'Josie's dosed with a flu. Marcella's not home until six or seven. She stays on in the library at school to do her homework. I'm doing my best, Teresa, cooking for my da and trying to keep him happy.'

'What has he to say about the state she's in?'

'Says she's astray in the head. She needs to pull herself together. Reckons that if she goes on like this much longer, she'll end up in the bin – stuff like that. He's staying out most of the day. He's slept on the couch for the past couple of nights.'

Poor Jimmy. It must have been hard on him too. And, sure, who the hell could sleep in that room and the state of it?

'What are we going to do with her, Teresa?'

'Don't worry, love. You've enough to be think-ing about with that wee babby due in a couple of months. I'll tip down and have a word with the doc.'

'Thanks.'

'Just have a seat there, Miss Reilly. Shouldn't be too long.'

It was the last place I'd planned on being that day, stuck in a stuffy waiting room and my stomach in knots wondering what I was going to say. I had to get them; I couldn't leave without that script. There were two other women sitting together when I went in.

'Howayis?'

Neither answered, the pair of ignorant bitches, just looked me up and down. They went on talking, so I picked up a *Woman's Way* and pretended to be reading it.

'Who's that man that's just gone in to the doctor?' one asked the other.

'That's Harry Agnew, lives up in Fairgreen, works in the council offices.'

'Oh aye. Isn't he fierce shook-looking?'

'He is, God bless him. I think I heard Siobhan saying that he was up in the Mater Hospital for a few weeks. She's pally with his daughter; they were at Loreto together.'

'Oh, right.'

'The daughter's doing nursing up in Drogheda. Nice young lassie she is too.'

'And what's your Siobhan studying?'

'Marketing.'

'Marketing! What does that entail?'

Good question. I'd never heard of it.

'It's all about . . . eh . . . business.'

'Business?'

'Yes, Phyllis, the selling end of it – testing the market and that kinda thing.'

'Testing the market?' With her index finger, Phyllis pushed the bridge of her glasses farther up her nose and looked up into the other woman's face.

'That's right.' She shifted in her chair and straightened herself up.

'Oh.' Phyllis rubbed her chin, staring ahead of her at a blank spot on the wall. Then she turned to the woman again. 'And what sort of career will she get outa that, will you tell me?'

'According to herself, they're crying out for market researchers,' she said, reaching across to the coffee table and lifting a magazine from the top of the pile.

'Is that right? Market researchers.' Phyllis frowned doubtfully, stretching her legs out in front of her and examining her shoes. Her tongue made a mound inside her left cheek. 'She'll not be like one of these women standing outside Dunnes with a clipboard and pen asking people questions about how they spent their money, will she?'

Jaysus! Imagine having to go to college to learn how to do the like of that.

'Ah no, I don't think so.'

'Oh good, 'cos there's nothing as off-putting, I think anyway.'

'Mrs Hill, you're next,' the receptionist called and

Phyllis got up. She tapped on the other woman's shoulder and whispered loudly, 'Another few months and I'll not have to come here at all. My Philip will be fully qualified then.' She smoothed out her jacket with her hands. 'He'll be fit to write me out all the prescriptions I need.'

Another patient came in the door as Phyllis waddled out with a smug grin.

There was no more chat in the waiting room to distract me from my nervousness and I was too jittery to read. I had the runs twice before I was called in myself.

'How can I help you, Teresa?'

He was a lovely man, really, for a doctor. No snobbery about him at all.

'I'm a bit under the weather lately – nervous – finding it hard to cope.'

'Depressed maybe?'

'Sort of, I suppose. I can't settle the head at all – can't relax.'

'Are these feelings of anxiety constant?'

'Eh, not constant, I suppose, but—'

'When are they less apparent?'

'How do you mean?'

'Well, when you have a drink, does that help?'

'Yeah, sometimes,' I said, thinking there's a man after my own heart.

'Ever thought of giving up the drink, or maybe

cutting down? Alcohol can cause anxiety, make you feel unbalanced, edgy or even depressed.'

What? Was he serious? Drink never made me feel like that. In fact, drink helped me *not* to feel like that. Apart from the odd night when I'd had one too many and ended up with a splitting headache the next morning, the drink was a godsend. But I wasn't there to argue my case. I just wanted to get the script and get the fuck out.

'I've been trying to give it up altogether but—'

'You're not having much success this morning, then?'

Well, feck me, I said to myself, you don't miss much, do you?

'I thought maybe if I could get something to relax me a bit – it might make things a little easier.'

'Fair enough, Teresa, but you'll have to make sure you don't mix the drink with the tablets I'm going to prescribe.'

'Oh, I'll not, Doctor, honest I'll not.'

'Well if you *do* drink, Teresa, don't take the tablets. I'm going to try you out on some Valium, a very low dose.'

Phew!

'Right, Doctor.'

'Stick firmly to the dosage and if there are any problems, come back to see me straight away.'

'OK. Thanks.'

He started writing on my chart. I leaned in to have a look, but couldn't make head nor tail of his writing.

'These may make you feel a little drowsy,' he said, scribbling the prescription on the pad, 'but you don't drive, do you?'

'Apart from driving my family round the bend,' I said, unzipping my bag, 'no.'

'While you have your bag open,' he said, looking in a drawer and shuffling through some papers, 'slip that in as well and have a read of it some evening. It's a great place to get support, if you feel you need it.'

He handed me a leaflet. 'Alcoholics Anonymous' it read. My face began to burn. The cheek of him! I dropped it into my bag and tried to close it, but the bloody thing got wedged in the zip.

'Feck it,' I said, tugging at it.

'Are you all right?'

'Yes,' I snapped, pulling out the leaflet and shoving it into my jeans' pocket. I'd love to have thrown it back in his face. Trying to make me out to be some sort of alco. So I'd had a few drinks that morning, big swinging Mickey! It had been a bloody crisis.

'You know, sometimes we tend to think of alcoholics as being the poor, homeless people we see lying in shop doorways with noggins in their hands, but let me assure you, Teresa, there are professional men and women in this town attending those meetings. Drink can get a grip on anyone.'

'Yeah?' I said, putting on my jacket. 'Well, it hasn't and it won't be getting a grip on me.' I put my bag over my shoulder.

'Teresa, I—'

'See ya, Doctor.' I marched out, leaving the door open behind me.

Feck you, Mary, and your bloody Valium, spoiling my day like that. I couldn't get out quick enough. That was it, good deed done for the day, mission accomplished, time for a long cold drink, a well-deserved drink, and fuck the lot of them.

'I'm sorry, Clint.'

'Don't say that, Mam.'

'Oh, listen, son, I never intended going to the pub, I swear to God. It's just that—'

'Don't, Mam. Stop. I don't want to listen to your crap any more.'

'Please listen, love, just let me explain—'

'Shut up, Mam,' he shouted. 'Shut up, shut up, shut up, shut up!'

'Oh, sonny—'

'Shut up, shut up, shut up!' he continued, walking away from me and up the stairs.

Then I heard his bedroom door slam and I cursed the fucking drink and all the hassle it caused. I dreaded the day ahead, the disappointment in his eyes, the silence in the house, the guilt weighing me down, the throbbing head, the unquenchable thirst. It was like doing time, it was the punishment for the crime and, although usually we didn't speak for twenty-four hours, I wasn't doing the time alone.

The doorbell rang.

'Is Clint ready?'

It was Hughie Clarke from across the street, Aggie's wee lad. Clint came running down the stairs.

'Clint, have you your homework done?' Hughie asked.

'Of course I have.'

He was a good boy, my Clint.

'Can I copy it?'

'It's a composition, you big eejit. You can't copy a composition.'

'Ah shite, I'm gonna be kilt.'

'Come on, we'll hurry. You might get a few lines done in the shelter before the bell goes. I'll help you.'

'You'd not get many friends who'd do the like—' The front door was pushed back in my face. 'Of that for you, Hughie,' I said, talking to myself.

I went to the window and peeped out through the curtains. The two of them were running along and I could see Clint was smiling now he had let his guard down and felt free of me, at least for a while. I went to the fridge, pulled out a bottle of Coke and took it up to my bedroom.

Sitting on the side of the bed, I started guzzling it down so I could feel the fizz, all the way from my tongue to my stomach. Turning to place the half-empty bottle on my dressing table, I got a glimpse of myself in the mirror. I moved closer, taking a longer look. The eyes staring back at me were lifeless, like a pair of dead fish floating on two stagnant pools. I started pulling faces, smiling, pouting, frowning but, no matter how hard I tried to pump some life into that face, the eyes remained the same, sapped of all enthusiasm.

'Fuck you, Father,' I said out loud, knowing that the dirty bastard was still hovering around, haunting me. 'It's all your fault. Why couldn't you just leave me alone?'

I closed my eyes and I took a tight grip of my hair in both fists. I pulled hard, trying to feel the pain, to pierce the stagnant waters and let the tears flow, and flow they did until I could no longer stand the pressure in my head and the heaving of my chest. I felt as if I was drowning, as though big strong waves of emotion were knocking me down, pounding me. I needed Clint. He was my lifeline. I made a dash for his room and threw myself down on his bed. Pulling his pillow in under my head, I inhaled his comforting smell, clung on to his love and rocked myself to sleep.

I didn't wake until twelve thirty and, although my hangover was still lingering, the crying was done and over with, or so I thought, and it was time to pull myself together. I made Clint's bed, not wanting him to know I'd been in his room. Tucking in his sheets, I came across his diary underneath the mattress. I sat on his bed wondering what to do. I respected his privacy and I would never have purposely gone looking for his diary, but now I had it in my hands, I longed to open it. When we fell out, Clint would be angry and not speak to me for a day or two, but he'd never tell me how he felt, not even when we'd made up and were friends again. All those feelings were here in this book, waiting to be read. I turned the pages, one by one.

Tuesday 25 Jan 1981

Teacher made Hughie cry at school today when she tapped her knuckles on his head and said, 'Get that through your thick skull.' Everyone laughed, except me and Hughie. I don't like teacher any more.

That's the bitch, I thought, turning the pages.

Friday 14 Feb 1981

It's Valentine's Day. I sent a card to Sharon O'Kane. I love her. She's gorgeous and she wears a bra. Mam says she's going out to celebrate but I don't know why 'cos she didn't get any cards.

Saturday 15 Feb 1981

Marcella stayed with me last night. We played Cluedo. I won. Then she made us toast and cheese. Don't know what time Mam came home at but she's on the aspirin today.

I skipped on a bit, trying to get to the more recent rows we'd had.

Saturday 6 Sept 1981

Slept in Auntie Mary's house last night. Uncle Jimmy battered Noel 'cos Noel battered Bernie. Mam was drunk. Marcella says it's worse she's getting. I wonder why she spends so long doing herself up to go to the pub, washing her hair and putting on make-up just to get pissed and end up looking all messy and stupid. Went to the ball alley this morning to pass the time until she slept it off.

There were tears in my eyes, and I cursed that wee shit-stirrer Marcella.

Sunday 7 Sept 1981

I hate Mam. No, I don't. But she sure makes me mad and sad. She was vomiting in the middle of the night and I could hear her cursing to herself on her way back to bed. I wanted to go in to her, to see if she was OK, but I was still mad at her because she promised to stay in and play cards with me and then broke her promise. What's new?

You stupid cow, I told myself, wiping the tears from my cheeks. I flicked back a bit and started reading again.

Sunday 6 June 1981

Had a great day today. Me and Hughie listened to tapes all day at his house. He says he's in love with Blondie and he has a big poster of her in his room. He says sometimes he can't

sleep at night when he's looking at it 'cos it gets him all randy.
He thinks Marcella is sexy too 'cos she's got big knockers.
Mam took us down to the amusements after tea. She gave us
£3 each. Hughie said my mam's lovely. That made me feel
really happy.

I should have stopped there and then, left it on a
high note. Just one more, I thought, and that's it.

Saturday, 17 July 1981

I heard my mam bawling her eyes out in bed last night. She
was drunk again and I wonder was it the booze that made her
cry or was there something making her feel sad? Maybe she
was thinking about my dad and missing him and maybe the
sadness made her booze.

Shit. He was thinking about his father, the one I'd
invented for him. It had seemed like a good idea at the
time. A couple of years earlier, he'd asked me about his
dad. I had nothing for him – not a name, not an address,
not a face or an age, not even a love story. I didn't want
him to know he was the result of a drunken romp with
a stranger whose identity was a mystery to me. I didn't
want him to think of sex in that way. He was just ten
years old then, an innocent boy whose only experience
of romance was the kind he'd read about in fairytales.
So I told him, like I'd told all my family, that while
living in London I had fallen in love with a man whose
wife was an invalid. We had been very much in love,

but neither of us thought he should leave a woman who was ill.

'Will he come and get us when she dies?' he asked.

'It's too late for that now, son,' I told him, stroking his cheek. 'Our life is here now, in Ireland, among our family and friends.'

He seemed to accept what I'd said and never mentioned his father again. But clearly he hadn't forgotten about him. My life was one big sordid secret: the carry-on with Da, Clint's father, my affair with Jimmy. But I'd have to live with the lies, try to forget the facts because, if the truth got out, I'd lose the little bit of dignity I'd managed to cling on to over the years. And without that, I didn't think I'd make it out of bed in the morning.

Right, Teresa, I told myself, from now on, no more binges and no more breaking promises.

I'd have a talk with Clint in the evening, put things right, even stay off the drink for a couple of weeks to prove to him that I could do it, that I was no alco.

I waited at the school gates in the rain, cursing the bloody umbrella I was struggling to keep upright in the wind. I heard the bell ringing. Then came the stampede, the cheering and yahooing, as if the kids had just been released from jail. Clint came sauntering out about three minutes after the rest. He gave me the cold eye; he wasn't pleased to see me.

'Put up your hood. You're getting soaked, love.'

He ignored me, just sailed past as if I wasn't there.

'Hang on there, Clint. I'm taking you to the chipper for your dinner.'

He kept going.

'Cheeseburger and chips – your favourite. What do you say?'

No response. We got as far as the chipper, me a couple of paces behind.

'Well, are you coming in?'

Obviously not. I hated the way he could do that, put the barrier up, shut me out. I stopped at the butcher's instead, got the burgers there and headed home. He'd already let himself in and was up in his room listening to music. I let him be. Maybe a bit of space was what he needed. But surely, I thought, when he smelt the fried onions, he'd not be able to resist. I brought his dinner up to him on a tray with a glass of Coke, thinking it was best to let him come down in his own time. Later, when he'd see I was staying in for the night, we'd get the chance to talk.

'I'm not hungry,' he announced, when he saw me standing in the doorway.

'You need to eat, love.'

'Are you deaf? I said I'm not hungry.'

'Just eat what you can,' I told him, putting the tray down on his bed.

I went back downstairs to have my own, managed a couple of bites of my burger and dumped the rest. As I was washing out the frying pan, I heard the front door slam. I peeped out the window and saw Clint on his way down the street, anorak hood down – it was still raining. He'd never before left the house without telling me. The tray was on his bed, exactly where I'd put it, the food untouched. He was breaking my heart. I was breaking his.

An hour passed. There was no sign of him. Two hours. Still no sign. I had the telly on, volume down, waiting to hear the sound of his footsteps or the front gate open. I could hear nothing but the bloody rain battering against the window. I went out to the kitchen to get my fags. On my way back to the sitting room, I heard the key in the door.

'Oh, thank God you're back, pet, I was—' I stopped when I saw Marcella stepping in behind him.

'Hi, Mam. Marcella wants to talk to you.'

'Right, come into the sitting room so,' I told her, 'and you go up and get out of those wet clothes.'

'Is there something up with your ma?' I asked her, closing the door behind us.

She let out a sarcastic little snigger, the bitch.

'There's always something up with my ma, as well you know, but that's not why I'm here.'

The cut of her, standing glaring at me, hand on her hip.

'Right.'

'Afraid she might be on to you, were you?'

'Cut the crap and get to the point,' I told her, beginning to see red, but not wanting to raise my voice.

'Clint.'

'What about him?'

'He's miserable, or haven't you noticed?'

'He's not miserable. We've had a bit of a falling out, not that it's any of your goddamned business.'

'A bit of a falling out – is that what you call it?'

'Would you ever fuck off? Who do you—'

'You were pissed out of your brains at six o'clock yesterday evening, you stupid tramp,' she interrupted me.

Feck you, Clint, I thought, why did you have to go confiding in this wee bitch? Why couldn't you come to me?

'Yeah, well, that's for me and Clint to sort out, not you, so don't you dare come in here shouting the odds, you arrogant little scut.'

'Personally, I couldn't give two fucks about you and your boozing. You could drink yourself to death, for all I care,' she said, the hurtful cow, 'but for Clint's sake, you'd want to cop yourself on and—'

That was it. The face was pure flying off me; I could have split her in two. But instead, I opened the sitting-room door, grabbed her by the sleeve of her poxy school uniform and tried to shove her out through it.

'Bernie's wedding.'

'What did you say?'

'You heard me.'

'What about it?'

'Give it to me, Jimmy, go on, give it to me,' she mimicked me.

I closed the door behind us.

'Shut your cakehole.'

'I will,' she said, real calm and triumphant, 'on one condition, yoyo knickers.'

'Fuck off.'

'Temper, temper, Teresa.'

'Say what you came to say, you blackmailing wee bitch, and get out.'

'If you let Clint down one more time with your drinking escapades, I'm telling Ma about you and my da.'

'Oh yeah? That would do her a whole pile of good, upsetting the poor woman over a one-off mistake.'

'Say what you want, that's the deal, like it or fucking lump it, but let me assure you of one thing, Teresa: that's not a threat, it's a fucking promise.'

She opened the door and marched out into the hall, 'I'm away now, Clint,' she shouted up the stairs.

'Watch that wind doesn't blow your halo down, Saint Marcella,' I said, closing the door behind her. Yoyo knickers! The fucking cheek.

Marcella

Silence at last. Mother of God, it wasn't as if I wasn't well used to domestic chaos, but this place took the biscuit. No, the whole flaming packet of biscuits. No wonder Josie was piling on the weight. If I were stuck with those two children of hers twenty-four hours a day, seven days a week, I'd be crying into my packet of chocolate digestives too. Entertaining them would make vacuuming our own house, top to bottom on one leg with a sack of coal on my back, look like a doddle.

At one point, at the height of all the furore, with the temperature and the volume rising rapidly, it felt as though I was trapped inside some sort of capsule about to erupt with all the pressure and launch itself into space. There was no way I was ending up like Josie, living in a dingy mobile home with Ken Dodd and two of his Diddymen. Spare me.

Thankfully though, the pair of them had finally passed out from a mixture of exhaustion and the stifling heat from the gas heater and were in bed and asleep by nine.

I decided to have one last look in on them before getting out my school books. Little Jimmy's mouth was wide open, but the only noise coming out of it was the soft sigh of his breathing. Sammy had kicked the blankets off herself already. I covered her up again and kissed her pink podgy cheek. The nappy didn't look too secure around her butt, but feck it, I wasn't going rooting at it now. If she didn't twist and turn too much, she'd be grand.

'War is never justified.' That was the motion for Monday's debate and I was captain of the team to oppose the motion. Thank God. And for two very good reasons. One, I disagreed in principle with the statement; it was too inflexible, too presumptuous. I could think of plenty of things worth fighting for. And two, that conceited little stuck-up cow, Leona O'Brien, was proposing the motion and I wanted to take her pompous arse down a peg or two. I just couldn't help it; I hated the bitch. Not once since I'd started at Loreto almost two months earlier had she acknowledged the fact that she knew me and had been in my class in primary school. In fact, she ignored me completely, which in my book was worse than fighting with me or telling me straight what she thought of me.

The other town girls I'd been in primary school with, while I didn't end up hanging around with them – I'd always had a different set of friends coming from Fatima Hill – did, at least, treat me as though I had as much right to be at Loreto as they had. But, right from day one, Gabby and I really clicked and I was having great gas with her and her friends. They'd gone out of their way to make me feel welcome. So, for the most part, I was happy at my new school, except for the annoyance of Leona O'Brien, niggling away at me.

'Ah Jesus, sorry, Marcella, we lost track of time. Are you bucking?' Josie asked me, coming through the door, bringing PJ and the smell of chips with her.

It was a quarter past twelve. I couldn't believe it. Over three hours racking my brains and jotting down about eight or ten points.

'No, youse are grand,' I told her, trying to fold away my stuff in a hurry. I knew if Josie got a gawk at what I was at with a few drinks in her, she'd make a right skit of me.

'Here, want a bag of chips?'

'Too right I do. I'm starving.'

With a bellyful of beer in him, PJ's grin was wider than ever, revealing even more of his prominent teeth.

He leaned over me at the counter to reach into the cupboard and grab a couple of plates.

'Where are you going with the plates, you oul eejit?' Josie said. 'As if I hadn't enough washing up to do.'

'I thought Marcella might want one,' he said, still grinning but putting the plates back straight away.

'Oh, go way outa that. Our Marcella never ate chips from a plate in her life.'

PJ was at the cutlery drawer now.

'Arragh, for fuck's sake, will you sit your arse down and ate your chips and stop your flapping. She doesn't want a fork neither, do you, Marcella?'

To be quite honest, by then my mouth was watering. I could have eaten the bloody chips with my hands tied behind my back, I was so hungry.

'No, no, you're grand, PJ.'

She could say what she liked to him. Did. She'd slag hell out of him, make a right gobshite of him at times in front of others and, the poor divil, he'd say nothing. Just keep smiling. Josie couldn't have found a man more opposite in character to my father, not if she had travelled to the ends of the earth to do so. Luckily for her, he'd been waiting for her all along, just a mile out the road.

'You walk Marcella home,' Josie told him as we were finishing our chips.

'Aye, I will surely.'

I dreaded going out into the cold and back to the house for another sleepless night. Bernie was becoming restless in her last few weeks of pregnancy.

'Or if you like, love, you can sleep here with Josie. I'll bunk in beside the childer.'

'Are you sure you don't mind, PJ?' I asked.

'Not at all. Sure, there's plenty of room.'

There wasn't really, but I said nothing.

I could smell the Bacardi and the fags off Josie when she rolled into the bed beside me.

'Ah, it's great to get lying down.'

'Did youse enjoy yourselves?'

'We'd mighty crack. Met up with all the lassies I used to work with down the factory. There was a gang of them in the Thatch. Headers, they are, the whole bloody lot of them. I must meet up with them more often; they're a great oul laugh.'

'You can go out again tomorrow night, if you like. I don't mind babysitting any time.'

'Marcella Buckley, since when did you turn into Mary fucking Poppins?'

'I'm just saying—'

'Come on. You don't fool me. What's up with you?'

'Nothing.'

'Nothing, me backside. It's home, isn't it? What's going on now?'

I didn't want to start complaining about them all, especially not about Bernie. And especially not to Josie. She'd a fierce gob on her. They'd hear it all back.

'Go on, you can tell me.'

'And you swear you'll not say anything?'

'My lips are sealed. Now, will you go on?'

'Look, I know you think I'm daft taking school so seriously and all, but it's the Inter – it's really important to me.'

'I know.'

'And I need to work really hard.'

'But sure you are, Marcella. For Jesus' sake, you're always at those books.'

'No, I'm not. I mean, I can't.'

'What are you on about? Sure, don't you spend most evenings in that library after school.'

'Not any more. Sister Goretti says she doesn't like to see me cycling home in the dark, and it's dark now these evenings by six o'clock.'

'So, what's wrong with home?'

'Bernie's stuck inside all day with Ma and Da for

86

company, so by the time I get home, she's going up the bloody walls with boredom.'

'Yeah. And?'

'The minute I go upstairs to my bedroom to get my lessons done, she's on my heels chatting, and I don't want to ask her to leave 'cos I'd not like to be in her position myself and if I was, I know she'd be there for me.'

'Huh! If you can't get any peace now, wait till the babby arrives: you'll have no hope, neither day nor night.'

'That's just it – I can't sleep at night either. It's not Bernie's fault or anything, but she's twisting and turning most of the night, trying to get herself comfortable. Or else the baby starts doing bloody cartwheels in her tummy and she nudges me to tell me that she thinks maybe it's on the way.'

'What?' Josie sniggered. 'You mean she thinks a few wee kicks is the start of labour? Ah, God help her foolish wit.'

'What do you mean?'

'I'll put it to you this way, love: when she's in labour, she'll know she's in labour.'

'I saw a woman giving birth on television once. It looked gory.'

'It's no picnic, I'll tell you that. Let's just say, she should practise screaming.'

I was horrified. The thought of Bernie in terrible agony made my stomach muscles tighten with fear. Much as I tried, I just couldn't imagine a baby battling to make its way into the world, down through Bernie's tiny hips. What if it got stuck, trapped in the passage? What if it couldn't get out to draw its first breath? What if Bernie panicked and wasn't able to push? I couldn't see her coping with the pain; it would scare the wits out of her. She'd be screaming and there'd be nobody with her to hold her hand, only some nurse she wouldn't know from a hole in the ground.

'You know what you should do?'

'About what?' I asked, still in a bit of a trance.

'About getting some space for yourself.'

'What?'

'Ask Teresa if you can use her box room.'

'No way.'

'Why not? She'd not mind.'

'I'm not asking that old trollop.'

'Hey, that's Ma's sister you're calling a trollop. And Clint's mother. What the hell is it with you two anyway?'

She had it off with Da at Bernie's wedding, I wanted to tell her. If I had done, Josie would have legged it there and then down to Teresa's and flattened the bitch with a box. I couldn't tell, for Clint's sake . . . for all our sakes, really.

'Is there something you're not telling me?' Josie said.

'No, no. It's just the way she drinks – upsetting Clint like that. She's a fucking useless mother.'

'Ah now, Jaysus, that's going a bit too far. She's mad about that boy, you know she is.'

'Yeah, so she'd like us all to think. It doesn't stop her making his life a bloody misery though, does it?'

'OK, OK, so she's a bit too fond of the booze, I'll grant you that, but she loves her son and there's no denying it. You can't take that away from her, Marcella. Fair is fair.'

'Whatever you think.'

'Anyway, she seems to be laying low these days. According to Ma, she's been on the wagon this past few weeks.'

Exactly three weeks to the day. I knew; I was counting. I was surprised she'd lasted so long, but I was glad for Clint's sake. I didn't relish the thought of telling Ma about the wedding incident either because, if I found it hard to get the dirty deed out of my head, it would be even worse for her. And she'd have nothing else to do but dwell on it and let it drag her down even further. Teresa and I had been avoiding each other since the blackmail, as she called it. I disliked the idea of blackmailing anyone, even Teresa, but I detested the thought of Clint being made to suffer a lot more. So the end did justify the means, just as I'd been struggling to explain in my speech for the debate.

'So how did we get around to talking about the bould Teresa?' Josie asked through a yawn.

'Forget.'

'Ah, here, goodnight, Marcella. I'm knackered.'

'Goodnight.'

'Just do us one favour, will you?'

'What's that?'

'Lighten up, love. You take things far too seriously for a young one.'

Typical – that's what they all thought of me, the whole bloody lot of them: Ma, Da, Josie, Teresa even Bernie. And the more I thought about it, lying there in the dark with Josie's big fat arse parked in my stomach, the more I wondered what the hell they thought was so wrong with taking life seriously. I just couldn't buy into the idea of whatever happens happens, or don't worry about the future it'll take care of itself, or sure aren't we grand as we are? Bullshit. I didn't want to leave my life to chance, falling into potholes and stumbling over humps along the way. Fuck that. My old principal Mr Dermody used to say we should broaden our horizons, and that's exactly what I intended to do. I wanted to take my time, look around me, see a bit of the world, consider my options and then choose my own destination. Josie was snoring away now, not a care in the world, leaving me to wallow in my frustration at not being understood. I needed to sleep. The tiredness was there, but the anger disturbed the sleep and the sleep disturbed the anger. It was probably the fumes of Josie's breath that knocked me unconscious in the end.

I hadn't planned on taking any money off Josie for babysitting. After all, it suited me to get out of the house, and she had bought me chips. But when she handed me two quid, I took it. Not for myself really; for Clint. He was turning thirteen the following week and I wanted to buy him something. I'd be able to pick up a couple of singles with that. I went shopping that afternoon and got 'Hungry Like the Wolf' by Duran Duran, and 'Layla' by Eric Clapton. Even though the rain was now seeping through the shoulders of my denim jacket, I couldn't but smile at the thought of his reaction when he'd open the present.

'Hey, Marcella, come here.' Gabby, my friend from school, was standing at the door of Katie's Coffee Shop. I could see through the window that there was a gang of them in there, Leona O'Brien included, and some lads I'd never seen before.

'Hiya, Gabby,' I said, standing in the porch out of the rain.

'Come on,' she said, dragging me in by the elbow.

Their tables were full of coffee cups, empty ice-cream bowls, full ashtrays. Clint's records had cost 99p each. I had two pence left in my pocket, not even the price of a cup of coffee.

'Another time maybe, Gabby. I'm in a hurry,' I tried to protest, but by then I was standing at a table next to some spotty fella with glasses.

'Hey lads, this is Marcella,' Gabby announced. 'Sit down, will you?'

Leona O'Brien was at the next table, looking the other way, the arm of a fine-looking fella around her shoulder. The bitch. He smiled and nodded at me, but I blanked him. Any guy latching on to that snotty cow wasn't worth speaking to. The spotty fella was grinning at me like an imbecile.

'I'd love to stay, Gabby, but I promised my sister I'd babysit for her,' I lied, trying to sound cool and confident, but really feeling embarrassed and self-conscious.

'I'll keep you company, if you like,' Spotty piped up, sending them all into fits of laughter, Leona's guffaws loudest of all. The wagon.

'No thanks. Two children are more than enough to look after. I don't need a third.'

There was cheering and slagging.

'Hard luck there, four eyes.'

'What's wrong with you, Adrian – the cat got your tongue?'

I caught a glimpse of Leona's boyfriend and realized he was smiling at me or maybe laughing at me, I wasn't sure which. But one way or another, I started to blush profusely. My ears were stinging, I felt like such a moron. It was time to escape. I couldn't bear it any longer.

'I'll see you Monday, Gabby. Have to go.'

'Come on, so, I'll walk you to the door.'

There was a chorus of, 'See you, Marcella,' ''Bye, Marcella,' 'Where have you been all my life, Marcella?' I wasn't sure who said what. I didn't turn to look, just kept heading for the door.

'You'll have to meet up with us next weekend. We always get together here on Saturday afternoons; it's wild crack. The lads are mental.'

'Who are they? I've not seen them around before.'

'Saint Michael's boarders. A few fine things there today, aren't there?' she said, nudging me excitedly.

'Oh yeah.' I laughed. 'That spotty geek really made me go weak at the knees.'

'Ah, poor Adrian. He does his best, the poor eejit. Of course Leona nabbed Cormac, the sexy beast, the very first weekend we met up with them. Isn't he gorgeous?'

'Never noticed,' I lied.

'The fella with the denim shirt and black leather waistcoat. Oh, Marcella, how could you miss him? He's a ride and a half!'

An irate woman with a pram was trying to get past us as we stood in the doorway, the perfect opportunity for me to move.

'Look, I'm away. Talk to you Monday,' I said, stepping out into the street.

As I headed up Fatima Hill, the rain pelted my face. The smoke from the chimneys of all the narrow grey houses blew horizontally over the roofs. It was getting dark, but the street lights were not yet on. The farther I climbed up the hill, the stormier it became, making me gasp for breath. I closed the top button of my jacket and turned up the collar, trying to protect myself from the harshness of the weather. I even walked backwards to keep my eyes from watering. Looking down the hill onto the town again, I started thinking about the gang in the coffee shop: all of them in their best gear, trying to look and act really cool; the girls competing with each other to impress the boys, flashing their smiles and their sexiness. And, of course, Leona gets first prize: the best-looking lad there, the one the other girls will ooooh and aaaaah over, putting her in a position of envy and admiration. I tried to comfort myself by deciding she wasn't all that beautiful, but I couldn't. I thought about the Christmas card my ma had received from a cousin in America when I was about six years old. It had had a beautiful blonde angel on it and I had called her Leona. Every day after school, I'd rearrange all the Christmas cards on the mantelpiece, always placing my angel in the centre. And when the wind blew down the chimney and a big puff of black smoke rose from the hearth and showered my angel with soot, I'd pick her up, wipe her down and place her back on her pedestal. I remembered asking Ma why none of the angels had red hair like me. 'Redheads are too fiery to be angels,' she'd told me.

She never knew how much that had hurt me, scared me even, because the only sense I could make out of her remark at six was that 'fiery' had something to do with fire and hell and the devil and burning for ever. I hated my red hair, and right through primary school had kept it as short as possible. Now, I quite liked it with its unruly curls, a stark contrast to Leona's perfectly straight, silky blonde strands, the likes of which I'd only ever seen on children from well-off families. Why that was I couldn't figure out, but I knew for sure that there wasn't one kid living up Fatima Hill with hair of such a rich and glossy texture.

The street lights flickered and lit up. I could hear a rip-roaring row going on in Number 66 and just as I passed by, the shouting turned to smacking sounds, followed by whimpers. As I backed away from it re-luctantly, a man emerged from the front door and tore down the hill, leaving his sobbing victim to her humiliation. The pig.

'Oh, there she is, Miss Loreto herself.'

I recognized the voice straight away – Cathy Sheridan. She was on her way down the hill with her cousin and Ricky, Noel's younger brother.

'Turning your back on us now, are you?'

'What the fuck are you on about, Cathy?' The silly cow had recently earned herself the nickname Hill's Angel, and by God, did she not love it!

'You, ya high and mighty wee bitch,' she said, standing in front of me, hands on her hips. 'You tink dat poxy Loreto uniform makes you someting special? Well, let me tell you someting—' She was poking me on the shoulder.

'Get your fucking hands off me, Cathy.'

'Make me.'

Jesus, she was really pissing me off now. I could sense Ricky enjoying every minute of this confrontation, standing there with a dirty sneer across his ugly mug.

'Well go on, make me,' she said, still poking at me.

'Cathy, Cathy, your mother's on the way up the hill. Come on,' her cousin said.

'Just remember one ting, Miss Loreto College: once a Buckley always a fucking Buckley. All de education in the world won't change de like of you.'

'Ah, will you cop yourself on?' I said, turning on my heel and walking away.

She said no more. Her mother was within earshot.

Just as I walked into my backyard, the neighbour's

95

cat leapt out suddenly from behind the bin and frightened the shite out of me. Without thinking, I drove my boot straight up its hole and sent it flying. It let a screech out of it like a deranged banshee.

'What the fuck is going on here?' Da muttered, opening the back door.

He looked as if he'd just woken up. I brushed past him, ready to burst into tears, but not wanting him to see me upset.

'Where's Bernie?' I asked.

'Gone down to the doctor's with your ma.'

Damn her, I thought, heading up the stairs. The one time I really needed to talk to her, lean on her. Throwing myself face down on my pillow, I started to sob uncontrollably. I pulled the second pillow over my head to try to drown the sounds of my pathetic sobbing. I cried over Leona with her sleek hair and her gorgeous boyfriend. I cried for the woman in Number 66. I cried over Cathy halfwit Sheridan. I cried over my dirty old sod of a da. And then I went on crying when I rolled over and my two coppers fell out of my jacket pocket onto the bedspread and I realized that I must be the only poor gobshite in the world who literally had just two pence to rub together. Even when I calmed down half an hour later, lying on my tear-soaked pillow, the hiccuping went on and on until exhaustion finally took over and I fell asleep.

I could hear the signature music to *Dallas* when I woke up, so it was either just starting or just over. I should have been hungry because I'd had no tea, but I wasn't. All I felt now was raw, fresh anger. Anger that gave me energy, ideas, vengeful thoughts. I pulled a copybook from my schoolbag. 'War is never justified!' I scrawled at the top of the page and I just kept on writing.

Two-thirds in favour of the motion! I couldn't believe it; I was sickened. Having to endure the smug expression on Leona's face was making defeat that extra bit harder to bear. I tried not to let it get to me. As I travelled home on the school bus, I considered the wisdom of Josie's advice not to take things so seriously, and was beginning to calm down by the time we reached town. But, as I stepped off the bus, I overheard one of my classmates sucking up to Leona, saying, 'The best team won in the end. Your speech was fantastic.'

Feck Josie and her crappy advice, I thought, as I stormed up the hill in a rage; no one will ever get the better of me.

That was my state of mind when I plodded in through the back door on the Monday evening and sent my school bag flying across the sitting room.

'Jesus Christ Almighty, who the fuck rattled your cage?' Da roared, poking his head out over the top of the armchair. The school bag had landed with a thump into the coal bucket straight in front of him. He'd been slumped down in the armchair, out of sight.

'Sorry, Da,' I said, trying not to explode with laughter at the state of the dopey-looking head on him.

'You frightened the bejaysus out of me. What the hell is wrong with you?'

'Our team lost the debate at school today. I'm pissed off.'

'Oh, I see. Lost your debate, did you? Well, sit your arse down here right now, madam, because you're about to lose another one,' he shouted, nodding towards the other armchair.

'All right, all right. Keep your hair on.'

'Don't give me any of your oul guff, Marcella,' he said, pointing his finger at me. 'You just listen to me and don't open that cheeky gob until I'm finished talking.'

Me and Da rarely had a conversation. And when we did, it was usually an argument, but I'd never felt frightened of him before. This was different. We weren't on a level pegging. He had already assumed the role of aggressor, determined to impose his will. When my bum hit the armchair, I felt as though I'd been pushed down into it, even though he hadn't touched me.

'I've had two very upset women here today. Your ma and Teresa. Now, for some reason, your ma thinks Teresa is avoiding her.'

'Huh!'

'Don't open your mouth, smart aleck, just listen. I arrived home at lunchtime to find the pair of them in tears in the kitchen, your ma accusing Teresa of deserting her and not calling to see her as often as she used to. Poor Teresa's trying to tell her that it's nothing to do with your ma, that she's feeling a bit down these days herself. When she leaves, your ma says she doesn't believe her. She's in a very distressed state.'

'So? What's that got to do with me?' I asked, worrying where all this was heading and feeling frustrated at not being allowed to speak.

'Shut up,' he roared, standing up and towering over me, making me feel so intimidated I wanted to cry. I tried hard to push back the tears, not wanting to show him any signs of weakness.

'Now, I call down to Teresa in the afternoon to try to find out what's wrong with her and what do you think I discover?'

I said nothing.

'Well?' he shouted. 'Answer me.'

'You told me not to speak.'

'Jaysus, Marcella, don't push me.'

I knew what he meant: don't push me or I'll hit you. He didn't have to say it, I just knew by his body language, his squared shoulders, his bent elbows, his legs apart, his head tilted forward, eyes like daggers.

'I'd a row with her a couple of weeks ago,' I told him, trying but failing miserably to make my voice sound confident and strong.

'Correct. And what would this row have been about then?'

'I can't remember the details.'

'*Try.*'

'Em . . . em . . . about her drinking.'

'And what were you going to do about it?'

'I think she's already told you that, Da.'

'Oh, she's told me all right, and now I'm telling you. You leave Teresa alone from now on and don't be trying to drive a wedge between the two sisters. Your ma needs Teresa: she's a good friend to her.'

'No, she's not. Aggie Clarke is Ma's only true friend.'

'This argument is not about Aggie Clarke. It's about you having the gall to stick your nose in Teresa's business.'

'I was looking out for Clint, that's all,' I said, half crying.

'If Clint has a problem with his mother, it's up to him to sort it out, not you, you silly little bitch. Now you've already got your pound of flesh over that incident at the wedding and—'

'Incident. Is that what you call it?'

I'd no sooner blurted it out than I realized it wasn't the cleverest of questions to put to a man on the verge of flipping his bap. I squirmed. But then his foot changed direction and the coal bucket got the full force of his wrath, which by now had reached its crescendo. There was coal everywhere, scattered all over the fireplace and on the carpet; there were even big marks on the wallpaper where a few lumps had hit the wall. Tears were streaming silently down my face. I was afraid to make a sound.

'Don't you ever, ever, blackmail Teresa again. Don't you mention Bernie's wedding to her or to anyone else, and don't you dare badmouth Teresa to Clint. I mean, who the fuck do you think you are anyway?'

'I just felt bad for my ma and Clint, that's all.'

'Don't give me that! You used that situation to suit

yourself, you selfish yoke. You didn't keep your gob buttoned for your ma's sake.'

'I could have told her, but I just didn't want to hurt her.'

'You knew well she'd not have thanked you for telling her. And what about Clint? How do you think he'd feel if he heard you were blackmailing his mother and lashing insults at her along with it? Well?'

'I care about Clint.'

'And you think his mother doesn't?'

I wanted to argue, to try to explain how angry I sometimes felt when I saw the people I loved being treated badly. But he was right: this was one argument I wasn't going to win, so all I wanted was for it to be over.

'He's *her* son, *her* responsibility and *her* fucking business. Not yours. And I'll tell you something else: she's doing a lot better job on him than your ma's doing on you, you brazen bitch.'

'Right, right, I'll not say anything to her again. Can I go now?'

'You don't move. I'll go, and when I do, you clear up that mess. Just one last warning: any more buck from you and out that door you'll go, you and your fucking Loreto uniform, and you'll not get back, believe you me. I don't make idle threats. Got it?'

'Yeah.'

As he headed towards the door, I realized what hatred meant and it frightened me. Sure, I thought I'd hated him before that moment; in fact, I thought

I'd always hated him, but no, that was dislike, disgust, lack of respect. This was different. This hatred felt like a living, breathing, ugly monster.

'And apologize to Teresa by the end of the week. I'll be checking.'

Then he was gone.

From that day on, I did what I was told. He had won, at least in the short term. But the hatred remained as sizzling-hot as ever, staring me in the face everywhere I turned. I didn't know what to do with it, how to offload it, so I accepted it, welcomed it even, in all its ugliness, and began to use it as a shield to protect myself from all the pain a family can cause. I'd love to have walked out that day for good, but I had nowhere to go. I'd love to have told Ma what had happened, so she'd throw him out, but I knew she wouldn't have. The only way I could survive my family – the fear, the hatred and the love – was to separate myself from them, if not physically, then emotionally. And that I did.

From Monday to Friday, I'd spend the evenings in the town library studying, until it closed at six. I got myself a Saturday job in Katie's Coffee Shop, so I could hang out with the girls from school and their boarder friends. Most Sundays I'd try to stay in my bedroom while Bernie was out or downstairs; otherwise, I'd call down to see Josie. Da started to speak to me again a little bit, probably feeling I'd learned my lesson and pulled back my horns. Sometimes Ma would tell me to make him his tea and I'd do it, knowing that one day, when I'd be free of all the mess, I could walk away and never make him tea again. I spoke to no one about the row. I apologized to Teresa, as he'd told me to. She said she was sorry too and she'd never meant to get me into trouble. Lying tramp. As for Clint, I tried to remain as friendly as I could with him without getting involved. He'd just have to fight his own corner. I was staying out of it.

'You're very quiet,' Bernie would say to me from time to time.

I'd have liked to confide in her, but I felt she couldn't have coped with any more hassle. I figured that as long as there were no rows in the house, Bernie would settle down at home and stay away from Noel.

Josie organized a girls' night out at the bingo one Monday evening. Seemingly, there was a big jackpot to be won down in Ballylogan, thirty miles away.

'It'll do Ma good to get out of the house,' she said.

They were all set to head off for the minibus at seven o'clock, leaving me alone with Da, when Bernie announced she was having second thoughts: she felt tired and dizzy.

'Ah, come on to fuck,' Josie told her. 'You'll be grand. Sure, you're not due for another three weeks yet.'

'Don't be daft, Josie,' I said. 'If she's feeling dizzy, the last thing she needs is an hour's bus journey.'

So Bernie stayed and, as it turned out, it was just as well because within a couple of hours her waters had broken and she started labour. I was upstairs doing my homework when I heard my father say, 'Holy Jaysus, not tonight of all fucking nights,' and then Bernie's panicky voice, 'Oh, help, Da, it's coming. The baby's coming!'

I raced down the stairs to find Bernie leaning across the back of the armchair groaning, and Da rooting in the change jar to find ten pence to phone for an ambulance.

'Never mind that, Da,' I said. 'If you run down and get Charlie Clarke, it'll be quicker.'

'You go. You're a lot faster than I am,' he said. 'But get your skates on, will you?'

I ran all the way there, whispering to myself, 'Still hate you, you bollocks. Still hate you, always will, macho creep, ugly fucking bollocks, I'll have the last laugh, you'll see . . .'

Even in a crisis, when Bernie should have been the only one on my mind, I was determined to keep my guard up and not be swept away by the strength of emotion that surrounded this situation. Any time I got the chance, I'd secretly indulge my hatred, nurture it, smile at it. So when Charlie answered the door he said, 'You look like a very happy girl.'

I snapped out of it, got back into action and dealt with the crisis.

My father didn't even bother to get off his arse to come with us. He just told me to ring him at the Horse and Jockey if there was any news. Bernie was whisked away as soon as we got to the hospital, leaving me pacing the corridor outside the delivery ward alone, cringing every time I heard her cry out.

'Are you sure she's all right?' I asked the nurse, who'd been in and out of the swing doors several times.

'Yes,' she said. 'She shouldn't be too long now.'

'Marcella,' I heard someone call and when I turned round, I saw Noel and his mother, Lizzie, rushing down the corridor towards me.

'What are youse doing here?' I asked.

'What do you think?' Lizzie said. 'My Noel has a right to be here when his wife's about to have his baby, or did she have it yet?'

'No, she didn't.'

'You can piss off home now. There's no need for you to stay,' he piped up.

'Bernie doesn't want him around,' I said to Lizzie, ignoring the arrogant creep. 'She'd freak if she knew he was here.'

Your man sniggered before announcing that Bernie had in fact told him, just a few days before, that she wanted him there when the baby was born.

'Go on, go and axe her,' Lizzie said, 'if you don't believe him.'

Dirty liars, I thought. They couldn't possibly be telling the truth. Bernie hadn't spoken to him for weeks, not to my knowledge anyway.

'I can't ask her now, can I?' I said. 'But if I did, I know well what she'd say. If she'd wanted him here, she'd have told me on the way to the hospital.'

'Are you calling us liars?' Lizzie eyeballed me, raising

both her voice and the ears of the other people in the waiting area.

'Just ignore the stupid cow,' Noel told his mother. 'I'm going down to the smoking room for a fag. Are you coming?'

She followed him, wagging her finger at me as if to tell me she hadn't finished with me yet. I waited until they were out of sight, then made my way to the phone and rang the Horse and Jockey.

'Well, what's the news?' Da asked.

'The baby's not born yet, but Lizzie and Noel Doyle have just showed up and—'

Bleep, bleep, bleep.

I could just imagine him, bulling his way out through the crowd in the pub, swearing under his breath. Lizzie and Noel came back out to the waiting area a minute later and Lizzie enquired from one of the nurses if there was any news about Mrs Noel Doyle.

'Who?'

'Bernie Doyle, me daughter-in-law.'

'Bernie Doyle, Bernie Doyle,' the nurse was muttering to herself, obviously trying to figure out who this woman was talking about.

'It's Bernie Buckley,' I said.

'Doyle.'

'Buckley.'

'Doyle.'

'Buckley.'

'Yes, yes, Bernie Buckley. She's still in the labour ward,' the nurse said.

'We know that,' Lizzie said angrily, 'but will it be much longer or—'

'As soon as there's any news, we'll let you know.'

Oh, hang on in there, Bernie, I prayed, for just another few minutes until Da arrives. The last thing I wanted was Noel getting in to see Bernie and the baby and trying to soften her up when she was vulnerable.

Lizzie started filling in some old nosy biddy on the ins and outs and ups and downs of Noel's marriage to Bernie.

'They were always against my Noel, that lot. Never gave him a chance.'

'That's a fright.'

'The father's a bit of a lunatic. You know him, don't you – Jimmy Buckley.'

'Ah, say no more.'

A bit of a lunatic! You mean a total fucking lunatic, I thought.

'A fierce interfering lot, them Buckleys. Weren't satisfied till they'd split them up.'

'That's a holy shame.'

'You seem to be forgetting one very important detail, Lizzie,' I announced, loud enough for the rest of the curious audience to hear. 'The fact that your son is a wife-beater.'

'Shut your dirty little trap,' she hissed at me, as Noel stormed off in a huff. 'Now look what you've done, upsetting the lad like that.'

'The truth hurts, doesn't it?'

I could see the heads of the spectators turning from me to Lizzie and back to me.

'That black eye she got was an accident. Nothing to do with my Noel, and well youse know it.'

All the faces were staring at me now, waiting for a response. But, before I had the chance to open my mouth, they turned in the direction of a whole lot of commotion that had erupted down the corridor. A nurse came racing along, shouting to her colleagues to page a couple of the porters for help, saying that a row had just broken out at the hospital entrance.

'I think it's your son,' she told Lizzie. 'You'd better go and see if you can sort it out.'

'Oh, Jesus, Mary and Joseph, help us,' she cried, running off and waving her arms.

I didn't follow, just sat where I was, doing my level best to hold back an evil little smirk that was trying hard to grace my face with its presence.

The labour-ward door swung open again and this time the nurse headed in my direction.

'Marcella,' she said, smiling at me, 'your sister's just had a beautiful little girl. You can come in now.'

Teresa

I was beginning to get used to Mary's mood swings. She was becoming predictably unpredictable, so I didn't bother my barney arguing with her when she started making excuses about not being up to visiting Bernie the morning after she'd had her baby.

'Bernie Buckley?' I asked at reception.

'Saint Anne's Ward. Second on the right.'

Youse sneaky bastards, I thought, when I saw Noel, Lizzie and Noel Doyle senior all sitting round the bed, Lizzie with the baby in her arms.

'The pure spit of her father, Teresa,' she announced.

'Hiya, Teresa,' Bernie said. She looked worn out.

For a few seconds, I was speechless.

'Yes, darlin', you are – you're just like your daddy,' Lizzie blabbed into the baby's face.

'Your da and ma will be here in two minutes, love,' I said to Bernie. 'They just stopped off at the shop for a couple of bits and pieces they thought you might need.'

'Come on, woman,' Noel senior said dourly, 'it's time we left.'

'I'll not be threatened by the likes of Jimmy Buckley,' Lizzie retorted. 'Bloody madman.'

'Yes,' I said, 'only today he's a madman with a bee in his bonnet and a sockin' hangover.'

Bernie was looking very uncomfortable, poor thing. Noel pushed his chair back and stomped off like a child in a huff, the ignorant little runt, not even bothering to say: I'd better go, see you later, take care of yourself, kiss me arse, or goodbye. Lizzie went to put the baby back in her cot.

'I'll take her,' I said, my arms outstretched.

Noel senior was at the end of the bed with his jacket on.

'Mind yourself, daughter,' Lizzie said to Bernie, 'and think about what I said.'

I wondered what she was up to, the conniving bitch.

'Congratulations, petal,' I said, bending down to kiss Bernie, as soon as they'd left.

'Thanks, Teresa,' she said, in a shaky voice.

'Are you OK, love?'

'They said once the baby was born, I'd forget about the pain. They were wrong,' she told me, her bottom lip quivering. 'It was terrible, Teresa; I thought I was going to die.'

I put the baby back in her cot, drew the curtains around the bed, sat down next to Bernie and held her in my arms, trying to give her some of the comfort that I had longed for back in London, when Clint was born.

'That's it,' I whispered, 'let it all out.'

She said nothing, she didn't need to, just cried a bucketful.

'Oh God, I hope they don't run into Ma and Da on their way out,' she said finally, wiping her tears on her nightdress sleeve.

'Sorry, love,' I said, handing her a tissue; 'they're not

on their way at all. Your ma had a bit of a headache this morning.'

'Oh.'

'Just thought you'd want rid of that Doyle lot. Bloody cheek of them, turning up like that.'

She didn't respond, just looked at me with her big brown sad eyes, like a lost child.

'You didn't want them here, did you?'

'Dunno. I'm not sure what I want any more.'

'Bernie, don't let them get to you. You and that little lassie there, youse will be all right on your own. Because Noel won't change. The likes of him never do, and believe you me, I should know.'

'Lizzie says the baby will be the making of us and that she'll help us out any way she can.'

'Lizzie's the two ends of a gobshite; she'll say whatever it takes to soft-soap you.'

I could see the girl was distressed and confused, and that maybe with her hormones all over the place it wasn't the best of times to be trying to sort her out.

'Look, love,' I said, nestling the baby back in my arms, 'we'll talk about it some other time. Let's just concentrate on the one good thing that has come out of all of this – your wee girl.' I kissed the sleeping babe on the forehead.

'You'll not tell my da they were here, then?'

'Not if you don't want me to.'

'Promise me, Teresa, please.'

'I promise.'

*

Little Amanda Josephine arrived home to Fatima Hill the following Saturday.

'Will Amanda not know her father, the same way as I don't know mine?' Clint asked me, after his first visit to see his cousin.

I dreaded those awkward questions, not knowing where they were going to lead.

'Well, it's a bit different, pet. Amanda's father lives down the street from Bernie so, although Bernie and Noel don't live together, she'll still know who her father is.'

'She's lucky.'

'Damn the bit of her is lucky, having a father like Noel Doyle. He's a wrong one, the same fella.'

'So if we hadn't moved back from London, I'd know my father, would I?'

'Maybe, maybe not. I don't really know how things would have panned out for us in London. But I'll tell you one thing: I've absolutely no regrets about bringing you home.'

'Still, I sometimes wonder what he's like.'

'I wish to God I'd never got to know what *my* father was like,' I said, that creepy feeling beginning to descend upon me again.

'Was he never nice to youse, Mam?'

'Nice? It's not a word that comes to mind, although sometimes he'd pretend to be half decent.'

'How do you mean?'

'He'd act all nice if someone called to the front door, or if a neighbour was in visiting, or when he'd want me to . . .'

'What, Mam?'

I could almost hear his voice again. 'Come on, girl,' he'd say to me, when my ma would have us all ready for Mass, 'you stay behind and mind your old da.' And I'd look at Ma and she'd say, 'It's all right. Be a good girl now and I'll bring you back some sweets.' And I'd say, 'Will you get bullseyes, Ma?' And she'd say, 'I will.'

I could feel a lone tear meandering down my cheek.

'Mam, what's wrong?'

'I'm just thinking that the only time I ever saw my da look happy, no maybe not happy . . . satisfied, was when he'd made the rest of us feel miserable. Isn't that a shockin' way to be?'

'Well, I hate him then.'

'You see, love, some people are just born bad and that Noel boy, he's one of them . . . just like my da. And Bernie, she'd not be able to protect Amanda on her own.'

'If Granda Reilly was still alive, I wouldn't even visit him because I know he made you sad.' He came over and wrapped his arms around me. 'You're the best mam in the world,' he said with such honest affection that I burst into tears over both the utter joy that comes from loving a son and the complete misery that remains from having loathed a father.

'Pande-fucking-monium,' was how Jimmy described the state of affairs in the Buckley household over the next few weeks.

Mary was lamenting about her life, her nerves, her lack of energy and about the fact that Bernie wasn't taking too well to motherhood and was constantly trying to pass Amanda on to anyone who'd take her. Sometimes she'd disappear for an hour or two, without saying where she was going and without appointing anyone in particular to look after the child.

Jimmy was calling round to see me more often, giving out stink about the lot of them, looking for his bit of consolation.

'All the years I've been riding you,' he said, stretching out on my bed one afternoon while Clint was at school, 'and we haven't once had the chance to spend a whole night together. Isn't that a terra?'

It wasn't the sort of thing I'd have expected Jimmy to come out with. Right from the start, it had always been a 'seize the moment' kind of relationship.

'But, sure, there's no need. We're all right as we are, aren't we?'

'If I had my way, it's you I'd be climbing into bed with every night, not herself.'

At sixteen years of age, that would have been music to my ears. Back then I was besotted with the man, had been since I was ten years old when I saw him as the knight in shining armour who had come and rescued Mary from my da. Death finally rescued me from that evil man, but not even our permanent separation could protect me from the guilt, the pain and the shame. They were my secret, my sin, the part of me that was bad and dirty, the part that no man could wash away, not even Jimmy Buckley.

*

114

As a kid, Christmas had always made me feel nervous, because my ma would be in a flap, fussing around my da, trying to humour him. She'd be doing her mightiest to give us a good time, while he'd be doing his damnedest to ruin her efforts. And although, since I'd had Clint, Christmas had always been a great time for us, the anxiety about the whole occasion never left me. So when I went down the town one Saturday evening in December and saw the array of lights, I felt the same rush of nervous excitement that I used to feel twenty years before. On the one hand, it was the sweet expectation that everything could be perfect; on the other, it was the cold, shivery feeling that everything would not be.

As I was passing Katie's Coffee Shop, I wondered if I should drop in for a cuppa. Maybe Marcella would see it as an effort on my part to patch things up between us. I decided it was best not to dwell on it, knowing that time spent mulling it over would lead to finding lots of reasons to walk on by. So I marched on in thinking, here goes and fuck the consequences.

Marcella turned as soon as she heard the door open and glanced at me indifferently, as if I were a stranger. There were only two tables occupied: at one, a pair of old dolls were having a chinwag; at the other was a young lad, good-looking, trendy. She sauntered over to me with a notepad, after I'd sat down.

'Can I help you?'

'I'll have a coffee, please, Marcella.'

'Right.'

'And a scone.'

'Would you like the scone heated?' she asked me in a deadpan voice.

'Oh, lovely. Yeah, thanks.'

At least she was civil. Cold but civil. I would have liked a few friendly words, a bit of recognition, even a smile, but civility, I thought, was a start. I couldn't help but notice that the young lad never took his eyes off Marcella.

'Do you want a top-up there, Cormac?' she said as she went past him with my tray.

'Yeah. Thanks, Marcie.'

Marcie! Very cute and cosy. As the place got busier, his eyes continued to follow her as she walked between the tables. Whether she knew it or not, he had fallen for her, hook, line and bloody sinker. And I could see why. She had that haughty confidence which came as naturally to her as it did to a peacock. Her body was sexy: all the curves in the right places. To top it all, her long curly red hair made her look 100-per-cent rock chick. She was unaware of him watching her, and in his smitten state he was oblivious of me watching him watching her.

Then to my disappointment, a girl of about Marcella's age strolled in, kissed your man straight on the lips and plonked herself down beside him.

'Are you here long?' she asked him.

'Five minutes,' he lied. 'What are you having?'

'A coffee.'

'Right.'

He got up, asked Marcella for the coffee and headed

for the jacks. While he was there, she brought it over to the young lassie. They barely spoke. In fact, whatever passed their lips sounded more like the utterance of two sulky pigs.

'Would you like a refill?' she asked me.

'Yes, please. Thanks, love.'

'I thought you might say that.' She sighed, as if disappointed.

The young lad came back and, while he managed to keep the conversation going with the girl, he didn't succeed in concealing his interest in Marcella.

'What do you keep looking at *her* for?' the girl said. 'Do you want to order something else?'

'No, no, I'm all right.'

'Well then, keep your eyes on me, not on Miss Hungry Hill.'

Vicious little toerag, I thought.

'Leona, don't be such a snob.'

'I'm not a snob. I'm just fussy who I keep company with. She was in my class in primary school. You should have seen the state of her clothes, and the dirt of her fingernails – oooh gross!'

My hands were shaking with temper. I wanted to grab the little bitch by the hair and duck her head in a toilet bowl, but I had to hold my tongue. Marcella wouldn't thank me for sticking my oar in.

'Hey!' the lad said. 'Give the girl a break. I like her. She's cool.'

'Cool! I don't think so, Cormac. I mean the way she tries to fit in with our crowd – it's pathetic.'

Marcella had gone into the kitchen, so I made my move. I grabbed my jacket, walked over to the table, stood facing the girl and said, 'The only pathetic thing, Lady Muck, is that the likes of a toffee-nosed little bitch like you would think for one minute that you could ever compare yourself to the likes of her. Isn't that right, Cormac?' I said, turning to him.

I didn't wait for their shocked silence to pass, just flung my jacket over my shoulder, stuck my nose in the air and left with a smile that stayed on my face the whole way home.

'It's snowing, Mam, look,' Clint told me, drawing back my bedroom curtains on Christmas morning. 'Happy Christmas.'

'You too, love,' I said through a yawn, my eyes trying to adjust to the sudden brightness. There he was, my boy, standing with his back to the window, snowflakes falling behind him, excitement in his voice, a smile on his face.

'You know what, son: you're one hell of a handsome dude. Did anyone ever tell you that?'

'Stop, Mam. That's pure embarrassing, that is.'

'You should prepare yourself for the stampede.'

'What stampede?'

'The stampede of young lassies trying to break their way through my front gate in a couple of years time when you're old enough for the bit of coortin'.'

'Coortin'! I thought that was something they did in the olden days, like when *you* were young.'

'Hey! You cheeky wee beggar.'

'Come on, get up, will you? I'm going down to open my presents,' he said, walking away, smiling contentedly.

I felt good that morning, better than I had done in quite a while. Apart from not having another half-dozen kids and a corny husband, I could have been Mrs Walton herself out in the kitchen stuffing my chicken in my pinny and humming 'White Christmas', as I stared at the heart-shaped framed photo Clint had given me of both of us. Me and him. Our family portrait.

It all went hunky-dory until we were making our way back up the hill after Mass, Clint trying to scrape up the makings of a snowball off the car bonnets, me still recovering from hearing the children's choir singing 'Away in a Manger', which always made me cry.

'Me ma wants to know if you'll be calling into the Buckleys'?' Ricky Doyle said, standing at his front door.

'What does she want to know for?'

'She wants you to give these to the child,' he said, turning and picking up some parcels from the hall table.

I considered it for a second, feeling a twinge of sympathy for the old tart not getting to see her grandchild on Christmas Day, but then I had Mary to think about and the row that might erupt if Jimmy took it the wrong way.

'Och, I'd rather not get involved. It's up to—'

'You bitch,' he spat. 'Me ma's right about you. Tramp.'

'Your ma should have drowned you at birth, you cheeky bugger. You were an ugly wee runt then and fifteen or sixteen years on you're still the same – a slithery little slimeball.'

'Shut up, tramp. Me ma told us about you. She says Jimmy Buckley's bound to be getting his leg over, all the traipsing in and out of your house he does.'

'She's a lying whore, your mother,' I roared, making a swing for him with my brolly, but he jumped back, laughing, and slammed the door in my face. I was so angry, I hadn't even turned around to see Clint's reaction to what he'd just heard. I was about to press my finger on the Doyles' doorbell when he touched my shoulder.

'Don't, Mam, please. I know he's lying; he's always causing trouble. Hughie says he's a fucking wanker, 'cos Ricky always calls him a four-eyed blind bastard. Hughie really hates him and one day . . .'

Clint continued with his story, but I got stuck at the one day: one day Clint will catch me with Jimmy and never speak to me again; one day Mary will wake up out of her trance and cop on to the way Jimmy looks at me; one day Marcella will get even and tell Josie about the wedding and I'll end up toothless; one day I'll get exactly what I deserve and . . .

'Mam, are you going to tell Uncle Jimmy about Ricky Doyle?'

'No, son. Let's just forget about it. It's Christmas. It's no time for fighting. Right?'

'Right.'

'I love you.'

'You too, Mam.'

We stood outside Mary's back door and heard a chorus of crying from within. We looked at each other and laughed, not that it was one bit funny really. It was more an automatic nervous reaction to what sounded like a crisis.

'Look at the state of me fuckin' hoorin' bastardin' turkey,' Mary wailed, as we entered the kitchen.

Clint slipped past me quickly and went into the sitting room, where Amanda was struggling in her mother's arms, her tiny face hot and red from the crying. Jimmy was sitting watching the telly, looking all hot and bothered too. I could hear Marcella's footsteps upstairs.

'It's ruined, Teresa, it's fucking ruined.' Mary sobbed. 'I'm a useless dope so I am, I—'

'Will you calm down, for Jesus' sake. It's only a fucking turkey. Here, let me have a look.'

It was a disaster all right. Burnt on the outside, still that purply-pink colour in the middle. There was no way to rescue the big bird: he was well and truly fucked.

'Open the door there,' I told her, wrapping the tinfoil back around the fowl.

'What are you doing?' She sniffled.

'Never mind. Just open it.'

She obeyed and, before she had a chance to utter another word, I ran to the bin in the yard and pegged the bird into it.

'There you go,' I said, coming back inside and leading her into the sitting room to sit her down. 'No more fuckin' hoorin' bastardin' turkey to worry about.'

They all turned and stared at me: him, the contrary

cock on the couch; Bernie, the troubled teenager with the baby in tow; and him, my blushing, bashful boy. Even Marcella appeared downstairs to see what all the silence was about.

'That's it,' I said. 'Dinner's at my house.'

It had all been too much for Mary, who was in no mood for eating and was relieved to see the back of the lot of them and get a few hours' kip.

'And what about yourself, Jimmy? Will you stay here and keep an eye on Mary?' I asked.

'Do I have any fucking choice?' he grumbled, pulling a can of corned beef out of the press.

'Arragh, will you give over? Haven't you a fridge full of beer, the makings of a plate of sandwiches and all the films on the box you could watch in a day? What more could you ask for?' I said, putting Amanda in her pram. She was fast asleep by the time we got to my house.

'That was always a great way to get you off to sleep – a wee walk in the pram,' I told Clint.

I could tell he was delighted having company for dinner, especially Marcella, who was a little less frosty with me than usual.

Somehow the incident earlier on with Ricky Doyle drifted to the back of my mind, having been overshadowed by the more urgent business of trying to make the most of Christmas Day.

'You make lovely stuffing, Teresa,' Bernie said, obviously enjoying her meal.

'Yeah, it's really nice,' Marcella agreed.

'Thanks,' I said, smiling, wondering whether or not she had decided to let bygones be bygones.

'How's that Cormac fella?' I asked her, after I'd had a couple of glasses of wine and felt brave enough.

She was hard to embarrass, the same lassie, but this time I'd done it. Blushed from the neck up she did and, for a moment, I thought I'd blown it.

'Cormac who?'

'Your man who calls to see you in the coffee shop. Him with the wavy fair hair and the cheeky grin. Him that calls you Marcie.'

'Tell us more,' Bernie said.

'Nothing to tell really. He's a boarder at Saint Michael's who comes into town every Saturday to meet his *girlfriend*, Leona O'Brien.'

'So you don't fancy him then?' I said, knowing by the glint in her eye that she was quite happy, even excited, to be talking about him.

'No I don't,' she protested weakly. 'He's a friend, that's all.'

'Is he one of the fellas in the show?' Clint asked her.

'What show is this?' I asked.

'*My Fair Lady*,' Marcella said. 'It's on at Saint Michael's next month. He's Henry Higgins, the leading man, and Leona, his *girlfriend*, is Eliza Doolittle, the leading lady.'

'Oh, I absolutely loved that film,' I said. 'Audrey Hepburn was fantastic. Are you going to be in it?'

'I am,' she told me proudly.

'Good woman yourself,' I said.

'She's getting fierce posh, our Marcella, taking part in a musical,' Bernie said.

'Shut up. It's no big deal. I'm only in the chorus.'

'So you didn't fancy the Eliza Doolittle part then?' I asked, thinking that she could be a right good little actress. And she could sing too; she'd got that off her da.

'I did audition for it, but they gave the part to Leona. Worse luck.'

'Is she any good, this Leona one?'

'She can sing all right, but she can't act. Stiff as a poker, she is.'

'Yeah, I saw her with himself, yon day in the coffee shop. She looked a right fucking po-face.'

'Oh, a real Miss Goody Two Shoes. I don't know what he sees in her.'

'Eliza Screwlittle, that's what youse should call her,' I said.

'Mam!' Clint shouted out in shock and then burst out laughing along with the others.

I was merry by the evening, happy and merry. Bernie had had a glass too many and was fast asleep in front of the TV. Marcella listened patiently to every song Clint wanted her to hear on his Walkman and then played his new game, Escape from Colditz, with him in the kitchen. I stayed out of their way, knowing Clint was enjoying having a smoke behind my back. I changed and fed Amanda, examining every tiny little finger and toe, held her close to my face and inhaled that beautiful baby smell of warm milk, comfort and innocence. Then

I cradled her in my arms, her tiny head resting on my cheek like a ball of velvet. She lay there contented, breathing her peacefulness into my chest, my heart. For a while, I felt happy and almost worthy of that happiness.

With what I had in mind to do on New Year's Eve, I felt entitled to a stiff drink, although it was only half past eleven in the morning. Subconsciously, I think the shock of Ricky Doyle's accusations on Christmas morning had triggered off the beginning of the end for me and Jimmy.

I'd not had a drink at that hour since the last big row with Clint, over two months earlier. But these were special circumstances: a bit of Dutch courage was essential for what lay ahead. Anyone having to face Jimmy Buckley would have felt the same way. He wasn't going to make it easy for me, I knew that, the fecker, but I'd have to persuade him that ending our affair was best for everyone.

Fuck you, Jimmy, I'll miss you, I thought, pouring another generous shot of vodka into my mug.

I was going to miss the sex, but not just the sex itself: it was the waiting for it, the longing, followed by the heat of the moment and the hurried, fierce passion. Still, I thought, better be without all that than to ruin my relationship with my sister, my nieces and, most of all, my son.

Later on that evening, Marcella called for Clint, as planned, to take him to his first youth-club disco.

'You'll keep a good eye on him, won't you?' I said, putting my hand on her shoulder.

'He's only going down the town for a couple of hours, not to Timbuk-fucking-tu.' She eyed me suspiciously, maybe even copping on to the few scoops I'd had earlier.

When I hugged Clint and wished him luck, she shook her head and rolled her eyes to heaven.

'Some day,' I told her, 'you'll have a kid of your own and you'll understand how I feel.'

'Me, a kid? Spare me. Come on, Clint, before she has a nervous breakdown,' she said, throwing his peaked cap at him.

They headed for the gate, sniggering. I was glad me and Marcella were on good terms again. I'd hated all that aggro between us. It had bugged the hell out of me, because underneath it all I knew she was a good kid – brazen, temperamental, bitchy, but good.

'I don't want you thinking I've forgotten what happened, Teresa,' she'd said late on Christmas night, when I asked her if she could forgive me, 'but I don't want to be fighting with you any more either so, yeah, I do forgive you, I suppose.'

'Oh, Marcella,' I said, reaching out to hug her, but she withdrew, saying, 'Although what you saw in the hairy bastard in the first place is beyond my wildest imagination.'

Well, the hairy bastard would be arriving in half an hour and I was as nervous as a bag of kittens. The effects of the few drinks I'd had earlier on were beginning to wear off. Another one, I thought, might do the business, calm me down a bit.

You can do it, Teresa, I told myself several times over, while I paced the kitchen floor, chain-smoking and having the odd swig to keep the old courage topped up. When I heard him at the back door, I was tempted to make a dive for the front door and disappear down to the pub, where I wouldn't have to deal with the problem.

'God, but you're looking fierce sexy,' he said, rubbing his palms together.

'Now hang on a minute there, Jimmy,' I told him as he made a grab for me. 'We need to talk.'

'Ah, now, Teresa, Teresa, not all this again. Come on. God but I've been looking forward to this all day,' he said, making another move on me.

'Buck,' I said, that's what I sometimes called him in private, 'please, will you listen? It's important and I need you to—'

'You smell lovely, Teresa. You're driving me wild. Will you shut up, for fuck's sake?' he said, pinning me up against the wall and kissing me furiously.

I kissed him back, trying not to get carried away, trying to think what to do. Maybe it was best to let him go ahead, have a bit of fun; he'd listen to me then, when he wasn't so wound up, so distracted, so fucking horny. He was at the buttons of my blouse now, pulling at them impatiently, and I was weakening, on the verge of submitting myself to his lust, my lust. Come on, Teresa, I thought, pull yourself together.

'Get up them stairs quick,' he panted.

'But Jimmy—'

'But Jimmy nothing. I need you now. Come on,' he said, lifting me up and throwing me over his shoulder, like some sort of caveman. All I could do at that moment was laugh as he staggered all the way up the stairs and landed me on the bed.

'There you are,' he said afterwards. 'I knew I'd put a smile on your face.'

It was so bloody hard to finish with Jimmy. He just wasn't going to let it happen, and I lay there wondering how I could possibly go through with it, while he cuddled into me and went for a snooze.

I started to think about Clint again, and Mary and her girls. I prayed for strength, said one Hail Mary after another – the flipping cheek of me after what I'd just done.

'I know,' I said, looking at the picture of the Blessed Virgin hanging on my wall, 'that you probably think I'm a right brazen hussy talking to you now, and me lying here bare-arsed in the bed, but I'm trying, I really am, and if you can just help me find the strength to—'

'Who the fuck are you talking to?'

'You,' I lied.

'What?'

'Jimmy,' I said, sitting up, 'I want you to stay away from me. I think we should call it a day. It's not that I—'

'Yeah, yeah. I've heard it all before.'

'I mean it,' I said a little louder. 'I'm putting an

128

end to it, here and now. Certain people are getting suspicious.'

'What do you mean? Who's suspicious?'

'Never mind,' I said, not wanting to tell him about Lizzie Doyle's dirty conclusions. He'd tackle her over it and I didn't want that.

'I'm not changing my mind, Jimmy. It's no good, all this sneaking around. It's wrong.'

'It's been wrong for the past fifteen years, Teresa, but it didn't stop you before.'

'I'm not risking it any longer, Jimmy. I want to move on. Please don't make it hard for me.'

'What? You mean get another fella?' he asked, accusingly.

'Yeah. No. Maybe. I don't know, for fuck's sake. I just want it to be over between us. I'm fed up with the guilt, I'm fed up with—'

'Suit yourself,' he growled, leaping out of the bed and getting into his trousers, 'but don't come slobbering all over me down in the pub, looking for drink or an escort home, right? Because if you do, I'll—'

'I won't.'

'We'll see,' he said, slamming the bedroom door behind him, leaving me to my remorse, my loneliness and my tears.

'You're the woman that's staying very quiet these days, Teresa,' Josie said, coming up behind me in the town the following week. 'Have you given up socializing for the new year?'

'No, no,' I said, trying to sound casual. 'Just been busy with work. I had to do a few extra shifts for Mrs Pollock – she had visitors over the Christmas and needed muggins here to clean up after them.'

'So you've not heard the latest then?'

'No. What's up?'

'Our Bernie has only decided to give that scabby husband of hers another chance and—'

'Ah no!'

'Yeah. She's moving out tomorrow, only she hasn't told Da yet.'

'So when did she decide this?'

'Announced it to Ma only last night. I'm telling you, Teresa, if she goes back to him, that's fucking it as far as I'm concerned. She's on her own.'

'We'll have to talk to her, Josie. We've got to stop—'

'No point, Teresa. She's heard it all before – from me, my ma and Marcella. She doesn't want to know.'

'How did he get around her, the sly fecker?' I said, thinking out loud.

'"Bernie," I says to her, "you mark my words: within a month, you'll get a bating." But would she listen? No. "He's changed," she says. I says, "Bernie, will you cop yourself on? That snakey fucker, he'll never change." "Josie," she says, "don't talk about my husband like that. How would you like it if I called PJ a fucker?" I says, "Bernie, if my PJ ever raises a hand to me or either of the childer, you can call him whatever the fuck you like." So where do you go from there, Teresa?'

'Come on,' I told her, forgetting all about my shopping, 'we'll have a word with her together. Your da's not home, is he?'

'No. Probably propping up the bar in the Horse and Jockey. He's had a right sour gob on him this past few days.'

I felt a little twinge of pity for the poor sod and dreaded to think how he'd react if Bernie went ahead with her plan on top of all the annoyance I'd caused him.

'I'll follow you up, after I collect the laundry for Ma,' Josie said.

'Well, how's our wee Amanda?' I asked Bernie, who was folding a few Babygros into a plastic bag.

'Grown out of these already,' she said, smiling.

'Where's the ma?'

'Aggie's.'

'Oh right. Any sca?'

'Nothing much,' she answered cagily.

I picked the child up and sat down on the couch with her.

'You know,' I said, 'it's not so bad being a single ma. The council will fix you up with your own wee house. You have your deserted wives' allowance and when this wee fairy's a bit older, you'll be fit to get yourself a part-time job, like myself, and sure what more—'

'Teresa.'

'What, love?'

'I'm not gonna be on my own.'

'How do you mean?'

'I'm giving the marriage another go,' she said, looking guilty and embarrassed.

'Ah, no.'

'Yes. Everyone deserves a second chance. And Lizzie says Noel's learned his lesson and that me and Amanda mean the world to him.'

I could see Bernie wanted so badly for someone to support what she was doing but, in my heart of hearts, I couldn't. How I'd make her see sense, I just did not know. But I tried.

'Bernie.'

'What?'

'What do you think of me?'

'What sort of question is that?'

'Do you think I'm an eejit?'

'No.'

'A bit daft then?'

'A bit wild,' she said apologetically, 'with the drinking sometimes.'

'And do you want to know why that is?' I asked her, not yet knowing how I'd answer my own spontaneous question.

'Why?'

I thought for a moment. ''Cos of all those memories that are locked inside here,' I said, pressing my finger on my temple. 'The drink – it helps me forget, you see.'

'But, Teresa—'

'But Teresa nothing. You never forget the whacking sound of the palm of your father's hand on your mother's cheek – or the crack of her head against the wall.'

'Stop, Teresa.'

'Or the sound of fear – no not fear, the pure fucking terror in her voice.'

'I'm not listening to any more,' she said, starting to cry. 'It's not fair comparing Noel to Granda Reilly.'

'Is that the kind of life you want for yourself and Amanda? Why do you think your ma's the nervous wreck she is? A lifetime of misery – that's what you'll get if you go back to him.'

'What am I going to do?' she sobbed.

Great, I thought, maybe she's having second thoughts. Then Josie barged through the door and spoiled the moment.

'Well, did you talk any sense into her yet?' she said.

'Oh, *she* put you up to this, did she?' Bernie looked at me accusingly. 'Ganging up on me now, are youse?'

'No, love,' I said.

'Noel's right,' she said, taking the child from my arms, 'youse never gave him a chance. Youse have had it in for him right from the start.'

'We're only trying to help,' I said, not wanting to fall out with her, whatever she did.

'Interfering more like. If youse had kept your noses out of it all along, he'd probably not have hit me in the first place.'

'Is that what he told you?' Josie roared. 'If you believe that, you're a bigger eejit than I thought.'

I knew once it had turned into an argument, we were pushing her straight into Noel's arms.

'Don't come running to me when—'

'Shut up, Josie,' I said, trying to put my arms around Bernie, but she backed away from me. 'That kind of talk's not helping.'

'Can't you see? She doesn't want our help, for Jesus' sake. It's a waste of time talking to her.'

And right she was. Damn the bit of good it did, because Bernie was grasping on tight to the foolish notion that somehow the man would change, the badness would go away and, in the interests of happily ever after, a more caring man would emerge. In a way, I understood that she had to go back: she hadn't yet had her bellyful of grief.

'You know where I am if you need me,' was the last thing I said to Bernie before leaving.

Over the following couple of weeks, Josie went on ranting and raving and swearing to the Almighty that she was washing her hands of her younger sister for good. I didn't see much of Marcella, she seemed to be wrapped up in her schoolwork. Mary was becoming even more withdrawn and was showing no interest in anything or anyone. And Jimmy did what Jimmy always did in a crisis: he drank his way through it. I'd like to have been by his side, to comfort him over a drink or six. Instead, I drank alone – a gin here, a vodka there – but damn the bit of good it was doing me. I was lonely. I cursed the weight of the January blues leaning on my shoulders with its dreary weather and long eerie nights. So when Clint came home from school one Friday evening with Aggie's son, Hughie, both of them pleading with me to allow Clint to sleep over in Aggie's house for a midnight feast, I agreed. It seemed like the perfect opportunity for me to have a good night out on the piss and to kiss farewell and good riddance to the long, dull, boring hoor of a month I'd had.

I woke up gluey-eyed with a terrible sense of remorse hanging over me like a black cloud. Over what, I wasn't quite sure, until I realized I wasn't alone in my bed. Even with my back to him, I knew he wasn't Jimmy. He didn't smell like Jimmy. He smelt earthy, strong, sweet and rural, like . . . Oh, no, I thought, not the farmer. I tried hard to recall the night before, but my head was pounding and my tongue felt shrivelled for the want of a drink. I was glued to the spot where I lay in a state of shock, fear and mortification. Taking shallow breaths, I tried to remain as still as possible, terrified of his wakening and of seeing his face. He stirred. I heard him pick up his watch from the bedside locker and check the time.

'Hey, are ya awake there?'

It *was* the bloody farmer all right. He put his big thick hand on me and started to maul me. I wanted to puke.

'Get your fucking hands off me,' I shouted, leaping out of the bed and wrapping my dressing gown around my naked body.

He looked like the cat that had got the cream, the dirty creep.

'Jaysus, lassie, what's aitin' ya? You were quare and happy last night.'

'Fuck off and get out!'

'Jaypers, Teresa, but you're the right moody woman.'

'Just go.'

'Be God, you're a good one,' he said, walking bare-arsed around the bed to get his clothes. 'So there's no chance of an oul boilt egg or a few rashers then?'

'The only fucking egg you'll be getting, sunshine, is one cracked over your thick head if you're not out of here in two fucking minutes,' I told him, beginning to feel sweaty and panicky in case Clint arrived home early.

'All right, all right. Don't get your drawers in a knot.' He laughed.

Me, I couldn't wait to cry. I was having flashbacks of the shenanigans that had taken place down the town the night before. I remembered Gerry, the barman, telling me to take it easy; flirting with some young soldier, trying to join him and his mates in a game of pool – them laughing – the farmer at the end of the bar. I'd always hated farmers, or culchies, as I call them, with their thick necks and their big wellies and the hair poking out of their ears. This gobshite who was in my bedroom, I'd seen him lots of times before, ogling me, sending me over a drink and, when he'd catch my eye, winking at me. Not in a thousand sober years would I have ended up with him.

'I'm going downstairs,' I said, finding it unbearable to be in the same room. 'I want to hear the front door closing behind you in one minute.'

'You're not a morning person then?' he sneered as I left the room.

I was gulping down a glass of water when he stuck

his ugly mug around the kitchen door to tell me he was off. I didn't look up or answer him.

'Well, sure, thanks for last night anyway, Teresa. There's no doubt about it, but you're the great wee goer between the sheets.'

'Drop dead.'

He walked away, laughing to himself.

'Such a temperamental wee mare' was the last thing I heard him say before he shut the door.

I felt soiled, as though there was filth crawling all over me. It triggered off old feelings, bad feelings. The farmer was gone but his odour lingered in the air, on my skin. The mocking tone of his voice was ringing in my ears. In a state of both panic and revulsion, I ran a hot bath, pouring into it almost a full bottle of bubble bath. I watched the bubbles rise and froth as I leaned over the toilet bowl and dry-heaved myself into a state of exhaustion. I called out, begging for mercy, not mentioning any names, just throwing out the request to anyone up there who was willing to help. In the bath, I cried and scrubbed and cried some more. If only I'd left things as they were between myself and Jimmy, I thought, this would never have happened. He'd have taken care of me, kept an eye on me, seen me home, made sure I didn't get out of control.

After getting myself dressed, I ripped all the sheets and pillowcases off my bed, bunged them into a black bin liner and flung them into the bin in the backyard.

Right, I thought, filling the kettle, calm down. It's over, it's history – it was only sex, no big bloody deal.

The doorbell rang. It was Aggie, to tell me that her Charlie had taken the boys off pheasant-shooting and they'd not be back until one.

'That's grand, Aggie,' I said, walking her to the gate.

'You know what, Teresa?' she said, taking a drag of her cigarette. 'That's one hell of a nice kid, your Clint.'

'Ah, thanks, Agg—'

'Hey, Teresa,' someone shouted. I looked up and saw Ricky Doyle coming down the street with another young lad. They started to sing.

> *The farmer wants a wife,*
> *The farmer wants a wife,*
> *Heigho me addio,*
> *The farmer wants a wife.*

'What the fuck is wrong with that pair of eejits?' Aggie asked.

'Dunno,' I said. 'Anyway, I'm away in to light my fire, Aggie.'

I was safe behind closed doors before the pair of boyos reached the house. I remembered Noel Doyle senior in the pub the night before. I felt sickened at the thought of that Doyle lot having a right good laugh at me over their breakfast table. Damn them. Damn me. I reached for the cupboard. What else was a girl to do under such distressing and humiliating circumstances? I thought, unscrewing the cap of the gin bottle.

Marcella

'So what do you think my chances are, Marcella?'

'I don't know, Gabby.'

'Oh, come on, you're always chatting to my gorgeous Colonel Pickering, you must have some idea.'

I didn't – not a clue. When it came to sussing out who fancied whom, I was totally useless. I knew the fella I fancied – although fancied seemed a very inadequate word for how I felt about Cormac. I loved him so much it hurt. For a full month, he had been responsible for every good and every bad thought I'd had. But how he felt about me, or how Joe, who was playing the part of Colonel Pickering in *My Fair Lady*, felt about Gabby, was a mystery to me. Any of the lads who had fancied me from up the hill would have made it clear how they felt by either telling me straight that they wouldn't half mind getting into my knickers, or, like Ricky Doyle, trying the more direct route and making a pass, cheeky feckers that they were.

'I'll tell you what,' I said, as the school bus pulled up at the college gates, 'I'll ask the colonel, the jolly old chap, this evening at show practice, how he'd feel about having his wicked way with Mrs Pearson.' That was Gabby, Henry Higgins's housekeeper.

'Ah, don't you dare!' she roared. 'If you do, I'll tell Leona you fancy the pants off Cormac.'

'Fuck off. I do not.'

'Yes you do, and I'm telling you, it's only a matter of time. Oh, can't you just see the shock on Doolittle's face? I can't fucking wait.'

Contrary to what I had thought, Leona wasn't Miss Popularity after all. Gabby, for one, although nice to Leona's face, couldn't stand her. I detested her. She had the two things I could only dream about, Cormac and status.

'. . . Mary B a C plus, Mary C a B minus, Leona a B, Marcella a D minus. Better to get an A or a B in the pass paper than to fail the honours paper,' Mrs Curran, our Irish teacher, said. It was hard trying to keep up. Before Bernie moved back in with Noel, I had barely managed to get my homework done at all, having to share the bedroom with herself and Amanda. An hour and a half in the town library each evening and that was it. Now they were gone, I had show practice three nights a week. Cormac, too, was to blame for having the cheek to distract me, without even being there, any time I tried to get some studying done.

At Loreto, it was much harder to get good grades, and damn near impossible to stand out from the others. Even my English essays weren't attracting any attention the way they had in the tech.

As Sister Helena said to me about my science project, 'You might get away with that standard of work in the tech, dear, but it's not good enough for my class. I expect more from my girls.'

Painful, but true. In the tech, the teacher would have been grateful that I'd done my homework at all.

'Ma!' I shouted. 'Ma! Ma! Ma, for fuck's sake, are you deaf?'

'What? What's wrong with ya?'

'Never mind what's wrong with me. What the hell is wrong with *you*? You've been staring at that wall like a bloody zombie for ten minutes now. I just don't get it, Ma. What's the matter with you?'

It had been like that every morning for the previous couple of weeks. Everything about her seemed to droop – her shoulders, her head, her eyes, even the perm she'd had done for Christmas had lost its bounce and clung to her head like seaweed to a rock.

'Must be oul age, dawther,' she muttered.

'You're only forty-one.'

She didn't answer, just bolted up out of the chair and started searching for something frantically. She looked under cushions and in drawers and then went back and looked under the same cushions again.

'What are you looking for?'

'My purse.'

'Here it is,' I said, picking it up from the windowsill and handing it to her.

'I – I need . . . eh . . . spuds and a bit of frying steak. Will you hurry up? Your da'll be waiting for his – his dinner.'

'Ma, it's half eight in the morning. He hasn't had his breakfast yet. Will you calm—'

'Half eight. Oh.'

I didn't know whether to laugh, cry or scream at her, she was being so daft and dopey. No matter what I did or said, it had no effect on her. She sat back down in the armchair and lit another cigarette, almost singeing her hair in the process.

'I'm away off to school, Ma,' I said, heading towards the back door, feeling a pang of guilt for leaving her to her stupor, but relieved to escape from her and her queerness.

'Remember, Leona, you're a common flower girl,' Miss Trimble said. 'Try again, darling. This time with a little more rumbustiousness.'

Gabby sniggered and nudged me.

'Come on, Dover,' Leona shouted, with a little more gusto, 'move your blooming 'orse,' she continued, her voice dropping volume considerably.

'*Arse*, Leona, not *'orse*. Eliza would say that Dover was an *'orse*, but she wants the *'orse* to move his blooming *arse*.'

Everyone laughed, thank God, because if they hadn't, I would have exploded anyway. Seeing us all in stitches, Leona joined in, tittering nervously.

'OK, OK, settle down, we've only twenty minutes left. Let's start the scene from scratch.'

With upturned noses we paraded around the stage in our long gowns, flamboyant hats and white parasols singing 'Ascot Opening Day', me pretending to be a snoot like Leona, her pretending to be a common girl like me.

As usual, the boarders hung around the front of the school with us until our lifts had arrived to take us home. I always went with Gabby's mother. Leona's father was already waiting when we got there, so she was the first to leave.

'Oh, Father,' I said haughtily, trying to take her off, 'Miss Trimble is making me use a very naughty word in the show. What will I do, Father? I don't want to be rude. Oi'm a good girl, oi am.'

All the lads were laughing. Gabby was trying hard to communicate something to me, her eyes darting, indicating for me to look round, but before I had the chance I was grabbed from behind and tickled furiously. Although I hadn't seen him, I knew it was Cormac. I automatically struggled to free myself from his grip. I wriggled, I screamed, I laughed, he laughed and, eventually, I managed to utter through my gasps, 'I'm sorry, I'll never slag her off again. I swear.'

He released me, saying, 'OK, I won't tell her, if you promise not to tell her this.' Bending down he whispered in my ear, 'I'm bloody crazy about you.' He rubbed his lips against my earlobe, which sent a tingling feeling through me, all the way down to my toes. My face flushed. I was dumbstruck. And then, thank God, the headlights of Gabby's mother's car came into view.

*

I was much too tired to finish off my French homework when I got home that night and much too happy to sleep. Everything felt different – my pillow, the sheets, my skin, my hair. My body reacted to everything I touched. I wanted to be naked. I removed my nightdress, spreading my limbs across the expanse of the bed and wriggled underneath the sheets, with Cormac in my heart, in my head, teasing me with hope.

'Ma, I've got two free tickets for the show. It's on next week. Will you go with Josie?' I asked, handing her a mug of tea after the Sunday dinner.

'Och, I don't think so, lassie. I'd not fit in with all the other parents. They'd be used to going to the like of that.'

'Ma, they're just ordinary people going to see their children take part in a musical, that's all. It's no big deal.'

'Maybe Bernie'd like to go with Josie instead. Poor lassie could probably do with a wee treat.'

'So go with Bernie then. Josie'll go anyway, even if she has to pay for the ticket. Says she's dying to see me make an eejit out of myself. The bitch.'

'I'll think about it, love,' she said, but somehow I knew she wouldn't be there. I wanted so much for her to go so that she'd be proud of me up on the stage, strutting my stuff with the best of them. Surely that would make her happy; maybe put a smile back on her face?

*

Josie turned up on the opening night with PJ, although she didn't bother to tell me in advance. I was oblivious, until I made my entrance as one of the East End flower girls, a shawl draped over my shoulders and my basket full of carnations. I started to sweat through the thick layer of make-up when I heard her have a fit of laughter. I looked down. She was in the front row. Shut up, you tramp, I thought, and at the same time heard poor PJ shushing her. He was wasting his time. The wagon, she just couldn't help herself. Every time I had to re-enter in a different costume, I was waiting to hear her shout, 'Ah Jaysus, PJ, would you look at the state of our Marcella?' but she didn't, and the rest of the cast were none the wiser as to who the laughing jackass was, and I certainly did not enlighten them.

I met Bernie on my way home from school the following evening. I'd seen her from a distance, coming out of the Doyles' house.

'Where's Amanda?'

'Lizzie's keeping an eye on her for me. I have to go down the doctor's.'

'What's wrong with you?'

'I've a fierce headache this past few days. Can't shift it at all.'

'Do you want me to come with you?'

'No, no, you're all right. I'll be fine.'

'I don't mind, honest. Sure, I'll keep you company if nothing else.'

'Right,' she said, looking shiftily back at the house several times until we were out of sight.

'Where's Noel?' I asked.

'In the flat.'

'Why couldn't he look after Amanda?'

'He's busy.'

'Doing what? Watching TV?'

'No! He has to meet some fella at five o'clock. Now, will you shut up and stop trying to pick fault with him.'

'Sorry.'

In the waiting room, I told her about the free tickets and about Cormac and how he had told me that once the show was over, he was finishing with Leona to go out with me. Although she tried, she just couldn't share my enthusiasm.

'So will you go to the show with Ma?'

'Bernie Doyle,' the receptionist called, giving her no time to answer.

'So what did he say?' I asked her, as we headed out the door into a heavy shower of rain.

'Just to take it easy.'

'No prescription?'

'No.'

'Jesus, that was a waste of time. So,' I said, nudging her, 'what about—'

'Ouch! Jesus, Marcella, don't be so rough!' she said, flinching.

'Sorry,' I said, reaching out to put my arm around

146

her, but she backed off, protecting her upper left arm with her right hand.

My stomach hit my chest and fell back down again with a thud.

'So, this headache,' I asked her nervously, 'do you have it now?'

'A bit.'

'Oh, please, Bernie, don't lie to—'

'Don't start,' she cried. 'I know what you're thinking, but you're wrong, so will you get off my case?'

We were silent as we walked side by side, heads down under the umbrella like a pair of mourners at a funeral.

'What about the show then?' I said, as we approached the Doyles' house.

'If it was on any other week, I would, but—'

'Never mind. Forget it,' I told her, as the changing winds caused the rain to pelt me from all angles.

With Da not being around when I got home and Ma being in no fit state to cope with bad news, I kept my suspicions to myself.

'Bernie's not going to the show, Ma.'

'Why don't you give your tickets to Clint and Teresa?'

I knew Clint would be up for it; he loved anything to do with music. As for Teresa, a few weeks earlier she'd have had no chance, but it was hard for me to stay mad with her, being so close to Clint. On Christmas Day I had forgiven her because deep down I believed that, unlike Da, she was truly sorry.

'Yeah, you're right. I'll run down to see them now before tea.'

I was looking forward to a chat with Clint. I'd hardly seen him since Christmas, having spent so much time preparing for the show. I grabbed my umbrella and headed back out into the rain. Teresa, I thought, must be doing another spring-cleaning, when I heard Rod Stewart blaring from her house and me still several doors away. I could always tell when Teresa was vacuuming: her stereo would be on full blast. Mad bitch. There wasn't much point in ringing the doorbell, so I headed round the back and into the kitchen.

'Teresa.'

I opened the door into the sitting room. Ah, I was right, the vacuum cleaner was lying across the floor.

'Teresa. Clint.'

There was no answer. They obviously couldn't hear me. I climbed the stairs, singing along with 'Tonight's the Night', Teresa's all-time favourite. She knew every last word of it, though she was never too accurate when it came to hitting the right notes.

'Teresa,' I shouted, walking across the landing, 'you'll have the neighbours driven mad with—' I said, opening her bedroom door.

It was much worse this time. It felt like a punch in the guts, a blow that forced everything inside me to erupt and, as I dashed to the bathroom, the contents of my stomach spewed out all over the landing carpet. I could hear Teresa screeching and Da trying to calm her down. My heart was pounding. I could feel it galloping in my ears. I pulled a towel from the hot press, wiped my mouth, tried to rub the puke off my jacket, dropped it on the floor and ran all the way home.

Ma didn't even notice my dishevelled state.

'Well, are they going?'

'They weren't there,' I said, running past her and straight up to my room.

'What about a bit of tay?' she shouted up after me.

'Not hungry.'

I lay on the bed. I didn't cry. I couldn't. For years I'd tried to escape the sounds of my da's self-satisfied grunting late at night by humming to myself in my bed, or by covering my ears with the pillow. I'd try to focus on anything that would stop a picture of his hungry naked body developing in my mind. But now I could see it and it wasn't going away. I would never see him clothed again, not if he were to wear forty coats. I shivered when the realization hit me, like a smack in the gob, that I had been conceived in the middle of all that naked romping about. It wasn't that I didn't know the facts of life – I was well aware of them – but up until that awful moment I had only had the sound effects to contend with. Now I had a picture as well as sound, and it was foul. I felt cheap, cheated. I could never associate any of it with what other people called making love. To me, he wasn't doing it *with* my ma, he was doing it *to* her, and I hated him for it. Hate. It did away with the need to cry. It buried all feelings of sorrow. It was self-protection, a coat of armour, the Great bloody Wall of China, a wall I swore that neither Da nor Teresa would ever cross again.

At the show that night, I kept standing on my partner's toes during the ball scene. Afterwards in the wings everyone was slagging me. I was in no bloody mood for it and I couldn't wait for the final curtain to go down. As soon as it did, I ran off to the toilets for a good cry. When I came out, Cormac was standing in the corridor waiting for me.

'Hey, Marcie, what's up?'

'Nothing,' I whispered.

'So you've been peeling onions in there for the past ten minutes, have you?'

'I haven't been crying – honest. Just needed a few minutes to myself, that's all. Stop looking at me like that. I'm fine – I swear,' I said, trying to convince him and myself.

'Come here,' he said gently, putting his arms around me. I held on tight. That was our first hug: me with my face buried in his chest, sobbing my heart out; him with his cheek resting on the top of my head, while he ran his fingers through my curls. He led me by the hand into the school library. The blinds were already down. He switched on a reading lamp, leaving the main lights off.

'Gabby's mother will be here to collect us in five minutes,' I said.

'Don't worry. I'll ring Luke, one of the day pupils, to collect you in an hour. He drives his father's car.'

'But—'

'Right now, we need to talk.'

He sat on a chair and pulled me down onto his lap. He didn't try to feel me or maul me or stick his tongue down my throat.

'I hate to see you cry, Marcie,' he said, wiping my tears.

'I hate you to see me cry too,' I said, a smile trying to break through.

'So, are you going to tell me what it's all about?'

'I can't.'

'You can.'

'You wouldn't understand, honest. Trust me. You don't want to know.'

'Yes I do. Tell me. I care about you. You know I do.'

'It's . . . it's hard to talk about. It's too embarrassing.'

Part of me was bursting to tell someone, to let it all out. On the other hand, I thought, it might put him off me, knowing the kind of family I came from.

'I can't finish with Leona until the show's over. It would be too awkward with me and her performing together. But this time next week, it'll be just you and me,' he whispered, as he stroked my cheek. 'So trust me, please.'

I wanted to trust him. If I was going to be his girlfriend, I'd have to learn to trust him.

'Come on, Marcie.'

'OK, OK, but I'm not going to look at you. I don't want to see your reaction when I tell you.'

'It can't be that bad.'

'It is, so that's the deal. Take it or leave it.'

'OK, we'll sit on two chairs back to back, if that would make you feel more comfortable.'

'It would.'

I went right back to the start, to the day of Bernie's wedding, and let it all out bit by bit. He didn't speak, but I could sense his sympathy by the sound of his breathing and the odd expressive sigh. When I'd finished, he leaned his head back on mine.

'I'm sorry.'

For a split second, I panicked, assuming that it had all been too much for him, more than he would want to know about or get involved with. But before that thought had time to sink in, he whispered, 'I love you.'

He came and kissed me, first on the forehead. Then his lips ran slowly down my cheeks until they brushed over my mouth, where they stopped and searched, like a bee around a flower, looking for a way in. I welcomed him, my lips trembling. Inside our mouths, our tongues twirled and tickled and tasted. It was beautiful. It was frighteningly passionate. We stopped only when we heard loud footsteps coming down the corridor, the clinking of keys and the flick of a light switch.

'Shit, it's Father Mohan. He'll have locked all the main doors. You'll have to get out the window.'

I climbed up on a chair, giggling, while Cormac raised

152

the window inch by inch, until the gap was wide enough for me to slip through into the cold night air. We kissed again through the open window, before Cormac sneaked off to the payphone to ring Luke to come to my rescue.

It seemed like an eternity before Luke's car cruised quietly around the side of the college with only his parking lights on to avoid attracting any attention.

'Thanks a mil.' I beamed at him, getting in the front seat.

'All in a good cause,' he said, smiling.

My mind was racing from one blissful thought to the next. I could see how it would all turn out: our own house, in a respectable area, no council rent. We're standing in our kitchen (you can swing a cat in it), we have a dishwasher and a fridge-freezer and we're making coffee for Ma. She's in the sitting room – she's happy – she's admiring our velvet curtains – nursing our baby. Cormac says she's welcome to stay as long as she likes – she's—

'So ye finally got it together then?' Luke said.

'Mmm, yeah,' I said, my head still stuck in the clouds. He said he loved me, *me*, Marcella Buckley, redheaded pale-skinned daughter of a low life from Fatima Hill and *he* loved *me*. I'd never felt so high, so excited. I didn't know that feelings like that were possible, but I did know I wanted to stay up there, blissed out, where even the ugly discoveries of earlier that evening could not dilute my happiness.

*

Da was still up when I arrived home, a glass of whiskey in one hand, a cigarette in the other. I hadn't seen him since we'd all been at Teresa's house. He stood with his back to the smouldering fire, facing me. I ignored him and headed for the stairs.

'Marcella.'

'What?' I answered, without turning around to look at him.

'You'd better not open that gob of yours,' he said, threateningly.

'You,' I said, looking him up and down in disgust, 'and that trollop can go to hell for all I care. You deserve each other.'

He made a dash for me. I stood my ground. He pulled me back aggressively into the middle of the room, closing the door behind us.

'Get your mucky hands off me,' I roared.

'Shut up, ya bitch,' he spat, backing off, 'you'll wake your mother. I'm not asking you,' he said, pointing his finger, 'I'm fucking telling you, don't you—'

'I won't,' I said, smiling at him sarcastically, 'because as far as I'm concerned, you and that yoke you're screwing, youse don't exist. So your names will not pass my lips. Not now, not ever.'

I turned on my heels and didn't wait for a response.

Whether it was love or hate that gave me strength, I didn't know.

The word was out. Cormac McCairn was two-timing Leona with Marcella Buckley, of all people.

Leona waited until the final night of the show, when we had all gathered for our last farewell. Then she struck.

'Unlike where you come from,' she said condescendingly, 'where I come from we don't squabble over men. So as far as I'm concerned, you're welcome to him.'

She had rehearsed it. I knew she had. She wanted me to lose my temper, let out a string of curses, or threaten her with a hiding. If she was lucky, I'd make a swing for her. I wanted to. She was setting me up to let myself down, the scheming cow.

'That, Leona,' I said, starting to applaud slowly, 'was the best performance you put on all week. Bravo, darling.'

You could hear a pin drop as I walked out and shut the door behind me. I took a few deep breaths, then I heard her burst into tears.

There were dozens of lads queuing up to comfort Leona and step into Cormac's shoes, suckers that they were. Even, Joe, Colonel Pickering, chanced his gentlemanly arm, much to Gabby's disgust.

'That's the little whore,' Gabby said. 'I'd love to rearrange that stuck-up face of hers.'

Gabby was funny. She'd act tough, talk tough, but underneath it all she'd about as much courage as the lion in *The Wizard of Oz*.

I had my first official date with Cormac on the Friday night after the show ended. He had been due to go home to Ashbourne, but had arranged to stay at Luke's house instead so we could spend some time together. I wore a pair of denim drainpipes, and a jade-green Indian top with fringes.

'That's a very pretty colour on you with your hair,' Ma said. I was thrilled she'd noticed.

I sat down beside her on the couch while I tied my desert boots.

'Guess what, Ma?'

'What, love?'

'I have a boyfriend. I'm meeting him tonight at the youth-club disco.'

'Ah, good lassie yourself. So who is he, this lad?'

'He's a bit older than me, Ma, he's eighteen. And he's not from around here. He's a boarder at Saint Michael's, comes from Ashbourne in County Meath. His da's a dentist.'

'A dentist, be God.'

'Ma, he's gorgeous and he told me he loved me. I've never felt like—'

'Be careful, dawther,' she said, her ice-cold hand squeezing mine. 'Be careful.'

'Of course I'll be careful. You don't think I'd get myself pregnant, do you?'

'With your heart, girl. Be careful with your heart. The likes of them ones, moneyed people, they'd not settle for the likes of you.'

'Cormac's not like that. He's not a snob.'

'Give him time. He'll change.'

She was pissing me off with her doom and gloom. All I wanted to do was share my excitement with her, cheer her up a bit.

'Ma, if you don't have dreams, you have nothing.'

'If you don't have dreams, love, you won't have disappointments.'

'Mother of God,' I said, 'let me out of here, before I lose the will to live.'

She laughed, her hoarse chesty cackle revealing her nicotine-stained teeth and her bad breath. I knew what she was thinking, she didn't have to say a word: there goes our Marcella again with her high notions; she'll learn, poor eejit.

I laughed with her, I couldn't help it. Our whole conversation was so pathetic, it was funny, in a mad sort of way. I was angry and amused. I wanted to shake her and hug her. I almost loathed her but I didn't; I loved her.

That was the best weekend of my life. I remember every detail: his blue and white pinstriped grandfather shirt; the red patch on his Wranglers; our first fast dance to 'Heart of Glass'; our first slow dance to 'Romeo and Juliet'; the walk home; my thumb hooked into the belt loop of his jeans; his hand inside my back pocket; the echo of our footsteps in the ball alley; the coldness of the wall, even through my denim jacket; the warmth of his body wrapped around mine. He kept putting my hair behind my ears, pecking the tip of my nose, tucking me inside his jacket any time I shivered and rubbing my hands in his. We talked about music and school and parents. He didn't get along with his father either; said he was a dictator, a hypocrite and a social climber. He said he hated class distinction, reckoned there was a lot to be said for socialism. I wasn't quite sure what that meant but I knew he was on our side, that of the working classes, and I loved him all the more for it.

He called to the house for me on Sunday. We went to the Dandelion Market in Dublin. Luke had his father's car for the day, and told him he was going up to Trinity College with Cormac to have a look around and a chat with some of the students. Both the lads planned to go there that September. Luke asked Gabby to come along. She soon forgot about Colonel Pickering. He had a great selection of tapes in the car – Eric Clapton, the Eagles, Horslips, Clannad. We sang, we laughed, we kissed and we shared cans of Coke spiked with vodka. I had never touched a drink before, thought I never would, but when I saw Gabby taking a swig, I thought, why not? We were just having a bit of a laugh. And I didn't want to be the odd one out, not when I had finally reached the stage of fitting in. We were cool. I was cool. The more I drank, the cooler I became. By the time we reached the Dandelion Market, I was so fucking cool, I was floating, walking on air, several inches above reality, not drunk but happy.

There wasn't a person there over the age of twenty-one. The place was full of dudes, students, bikers, punks, hippies and musicians. The smell of incense made me feel as though we were on another continent, somewhere exotic, a lifetime away from Fatima Hill.

We split up for a while. The lads wanted to stay outside and listen to the buskers. Gabby and I browsed the stalls. I bought a red Indian scarf, some jasmine-scented Indian oil and a toffee apple. Gabby bought henna for her hair, some incense and a T-shirt with 'Fuck the System' written across it. It was my first shopping spree. We snogged the whole way home in turn. First Cormac drove, leaving Luke and Gabby in the back seat. We kept the music on full blast to drown the sounds of heavy breathing and groaning. I could hardly wait until it was our turn. I'd been daydreaming about sex a lot. I'd go through it all in my head, the kissing, the touching, the passion, losing control, getting naked. It made me feel wild to think about it and I enjoyed the fantasy, the private moments, alone in my bed.

I paid for my weekend's fun on Monday morning.

'This standard of work will not get you your honour in English, Miss Buckley. You're going to have to knuckle down. This won't do at all. Right?'

'Right, sir.'

There was a lot of talking in the house over the next couple of weeks – meetings and arguments. Josie and Teresa, Josie and my da, Teresa and Aggie Clarke, Josie and Aggie, the whole bloody lot of them – whispering, followed by shouting, then long silences. They'd change the subject as soon as I came into the room. They'd talk about the weather or the great value in Dunnes

Stores, or which of the young lassies was up the pole now, and how God knows some of them were doing it just for the welfare benefits, sure didn't it beat working for a living? Ma was never in on it. She was always upstairs, resting.

I got tired of being left out of it – whatever *it* was. I nabbed Josie one evening as she was leaving the house. She was at the back door.

'What's going on, Josie?' I asked.

'Nothing.'

'What do you take me for? Do you think I'm thick?'

'Sit down.'

I sat. She took off her jacket and lit a fag. She looked bothered – for Josie. She wouldn't sit down at first and looked out the window biting her lip.

'What is it, Josie? Tell me, will you?'

'OK, OK,' she said, parking her bum on the stool opposite me. 'It's Ma. We think she needs to go to hospital.'

'Why? What's wrong with her?'

I knew she was down in the dumps. I knew she had her tablets for her nerves, but that wasn't being sick, that was feeling unhappy. And being married to my da, who could blame her?

'She's not coping, love. She's getting worse.'

'We'll talk to her then, together, find out what's wrong, see what we can do.'

'It's not that simple, Marcella. I wish it was.'

'And what good would going to hospital do? What could they do for her in there?'

'Not the county hospital, love. Saint Andrew's.'

'The mental! No fucking way. No way, Josie, she's not going there, I don't care what youse say. No no no no no no no—'

'Marcella,' she said, grabbing my arm, 'stop shouting, she'll hear you. You'll upset her.'

I pushed her away. I wanted to batter her, pull her hair out; she was crazy, the bitch, talking about my mother like that.

'You're off your rocker, you're a sick bitch suggesting the like of that—'

'It wasn't my suggestion. It was the doctor's. Not mine.'

We were both crying now, sitting face to face at the kitchen table, looking at each other through our tears.

'I'm not letting youse bring her there, Josie. I've seen *One Flew over the Cuckoo's Nest*. She'd be scared in there with all those loonies. She's not a loonie, Josie. She's just sad, that's all.'

'Look, love, that was just a stupid film, set in America – the other side of the Atlantic Ocean, for God's sake. Saint Andrew's wouldn't be like that. Besides, it mightn't happen yet. The doctor has put her on some new tablets to see how it goes. He said he'd give it a week or two.'

'What does she say about it herself? Or have youse even bothered to ask her?'

'Ah, you know Ma, says she's going nowhere. Wants to be left alone.'

'I suppose Teresa thinks it's a fucking fantastic idea,'

I spat, suddenly feeling angry at the thought of her having anything to do with it. 'Or maybe it was Da's idea. Was it?'

'No. You're wrong, about Teresa anyway. She's totally against it. Look, all we can do now is pray to Jaysus that she'll snap out of it with these new tablets.'

Josie left and I spent the rest of the night in my room, my head feeling only seconds away from exploding with anger and confusion. I knew she wasn't strong or confident or reliable or beautiful or glamorous, but she was my *ma*, and nobody was going to take her away from me and lock her up.

Two days after Josie told me the news, Cormac rang me at five, as usual, on the public phone halfway down the hill. We talked about our day at school and arranged to meet up at the weekend. I didn't tell him about Ma. She was one of the sad things in my life, her and Da and Teresa and Bernie. Cormac was my happiness, my hope and, I prayed to God, my future.

Ma had now been on her new tablets for a full week. No improvement. But there was still time, a flicker, a hope, prayers to be said and to be answered. She was up when I got home, sitting on the couch, photos spread out before her. She looked distracted and frightened, worse than usual. I spoke to her calmly, though my heart was racing, skipping beats, like it was jumping over hurdles.

'Are you having a trip down memory lane, Ma?' I said, smiling.

She was rooting furiously through the box on her knee.

'It has to be in here,' she said.

'What does?'

'Ah, here it is,' she whimpered, clutching a small black and white photo. 'Look, it's me and Teresa. See,' she said, 'I'm holding her. She was only a few days old there – me, I was ten. God, but I loved that baby – used to tell her she was a real princess.'

'It's lovely, Ma,' I said, rubbing her back. 'You were very pretty.'

The little size of her, for ten; she was more like six, I thought. But she was beautiful, her two dark eyes staring out from under a crooked fringe.

'I'd take her out, you see, when it would start.'

'When what would start?' I asked, holding her hand. She was talking and it wasn't just chitchat; she was saying something and I wanted to, needed to, listen.

'The shouting, the fighting . . . and crying and all them awful noises. They'd have frightened her, see. So I'd take her out, in the pram.'

She was shaking now.

'It was one of them big yokes, near as big as one of them shopping trolleys you'd get in Dunnes – a big brute of a thing; wrecked it was too. Done us all, did that pram.'

'You were a good kid, looking out for her like that,' I whispered. I didn't want to make any loud noise to interrupt her train of thought. Maybe this was a good sign, opening up, getting things off her chest.

Maybe the new tablets were doing the business after all.

'We'd go for walks, way out on the back road there, as far as the old mill. Seemed like miles at the time. And I'd tell her stories – pretend we were running away, back to the castle where our real parents lived. We'd been kidnapped, see, by a bad man. But his wife was good and kind. She wanted to bring us back to the castle, but every time she tried to sneak us out of the house, he'd catch her and he'd get very angry and—'

'It's OK, Ma, it's OK,' I said, wrapping my arms around her, when the tears started to flow. 'You'll be grand. The tablets will make you feel better, you'll see.'

'There's things, Marcella,' she sobbed.

'What things?'

'Things I know about. Bad stuff. She doesn't think I know about it, but I do,' she gasped, her hand over her mouth, tears flowing out of her like a river.

'Who? What things?'

'Teresa. She thinks I don't know about all that carry-on. But I've always known about it – seen them at it, I did. Dirty old git.'

She knew! All that time I'd been keeping it from her and she already knew. And she was hurting, keeping it to herself, blaming herself, no doubt. Jesus Christ, I thought, she's fucking known all along!

'I know about it too, Ma. I'm sorry—'

'You! How? Teresa didn't tell you, did she?'

'Ssh, it's OK. You don't have to keep it a secret any

longer. I found out the day of Bernie's wedding. Caught her and Da at it in the jacks and—'

'What?'

'And then again a couple of weeks ago, in Teresa's bed – and I wanted to tell you, but you were in such bad form—'

'What are you telling me, dawther?'

'That I know about Da and Teresa. It's all right, you don't have to protect me – or them. I saw them, buck fucking naked, the cheating bastards.'

'No!'

'Honest to God, Ma, really.'

She looked shocked. She closed her eyes really tight, started rocking and put her hands over her face.

'No,' she gasped.

'What is it? You didn't want me to know? You thought it was all over between them? What, Ma?'

She started banging her knuckles on the side of her head, her eyes still closed. She was scaring me.

'What is it? Talk to me, please.'

The doorbell rang. She didn't seem to notice. With any luck, I thought, whoever it was would feck off.

'Come on, calm down, talk to me, please.'

I grabbed her wrists, tried to stop her knocking herself on the head. The doorbell rang again. She didn't resist. She let me hold her hands in mine. She let me rub them, but she wouldn't open her eyes and she wouldn't speak.

There was someone rooting at the letterbox.

'Are you in there, Mary?' It was a man's voice.

'My Teresa — she done that to me?' she uttered, her eyes opening, but remaining downcast.

I didn't know if it was a question or a statement.

'Mary,' his voice roared through the letterbox.

'I thought you knew,' I said, wiping her nose with my tissue.

'No,' she whimpered. 'No.'

'Mary. It's Derek, the barman from the Harp. Mick sent me up to tell you that there's something wrong in the flat upstairs — a lot of shouting and banging. Are you there, Mary?'

I nearly broke my neck tripping over my school bag in the hall as I dashed out to open the door. Ma was behind me, wailing. 'Where are you going, lassie? Come back. Don't leave me on me own. Please, dawther.'

'Stay here, Ma,' I said. 'You're in no fit state to go anywhere. Derek, go down to our Josie's, please. Tell her what's going on. Ma, get back inside. I'll only be a few minutes.'

I had to move quickly. I should have told Derek to take Ma with him to Josie's. I would have, had I been thinking straight. But I wasn't. All I could see was Bernie on the floor, bruised, bleeding. And Amanda — he'd better not have hurt her, the bastard. I got to the end of the hill. There were cars whizzing by, as close to each other as carriages on a train, damn them. I saw a gap. I had to get across the street, quickly, before the van got any closer. I'd make it. I ran. I heard the horn

166

– fuck off, you bollocks – the screech of brakes. I heard the thump. It wasn't me. I was still standing. Ma. Ma. Ma. I turned around.

'Maaameee,' I heard the scream ringing in my ears. It came from inside me. I was six years old again. My lips didn't move. There was chaos all around me, people appearing from nowhere. I sensed them, I didn't see them. All I saw was my ma, on her back – and blood, lots of blood. I was on my knees, bending over her. I don't know how I got there. I don't remember stepping off the footpath. She was motionless. The only part of her that was moving was the blood spurting out of the gash in the side of her head. I felt it, warm, sticky and thick, running over my hand, between my fingers.

'Ambulance.'

'Accident.'

'Mary Buckley.'

'Doctor.'

'Oh no.'

'Jesus Christ.'

'The priest.'

'Last rites.'

The words were up there, above me, in the distance, like an echo. There was a hand on my shoulder. 'She's still breathing.' I don't know who said it.

I felt her face twitch underneath my hand. Her eyes opened, just for a second. Sadness – that's all I saw in them, sadness. Her lips were moving. She was trying to speak. I held her hand. I watched her lips. What?

What was she trying to tell me? Her mouth hung open, stopped moving. I leaned in closer to her and whispered in her ear, 'I love you, Ma.'

Teresa

'Come on, Teresa, unlock the door, will you? Teresa?'

There was a gentle tapping on my bedroom door.

'Teresa, I'm going nowhere till I see you.'

'Fuck away off with yourself, Aggie.'

'Indeed and I'll not. I warned you yesterday evening I'd be back in the morning. I told your Clint I'd talk to you. I promised the lad last night. Poor kid's worried sick about you.'

'Well, then, tell him I'm all right. Tell him you've had a chat with me and that I'm grand – and so I would be if you'd piss off with yourself and let me get some sleep.'

'Teresa, if you were OK, he'd be able to come home, wouldn't he? He's not stupid, you know. He knows you're drinking.'

'He's all right over at yours, isn't he?'

'Well, yeah, for now – but he wants his mam back. He loves you, Teresa. Teresa! Teresa!'

I hated that he loved me. I wished he didn't care. It was a burden, him loving me, a responsibility, a fucking heartache. More pain to contend with, more emotion to overcome, more booze to help overcome it. I stretched my arm over to the bedside locker. Another swig. Another tear. I felt something inside crushing me. It hurt so bad. Another sip.

'Please, Teresa.'

Her voice was pleading. There was a long pause while she waited for me to respond. I'd nothing to say, nothing she wanted to hear anyway.

'For Clint's sake.'

I was in no fit state. I needed time.

'Maybe—'

'For Mary. You know she'd not like to see you like this. If she was here now, she'd be quare and worried about you.'

Mary. Mary. My head was spinning, my stomach turned sour. Mary. Gone. Panic attacked me. Flashbacks – ugly, eerie, agonizing images bombarding my brain, like a round of bullets: Mary, lying cold in the morgue, motionless; sounds of a banshee cursing me; Marcella, wailing; Mary's blue lips, thin blue icy lips on mine; our last farewell – a kiss from her betrayer, her Judas, me. Rap, rap, rap – your Mary, she's dead. Dead.

'Come on now, Teresa.'

I jerked. Who said that? Was it Aggie? Mary? Back to haunt me. Help!

'Oh Christ Almighty,' I whispered, 'I'm losing my mind.'

My eyes darted around the room, but there was no one there. I grabbed the bottle and sucked on it, like a starving infant in need of milk. Oh yes, that's better.

'Teresa.'

Aggie. Damn her. I had to get rid of her. She had to go, fucking pain in the arse that she was.

'Tomorrow, Aggie. I'll talk tomorrow.'

170

'That bastardin' drink. Will you stay away from it, for Jesus' sake?'

'Jesus. Hah! Don't talk to me about that fella. He's never around when you need Him, the same bollocks.'

'Oh merciful God, forgive you. That's blasphemy, you know, a very serious sin. He's here all right. You're just too fucking drunk to see Him.'

'Damned to hell now, am I? Well who fucking cares? It can't be any worse than where I am right now.'

'I know, love. You've had a rough time of it. But trust me, God will help you. He's got me through many's the tough time. He has.'

'If He was here, if He gave a flying fuck about me, number one, He'd not have let my Mary run out in front of a van, and number two – are you listening out there?'

'I'm listening.'

'Number two, He'd show a little bit of consideration and turn my water into wine, you know, like He did at that wedding. Probably wanted to get pissed Himself.' I heard her gasp. 'Sure He loved his wine, that fella – must have been plastered at that last supper 'cos, had He been sober, He'd have run like fuck, as far away from that lot as possible, instead of hanging around waiting for crucifixion. Gobshite.'

I started to laugh, thought I was being hilarious.

'Holy Mother of Jesus, God forgive you,' Aggie shouted, from the other side of the door.

I just kept laughing, loudly, wildly. That sent her packing. I knew it would. I could hear her heavy footsteps on the stairs. Probably cursing me, insulting her friend Jesus like that. A pure disgrace, that Teresa one, she'd tell her Charlie; there's no hope for her or that poor wee fucker, Clint. What did he do to deserve her?

What *did* he do to deserve me? Oh, my poor baby. Another pang. Another tear. Another swig. Sleep, I thought, come to me. Gulp, gulp. Alcohol-induced sleep – problem solved. For now.

I was awake again, alone with my thoughts. I didn't know what day it was. I didn't care. What did it matter? Mary was gone – gone from this world, but not from my head. I kept seeing her, lying bleeding on the street, head in tatters, drawing her last breath. And me, the tart, doing my stuff, the only thing I was any use at, screwing Jimmy, her man.

He was right, my father, what he said to me that day. I wasn't going to go to see him, I'd sworn I never would. I thought I'd seen the last of him the day they carted him off to the County Home. He died six months later.

'Just go and see him, one last time,' Mary told me. 'Say your goodbyes.'

'I don't want to.'

'He can't hurt us now, Teresa.'

'Can't he?'

He was an awful sight – pathetic. Fit for nothing but death. Gone were the strong arms, the bulky chest, the puffy cheeks. The eyes – they looked like they'd been catapulted into his face. I sat on a chair at the end of the bed, in silence, for ten minutes or an eternity, I'm not sure which.

'There's a few pound for you after I'm gone.'

The voice was feeble, the eyes still cold.

The bastard.

'Got a guilty conscience, have you? Hoping your pitiful few quid will save you from the fucking divil?' I spat.

Suddenly, he looked frightened. Ah! Gotcha.

'It wasn't all my fault, lassie,' he tried to protest through dry lips, 'you were . . . you were—'

'I was what?' I snarled. 'Six years old?'

'You were,' he muttered, struggling with his breathing, 'different from the rest of them.'

'What do you mean?'

He said no more, just turned his head and stared over at the poor sick creature in the bed next to him, moaning. What the fuck was he trying to get at? I had to know.

'Hey you, Father, what the fuck do you mean I was "different"? In what way?'

He looked straight at me. His face was so gaunt, so bony, he was halfway to being a skeleton. There was fear written all over it. I struggled to suppress the pity. Fuck you, you're not getting any sympathy from me, you humpy bastard. His lips moved. I couldn't hear the words.

'Speak up, will you? Answer the fucking question. Why was I different?'

He was beginning to get agitated.

'Well,' I said. 'Well,' a little louder. 'Well,' I shouted. 'I'm fucking waiting.'

'Gamier . . . always wanting to please.' He gave a couple of chesty coughs. 'You came to me, dawther. Remember?'

I wanted to slap his face. I would have, only there was no face to slap, no flesh to strike, nothing to hurt – not even a heart. It had turned to stone a long time ago. I walked away, got to the door of the ward and paused but never looked back. He died a week later. I've never said a prayer for him. 'You came to me, dawther. Remember?' I kept hearing him say it, in my thoughts, in my dreams. It haunted me – the blame. For years, I tried to convince myself that it wasn't my fault. I had been six years old. I'd witnessed my mother being beaten up, day in, day out. I'd heard her cry for help. I'd heard her fear. Other people heard but didn't listen. I wanted it to stop, stop, stop. I went to him one day after he had given her a hiding. She was lying on her side on the kitchen floor, holding on to her stomach, whimpering like a wounded animal. I went to him. Climbed the stairs and stood at the bedroom door. He was lying on the bed, breathless.

'Why did you hurt my ma? I love my ma. That was bold. I don't love you.'

'Your ma doesn't love me ayther. None of youse gives a damn about me, do youse?'

'Is that why you get mad, Da? Is that why you get cross?'

174

'Go away, will you?'

I felt sorry for him, in a childish sort of way – thought I'd put my arms around him, give him a big hug and he'd be happy. Wouldn't he? He'd not be angry any more and he'd not hit my ma. I inched my way towards him, treading carefully. I got to his feet, his tummy, lay my head down on his chest. 'If you don't hit Ma, I'll love you too, Da. Honest.' I felt his strong fingers around my wrist, pushing my hand down, curling my tiny fingers around this thing – the shock, confusion. What am I doing?

'That's the good lassie. Away with you now.'

I ran to the bathroom and washed the sticky mess from my hands. The water was so hot – too hot for six-year-old hands – but I had to get them clean, so I scrubbed and I scrubbed, that day and every other day after that. I'm still scrubbing. I never said no. I didn't run away. I didn't scream. I never told my ma. A little tramp. Even then. Yes, he was right yon day. I was different – I was gamier – I was asking for it.

It was early morning when I woke up. It was getting bright. I was bursting for the loo. I eased my way out of the bed. Stood up, wobbled. I sat down again and reached for the bottle. It was empty. Fuck. I staggered to the toilet. I needed to straighten myself out, make it down the town, stock up. I'd be down at the Well first thing, I thought. In and out in no time. Fuck the begrudgers; I was entitled to my period of mourning. I'd try a coffee first, to quench my thirst, wake myself up a bit. The kitchen was in an awful state. I hated the mess. I plugged in the kettle. The sound of the water starting to boil – I'd never noticed it before – was grating on my nerves. I emptied the bin. Bottles clattered off one another. That blasted kettle – screeching. My head was thumping. Click, it stopped. I rinsed out a mug, put in two teaspoons of coffee, three teaspoons of sugar. I needed the boost. I peeped through the sitting-room curtains and saw Clint, strolling up the street with Hughie, on their way to school. I could only see the back of him. His black shiny hair needed a cut. They had on their PE gear. Friday – that's when they had PE. I watched him until he was out of sight. He was happy; I knew by the walk. Love. I just couldn't escape it. My heart was full of it, pumping it all round my body, overwhelming me. It was a burden. I hadn't the space for it, but I was nothing without it. I was dead without it. The sooner I got down that town, the better.

I put on my grey tracksuit, didn't want to be drawing any attention to myself. I opened the front door to light, life, noises. I shut it again. I took a few deep breaths, opened it again and moved forward. I was conscious of every step. I kept my head down, tried to shut out my surroundings, stay focused on the task in hand – in and out in no time.

'Och, howaya there, Teresa?' Her at Number 82.

'Isn't it a terra about your Mary?' The postman.

'You never know, do you?' Old Sheridan.

'Sorry for your troubles, love.' Mrs McKenna.

176

'None of us knows the day or the hour.' Eileen, in her dressing gown, taking in milk from her front door.

I could cope with all that. I didn't need to answer them, just nod and keep walking. The young lad in the Well handed me my brown paper bag.

'That's fourteen pound, Teresa.'

I fumbled in my purse, a fiver, six, seven – oh good, another fiver, that's twelve – two ten-pence pieces and a few coppers.

'Hang on a second,' I said, searching my tracksuit pockets. 'I might have more here.'

'Don't worry about it, Teresa. I'll get you again. You're all right.'

My hands were shaking. He was looking at them. A few more condolences on my way back up the hill. I quickened my pace as I passed Mary's house.

'Teresa,' Jimmy called, coming out of his front door. He must have seen me from the sitting-room window.

I kept walking.

'Teresa, come here, will you?'

I turned around. He looked scruffy and tired. I hadn't seen him since the funeral and I'd hardly seen him that day either with all the people and drink coming at me from all angles.

'You look shockin',' he said.

'You're hardly the picture of health yourself. Are you on your own in there?'

'Yeah.'

'Right, I'll come in so. Just for five minutes. We'll have a quick drink and then I'm away.'

I stumbled through the hall and into the kitchen. Mary's apron was still hanging on a hook on the back of the door.

'Never mind the drink. A pot of tay will do rightly,' he said, filling the kettle.

'Jimmy Buckley, I've never known you to turn down a drink. Come to think of it, I've never known you to fill a kettle either,' I said, laughing nervously.

'You look like you've had more than enough booze. The cut of you! You're an awful-looking sight.'

'Hey, I didn't come here for a fucking lecture,' I said, standing up to leave.

'Will you sit down, woman?'

'No, I'm going.'

'She knew.'

'What?'

'Mary. She knew.'

Christ! Was he saying what I thought he was saying?

I sat down and started to unscrew the top of my bottle. It was snatched out of my hand. I went berserk: kicking, screaming, throwing things around the place. Jimmy grabbed me, but he couldn't hold on. I was like a mad woman. He caught me a second time, holding on with all his might. I struggled to free myself, but couldn't. I thumped him. I dug my nails into him. He flinched, but still held on, pleading with me, 'Calm down, for Christ's sake, Teresa. Calm down.'

'Let go of me,' I roared, and when he didn't, I grabbed his hair, pulling out a chunk of it.

With the force of me trying to escape his grasp and the suddenness of his pain, when he let go of me, I fell to the floor, knocking my head on the back door. I banged it violently with my head a few more times myself. I didn't feel the pain.

'You crazy bitch,' Jimmy spat, still shaken. I laughed at him, continuing to knock my head against the door.

'OK,' he said, his voice unusually soft. 'I'm going to pour you a drink. Look. See?' he said, filling a glass with my vodka. 'Now, come on,' he said, taking hold of my arm and helping me up off the floor, 'sit down and have a drink.'

I sat at the kitchen table and he put the drink down in front of me.

'Hold it with both hands,' he said, as though I was a two-year-old child using a glass for the first time.

'How long?' I asked. 'How long did she know?'

'I'm not sure. She told Marcella the day she – the day of the accident. Marcella told me at the graveside, just out of the blue.'

'What exactly did she say?'

'That her mother knew about me and you. She had told Marcella only fifteen minutes before her death.'

I gasped, remorse descending upon me like a black cloud.

'Marcella looked me in the eye and said, "I hope you're proud of yourself." She hasn't said another word about it since. She was trying to hurt me, I suppose, stick the knife in. Can't say I blame her, after what she's been through, watching her ma . . .'

I lit a cigarette, drained my glass and poured myself another. 'Maybe she was lying,' I said, clutching at straws.

'I doubt it.'

'That's it,' I said, starting to cry. 'It's all our fucking fault. We killed her. You and me. A pair of murderers.'

'How could it be our fault, Teresa? It was an accident, for Jaysus' sake.'

'She'd not have run out in front of the fucking van in the first place, if she hadn't been out of her tree on those bloody Valium. It's all falling into place now.'

'Teresa, you can't blame—'

'Shut up, will you, and listen. All that depression. Lying in the bed, day in day out, the endless tears. It makes sense now.' My heart was pounding. My breathing was erratic. I felt dizzy. 'I tried to finish with you,' I blurted. 'I told you to stay away – but you couldn't, could you? Always after your—'

'Hey! It takes two to tango, Teresa. I didn't exactly have to tie you to the bed, did I?'

'You kept chasing after me – turning up at my house uninvited.'

'You didn't throw me out, did you?'

'So what are you trying to say, Buck? That it was all my fault?'

'No, but it's hard for a man to resist that kind of temptation.'

'So it *was* my fucking fault,' I cried, feeling my stomach heave. I reached across to grasp the bin, but it was too late – I had vomited all over the floor.

Jimmy let a string of curses out of him as he leapt to his feet and dashed out into the backyard.

I sat with my head between my knees, swaying, staring down at my own puke. It was vile – like me. It stank – like me. It was bad, rotten – like me.

Jimmy came back with a mop and bucket. He was making a pig's arse of trying to clean up: started mopping with a dry mop, then dipped it into stone-cold water. Drunk as I was, I noticed that – me being the expert scrubber. But I said nothing, let him at it.

'Stay away from that vodka,' he said, when he saw me trying to fill my glass.

'What the fuck do you care what I drink?'

'Of course I care, you silly cow. Now put that bottle away. You're drunk.'

'So why haven't you made the pass yet? What's wrong? Guilty conscience?'

'Yes, I do feel guilty. That's what you want to hear, right?'

'Well it's too late for regrets now, isn't it?' I hissed.

'I don't regret the time we spent together, Teresa. No way. I was always mad about you. Still am. I cared about both of youse, you and Mary.'

'Hah,' I sneered, 'wasn't that very generous of you? Dividing your time between us – keeping us both happy.'

'Arragh, there's no bloody point in talking to you when you're in this state. Away home with you and sober yourself up,' he said, snapping my half-glass of vodka from my hand and pouring it down the sink.

I started to wail, like a baby whose lips had suddenly lost the grasp of its mother's breast.

'Come on,' he said, grabbing my arm. 'I'll walk you home.'

'Don't touch me!'

'Right,' he said impatiently, 'have it your way. But as soon as I've cleared up this mess, I'm away down the bookie's.'

I cried on, mumbling something about taking bets on how many men I'd had – how many more drinks I'd have downed by evening, shit like that.

He was not amused. He stormed out of the kitchen and slammed the door.

I gulped a few more mouthfuls of vodka from the bottle and got up to leave.

I felt as though I was standing on stilts. I tried to steady myself, holding on to the table. All my limbs were shaking. I staggered out the front door and sat myself down on the windowsill. Through bleary eyes, I could see Jimmy almost at the end of the hill. I got to my feet again, contemplating my next step.

Some woman pulled up in her car and offered me a lift home. I don't remember who it was, but she must have known me, because I recall her using my name when she helped me into the front seat. There was a musty smell in the car; it could have done with a blast of my air freshener. I remember thinking that. Pulling up outside my house, she said she'd help me out of the car.

'You're all right, missus,' I told her. 'I'll manage.

And thanks a million for the lift.' I closed the car door.

Come on, straight line, straight line, I told myself as I headed towards my front door. I fumbled with my key but couldn't get it in. I turned to signal to the woman to give me a hand, but she had driven away.

'Damn it – stupid blasted key . . .'

'Do you want me to do that for you?' It was some kid.

'Good lad,' I said, handing him the key. 'You're a life-saver.'

He got the door open.

'Here,' I said, rooting through my purse, 'buy yourself a few sweets.'

But the purse was empty.

'Sorry, kid,' I said. 'I'm sorry.'

I made it to the couch and collapsed in a heap.

I was alone again. Just me and my booze. At last.

Marcella

No one knew the truth but me. It was always there. It chased after me during the day, poked and prodded me – hey, Marcella, remember me? I tried to shake it off, keep busy. Tidy my room – flashback – do the dishes – flashback – try some school work . . . impossible. At night, it took me over, it had my attention and did jigs in my head with my memories: Ma, hands over her face; hands scrambling through photographs; the same hands with rosary beads wrapped around overlapping fingers that were cold now. The smell of incense, the sounds of grief, the chill in the morgue, the warmth of her blood trickling through my fingers.

I had told her. *I* had pushed her over the edge. She had been in a bit of a state that day. She'd been jumpy. There was something upsetting her, something she needed to get off her chest. I should have listened, shut my gob, let her finish. Blinded by hate I was. Couldn't wait to get my revenge and jumped to all the wrong conclusions. Wanted to. It should have been *her* moment, *her* time to spill out her guts, to roar and shout and curse if she'd needed to. I'd snatched the moment from her. Stolen it. Because I hadn't the patience to hold my careless tongue, mouthy piece of work that I am. 'Seen them at it,' she'd said, 'dirty old git.' I just thought – no, I just didn't think. I spat it out. 'I saw them,' I said, 'buck fucking naked, the cheating bastards.' It was my fault. I'd wanted to take it back when I saw the sadness in her. That bloody doorbell. Ding dong. Ding dong. Someone calling her to her death. Thump. She was down. I watched her die. I saw her face. Her sorrow. I wanted to tell her, 'No, it's not true, Ma, it was a lie.' But I couldn't. It was there, ready to come out, but the truth got past it. 'I love you, Ma.' And she was gone.

Cormac came to the funeral without permission from school. He missed his Pre-Leaving oral Irish to be there. I cried all day. I'd started the evening before in the morgue when they shut the coffin. They dragged me away, arms pulling me back out of sight. But I could still hear them clamp the lid down. Clunk click every trip, like that ad on TV. Fasten up, even for the short journeys – morgue, church, graveyard. How could they? Things like that, they made me cry. Six men in black – her husband, her brothers, her nephews, struggling to lay her on their shoulders. Straight backs, slow purposeful steps. Six men united, paying their respects. At last. I didn't want to look down into that hole. I was frightened of what I'd see – worms, creepy crawlies, old bones. I looked up over the drooping heads, into the clouds, wondering if she was up there, hoping she was. The crowd shuffled. Bodies trying to get to the graveside pushed their way in for a better view. Another shuffle. Da and me, side by side, arm against arm.

'She knew,' I sobbed. 'Found out about youse the day she died.'

'Ashes to ashes.'

'I hope you're proud of yourself,' I said.

Oh God, the pain, ripping through my heart.

Thud. The sound of clay on wood. No, don't do that.

'Dust to dust.' Stop. I can't stand it. I can't breathe.

I felt two arms around me. It was Cormac. 'Excuse me, excuse me, excuse me.' He led me through the crowd, wrapped his arms around me, rocked me, caressed my head, comforted me.

He called for me on the Sunday before I was due to go back to school. I was sorting out books in my bedroom. A bit of normality back in my life, it would do me the world of good, they said. I wondered what they meant by normality. I'd spotted him from my bedroom window, strolling up the hill, smoking. I smiled when I saw him and then felt guilty for doing so. I ran downstairs and opened the door.

'How's my girl doing today?'

I loved being *his girl*. It got me out of bed in the morning, kept me upright when the sadness tried to knock me down.

'Just getting my stuff ready for tomorrow.'

'Are you sure you're ready?' A little peck, just below my eye.

'No. But I'm going anyway. Beats hanging around the house.'

'Tough times?'

I nodded.

'Want to go for a walk?'

'Yeah, OK, when I'm finished what I'm at here. Come on up with me for a minute.'

'Are you on your own?'

'Yeah. They're all away on a mission today, trying to talk some sense into Teresa. She's been pouring booze down her throat since—'

'That's the one who—'

'That's her.'

He'd never been inside the house before, only to the front or back door. He followed me up the stairs and into my room.

'Do the three of you sleep in here?'

'Yeah.'

'God. Does the baby sleep all night?'

'Sometimes. Ends up in the bed between us some nights.'

'Fuck!'

'What?'

'How do you get any sleep – any work done?'

'Just have to try and make the best of it.'

The look on his face – it made me laugh. He seemed shocked.

'It must be hard though.'

'Well, I have to admit, I got used to having my own space when Bernie and the baby were living with Noel. But I'd rather have them here with me than be alone with that creep.'

'I think you're great.'

He was stretched out on the bed now, hands behind his head, his shirt untucked from his jeans, showing shiny sallow flesh. He was gorgeous. I mean really beautiful. It's not a word my friends would have used to describe him. No. Gabby'd have called him a hunk, a ride, a fine bit of stuff or a sexy bastard. And he was. But most of all, he was beautiful. Being with him again, it made me want to cry.

'Don't cry.'

'I'm not,' I said, trying to hold back the tears.

He held out his hand. I took it, lay down beside him and tucked myself into him. There was a long silence. A comfortable silence: my ear on his chest, listening to his heartbeat, his fingertips running through my hair. I watched him as he unbuttoned his shirt and flung it over the chair. I raised my arms and closed my eyes as he lifted my T-shirt over my head. Shoes and socks kicked off. Nothing said. Toes touching toes. Nothing to say. A kiss. A kiss that made me tremble and cry. His lips all over me – my face, my neck, my nipples. Sensations running through my body as if it was covered with butterflies, pulsating wings sending ripples through me. All those pent-up emotions of love and desire, anger and hate rising from within me. I wanted to be naked. I wanted to scream.

'I love you.'

'I love you too.'

His voice. Mine. A struggle with belts and zips. The moment I touched him, he squeezed his eyes shut and cried out with pleasure.

I was like a volcano, about to erupt. Touch me, I thought. He did. It happened – the rush – the explosion – tiny atoms of pleasure released from deep inside me. I felt beautiful, powerful, comforted. We lay together, almost naked, my arms wrapped around him, my soulmate.

I didn't make it to school the following morning. I couldn't. I hadn't slept, not a wink. They had taken Teresa away that night to St Andrew's, to dry out, they said. I should have been happy, her getting her comeuppance, the stupid bitch, but I wasn't. I felt sick – weak. Sick, for Clint. Weak, for caring. I was tired of feelings. They were confusing me, exhausting me.

'Will you quit your shifting about, Marcella,' Bernie complained, 'you'll waken the child.'

'Sorry.'

That bloody film again, *One Flew over the Cuckoo's Nest*, I couldn't get it out of my head. I went downstairs, shuffled across the hall like Jack Nicholson with short steps, bare feet and long gown. I could see Teresa, huddled up on her bed, frightened, the sounds of madness all around her. Long gown versus mini-skirt. I could almost hear her sobbing, *I'm sorry, I never meant to hurt her*. Too late now, you stupid fool. Da's bottle of whiskey was on the kitchen table. I unscrewed the cap, sniffed it. Will I? Won't I?

I took a swig. It tasted even stronger than it smelled.

*

I woke up on the couch, shivering. I could hear Amanda cheering and Bernie's footsteps on the ceiling above me.

Waking up was the toughest part of the day, because for the first few seconds I'd feel a false sense of calm. But then my brain would start ticking over and all the bad memories would come flooding back.

I called to Aggie's after breakfast to find out how Clint was doing.

'Come in, he's here. He didn't want to go to school this morning,' she whispered to me in the hall.

He was stretched across the sitting-room floor, a big drawing pad in front of him and markers scattered around.

'Hi,' I said.

'Hiya.'

'What are you up to?'

'This,' he said, holding up the sheet he was working on. 'It's a design for an album cover. What do you think?'

A big heart, broken in two, filled the page. One half was coloured red, the other half was light grey. There were droplets of blood dripping from the red half onto what looked like a pool of blood underneath. Little designs I couldn't quite make out were drawn underneath the other half.

'What are they?' I asked.

'Icicles.'

'Oh yeah, I see it now. It's really good.'

A slight smile.

'So is this going to be for *your* first album, then?'

'Hope so.'

Aggie called us out to the kitchen for tea and apple tart. It felt good being in her company. She was big, motherly and comforting. She was also in charge. I liked that about her.

'Time's a great healer,' she said, and, 'God is good,' and, 'When you've hit rock bottom, there's only one way to go, and that's up.'

She patted my head. Then Clint's.

'I've to be down in the laundromat for twelve,' she said. 'You'll keep him company till I finish my shift at three, won't you, Marcella?'

'Yeah.'

When she left, I asked Clint to come down to Katie's Coffee Shop with me. I wanted to let them know I'd be back at work the next Saturday.

'What if everyone knows about my mam?'

'Clint, you can't stay cooped up indoors till she gets out of hospital. Anyway, you've got nothing to be ashamed of. It's not *your* fault.'

'It's not her fault either, you know.'

I didn't answer.

We were walking down the hill together in silence.

'You think it's her own fault, don't you?'

I still didn't answer. Couldn't. What I had to say, he wouldn't want to hear. But my silence made him angry.

'I know what you're thinking, but you're wrong about her,' he snapped. 'Aggie says it's a disease – that she can't help it.'

'Well, if—'

'And that your ma's death has been very hard on her.'

191

I was seeing red now – Ma's death being used as an excuse for that bitch's drinking. Her getting all the sympathy, acting like the chief fucking mourner. The two-faced cow.

'Your mother,' I said, standing in front of him, 'didn't give a continental fuck about my ma. If she did, she'd not have—'

'Not have what?'

I couldn't say it. 'Disease, my arse. Cancer, TB, diabetes, they're diseases. People with cancer don't have any bloody choice in the matter, do they? They don't go pouring poison down their throats to make themselves ill and they—'

'Aggie said—'

'Aggie's doing her best to make you feel better, Clint. Your mam, I'm sorry to have to say it, but she's a selfish bitch.'

I saw the hurt in his face. An expression that said, how could you? We were almost at the end of the hill.

'I hate you,' he said, turned and walked away, shoulders drooping, head down.

'Clint,' I called after him. 'Clint.'

There were footsteps behind me. Click clack click clack. It was Ricky Doyle.

'What's wrong with sissy boy? Crying 'cos his oul doll's in the funny farm?' he sneered, then started singing 'The Lunatics are taking over the Asylum.'

Clint heard him. He turned round. His face was pale, his dark eyes like two daggers. He came charging back down the hill towards Ricky who was right beside me. Clint was going to hit him, but he'd have had no chance. Ricky was wiry and well used to fighting. He would have pasted Clint to the wall. It was a split-second decision. I lifted my leg and swung it as forcefully as possible in the direction of Ricky's crotch. I hurt my foot. He fell to his knees, mouth wide open, tears pouring from eyes that were almost crossed.

'Don't you ever talk about Teresa like that again,' I said. 'Wanker.'

'Thanks,' Clint said and burst into tears.

'You're welcome,' I told him, putting my arm around him and heading back up the hill. 'Let's go back to Aggie's house. I'll call to the coffee shop later on.'

'Thanks.'

'And I'm sorry, Clint, for saying those horrible things about your mam.'

'It's OK. What you said, sometimes I think that about her too. I don't know what to believe any more, Marcella.'

'Me neither.'

'They should have locked you up along with her, you crazy bitch, Buckley.' We heard the roar from behind us.

Neither of us turned around.

'Do you miss your ma?' Clint asked.

'Yeah. Do you miss yours?'

'Like mad. Do you think we'll ever be happy again?'

'Dunno.'

'I dunno either,' he said with a sigh, 'but I hope so.'

Teresa

I thought at first I was dreaming when I woke up and heard footsteps – squeaky footsteps: rubber soles on a tiled floor.

'Good morning, Madge.' Swish. Squeak, squeak.

'Good morning, Joan.' Swish. Squeak, squeak.

'How's Martina this morning?' Swish.

'Ah fuck off, nurse.'

Nurse – nurse – yes, that's what she'd said. What the hell was I doing in hospital? I opened my eyes and saw floral curtains drawn round the bed where I was lying in a state of confusion and panic. Then I remembered something: it was dark, raining. I was in a car – Aggie was there. I wanted to sleep but I was being dragged from the car into the cold. Then I was inside. It was warm again and there were strange voices. Aggie was trying to get me to drink coffee – I didn't want it. Then what? Think, Teresa, think. Aggie undressing me – crying. 'You know where you are, don't you, Teresa, love? Oh God, no, that's it – Saint Andrew's – the bloody mental! The footsteps were coming closer.

Squeak, squeak.

'Good morning, May.' Swish.

I curled up, pulled the sheets over my head and

lay still, beads of sweat trickling down the small of my back.

Squeak, squeak. Swish. 'Feeling any better this morning, Alice?'

Squeak, squeak. 'Good morning, Teresa. Teresa? Are you awake, Teresa?'

I could sense the brightness all around me, though I was still huddled under my linen shell.

'Go away.'

The mumbling of the other women came to a stop as soon as I'd spoken, and I felt as if eyes were boring holes through the bedclothes, through my skull into my head. They could see my fear, they could smell it, taste it; it was warm and salty and fresh. They could hear my heart pounding – thump, thump, thump. My body was gone. There was nothing left but fear, and a heart racing – faster, faster – trying to escape before the fear exploded.

Someone coughed, and like a stick of dynamite the fear ignited and I bolted out of the bed and raced through the ward and down a corridor, screaming like a mad woman. Yes, that's what I was. Locked up for my own good.

The nurse from the ward was chasing after me. As I approached the double doors that led to the reception area, another nurse hurried from behind her station and stood in front of me.

'I'm sorry,' she said. 'You can't leave. You signed yourself in. Seventy-two hours' notice. Then you can leave.'

'But I want to go home. I need to see my boy. Give me my clothes.'

'I'm sorry. I can't do that.'

I made a dash for the doors, but they were locked. I shook them furiously, looking through the pane of glass into the corridor that led to my freedom.

'Come on, Teresa,' one of them said, 'take it easy.'

I pressed my forehead against the glass and started to cry.

'At least let me go for a walk.'

'I'm sorry, dear, but rules are rules.'

'You can stick your rules up your arse.'

They wouldn't leave me alone. They were constantly nagging, 'You need to take your medication – you need to eat – you should mix with the other patients – try to settle yourself.'

I wasn't having any of it. They wanted to trick me, like that doctor and Aggie had done when they got me to sign myself in. Bastards.

'What day is today?' I asked the nurse who was writing something on my chart.

'Tuesday.'

'I'm going home on Friday. I'm giving you my notice now. What time is it?'

'Ten past nine.'

'Morning or night?'

'Night.'

'Ten past nine Friday night, I'm leaving. You got that?'

'You'll have to speak to Doctor Kennedy.'

'Take me to him.'

'He's not here till tomorrow.'

Tomorrow came. 'Can I speak to him now?'

'He's at a meeting.'

A couple of hours later. 'Now can I talk to him?'

'He's gone home for his lunch.'

'He's seeing his outpatients.'

'He's on his day off.'

'He's gone to a conference.'

One bloody excuse after another.

For the first week, I felt as though I'd landed on the set of a horror film – strange goings on and creepy sounds – only *I* wasn't part of the cast. I couldn't separate night from day, dreams from reality, madness from sanity. I watched some women in the ward making themselves at home: flowers in their vases, books on their lockers, coffee with their neighbours, cosy chats, having a laugh, having a cry, preparing themselves for their visitors, combing their hair, powdering their noses – home from home. Were they blind? Deaf? Dead? Could they not see what I could see, hear what I could hear, feel what I could feel?

'Would you like to come and watch TV with us?' one of them said. '*Coronation Street* is on.'

'No.'

'OK, maybe next time,' she said smiling.

Huh, I had them sussed, coming on to me like that, trying to soften me up, sweet-talk me, like that mad religious cult I'd read about, the Moonies. Same tactics: target you, lure you, brainwash you – ha ha, gotcha, sucker. They weren't going to get to me, the pyjama brigade, mad as brushes, the whole lot of them. I wanted to go home so badly, I could think of nothing else. I never left my bed except to go to the loo. There were no locks on the cubicle doors. An old woman barged in on top of me one day and pissed on the floor in front of me, with me screaming at her to get out. She lay on her bed afterwards sucking her thumb and whimpering for the rest of the evening. Mad cow.

'Why are there no fucking locks on the toilet doors?' I roared at some nurse.

'In case anyone tries to harm themselves. It's standard practice in all hospitals.'

'This bloody hellhole,' I said, beginning to sob, 'no privacy, no dignity, no goddamn peace.' The nurse was already halfway down the corridor. What did she care about my rantings and ravings? She was well used to it, I guess.

By the time I got to see Dr Kennedy, I was all fired up for a row. I sat on a bench outside his office waiting to be called in, lips pursed, fists clenched. I'd have loved a drink.

'Teresa Reilly,' he called. I remembered his voice when I heard it. Soft, calm.

'Take a seat,' he said, as I walked across his office on rubber legs.

He looked at my chart, then at me. He was handsome and gentlemanly.

'So you've done it cold turkey, I see.'

'What?'

'You didn't take the medication I prescribed.'

'No way. I've seen what that shit does to people.'

'Librium is well established as a very effective drug in combating alcohol abuse. It minimizes the withdrawal symptoms. But you've managed without it and that's OK. However, I would still recommend—'

'Hang on a second, Doctor Do-Gooder, I'm not here for your advice. I came to give you my notice. Seventy-two hours, right?'

'I see. So you feel you can cope with your life without a drink and without support? Can you honestly—'

'I'll be fine,' I snapped, trying to control my shaking hands.

'I have you down on the list to start therapy tomorrow. It's a vital part of the recovery programme. I'm also concerned about your lack of appetite. You're underweight, Teresa. That can cause—'

'I've tried to eat. I can't. The food gets stuck in my throat. It's the smell in this kip. I hate it. That sick stench of lukewarm mushy cabbage-smelling slop. It brings back old memories – cruel ones – of a place I visited once, a bad place – and that smell, it sticks to my nostrils like scum.'

I didn't realize I was crying until he handed me a tissue.

His sincerity and concern disarmed me. I no longer felt angry or threatened, just very sad. I couldn't stop crying. Through my tears, I heard him speak to me in a comforting tone.

'I'd advise you to give the medication a go. It will

help you relax, rest a little bit. You're tired. Your appetite would improve too. Be patient; these things take time. Just go away and think about it and if you change your mind and still want to give me your notice, I'll be in the hospital until five thirty.'

'Thank you,' I sobbed.

'For what?'

'Giving me a choice.'

I left and made my way down the corridor, still sniffling, still shaking, my body feeling like a bagful of weary bones. There was a parcel on my bedside locker when I returned to the ward. Inside there was a nightie, toiletries, three pairs of big grannyish knickers, a packet of Benson and Hedges and a couple of letters. My heart skipped a beat when I spotted Clint's handwriting on one, with *Mam* written inside a big heart. I placed it on my lap and opened the other one, from Aggie.

Dear Teresa,

I hope that by the time you receive this letter, you will have forgiven me. What I did, I did for you, and of course for Clint. Don't worry about the lad, Teresa. Hughie and him are having a whale of a time. The'yd a spelling test last week and your fella got nine out of ten. Brainy wee lad. Hughie says he copied your Clint, but he only managed five out of ten. It mite be his glasses, there probibly not strong enouf. The pair of boys went fishing with Charlie on Saturday and Clint caught a trowt. Mrs Galvin from number 44 has had her sixth child, which is highly suspishous considering her husband has been working in the Shetland ilands for the past twelve months. I haven't seen the kid myself yet, but from all accounts, it has a head of pure orange hair. Are you thinking what I'm thinking – that likely it's that McCorley, the parish bull himself. I'm saying nothing, Teresa, but between me and you, I'd say I'm rite. Anyway, love, that's about all the news. I hope you're feeling a bit better and that you're making progress. I want you to know that I'll always be here for you, Teresa. Me and your Mary, we were the best of freinds and I know she'd be wanting me to keep an eye out for you and that I will. I'll call to see you Wednesday. Take care of yourself and put your trust in God.

God Bless, Aggie.

The tears were streaming again. Without realizing it, I'd picked up a pair of the big knickers and wiped my eyes. I laughed when I noticed what I'd done and almost felt human again, just for a moment.

I ran my finger along the shape of the heart Clint had drawn so beautifully. I had to take several deep breaths before I finally plucked up the courage to open the envelope and read the letter.

Hi Mam, it's me. I hope you are well. Sorry I didn't get to say goodbye to you before you left, but it was late and I was in bed. I'm sleeping in Hughie's room, in the top bunk. I caught a trout on Saturday, helped Charlie clean it out and Aggie cooked it for our tea. She makes us all kneel down and say the rosary every night. Hughie, the plonker, keeps trying to make me laugh, but I close my eyes and think of you. I miss you, Mam, and I think you might miss me too. But don't be sad,

Mam, 'cos soon you'll be better and we can spend more time together. Maybe we could go to Bundoran again for a few days, like we did a couple of years ago. That was great fun, wasn't it, Mam? And we'll be happy then. I'll write again soon, Love Clint. xx

I sat on the edge of the bed rocking, holding Clint's letter to my cheek, inhaling deeply, trying to breathe him in – smell him, feel him, touch him – my baby.

'I have some medication for you, Teresa,' a nurse said, coming through the curtains. 'I hear you've had a change of heart.'

I looked up and nodded. I couldn't see her face through the tears.

'Are you OK?' she asked, sitting next to me. 'You're shaking like a leaf. The letter – it's not bad news, is it?'

I couldn't speak; my mouth was dry, my head was overloaded with feelings, raw feelings, emerging from deep within me, clinging to my skin, making my flesh tingle, curling like ivy around my body, gripping me, strangling me. I panicked. I ran to the toilets and tried to throw up. But there was nothing there, only phlegm and gas and sounds of hollowness from a stomach that was buckled with pain.

'The pills,' I gasped to the nurse who was holding me upright. 'I'll take the pills.'

Back in the ward I lay on my bed waiting for comfort, for sleep.

Minutes passed. My eyelids became heavy, my muscles relaxed.

'That's it, Teresa, take it easy. Try and sleep,' I heard the nurse's voice falling on my ears like snowflakes, as calmness swept through my body like a silk veil.

My first therapy session was with Julie, a woman of about my own age. It lasted only fifteen minutes and I did most of the talking.

'Tell me about your son.' That was all she said. I told her about his birth, his colic, his first words, his school, his love of music, his affectionate nature, his shyness, and that was it. Time up.

'That wasn't so bad,' I said to Madge, the woman in the next bed.

'It'll get tougher,' she said. 'Mark my words. But you have to go through with it.'

She was discharged the following day.

Two days later I had group therapy. Aggie was due to visit that evening. I felt like a right moron, sitting there in my dressing gown in front of a dozen strangers about to discuss matters that were, in my opinion, none of their fucking business. I had my mind made up to keep my ears open and my gob shut. I sat chewing my nails, avoiding eye contact with anyone as a couple of women, in turn, spoke with foolish honesty about their drink binges, their blackouts, spending their housekeeping on noggins of gin and, in one case, an attempted suicide. Hard cases, I thought, God love the pair of them.

Then a man, about forty, cleared his throat, looked around the room and started to speak.

'First of all,' he said, 'I'd like to congratulate and thank the two ladies for their courage and frankness.'

Well, be the hokey, I thought, there's a gentleman.

'Absolutely,' the therapist agreed. 'Well done, Joan and Rosetta. Go ahead, Seamus.'

'It has taken me some time,' the man continued, 'as those of youse who've been attending these sessions over the past few weeks will know, to come to the conclusion that I am an out and out alcoholic. Booze. I couldn't get enough of it. Love the cursed stuff, I do. And that's a fact.' He spoke slowly and clearly. 'And let me tell youse,' he said, 'how low the same bloody booze made me sink.'

He bowed his head, shaking it, like he was ashamed of what he was about to reveal.

'I have a young lassie. She's eleven. She's tall for her age and I suppose you could say ... eh ... well developed,' he said, reddening. 'Her mother, a great woman, decided to throw a birthday party for her. I'd been on the piss the night before and was lying in bed, when the wife came up and asked me to go into town and collect the birthday cake in the bakery. "You'll not be long, will you?" she said, handing me a twenty-pound note. Well, to make a long story short, they didn't see sight nor sign of me again for hours, 'cos I went straight to the pub and ordered a whiskey.'

He sighed, looked around him and continued. 'I ordered another. And another. And another. Knowing my form, the wife rang the pub – it was my local, and the barman told me to drink up and go home. "I will," says I, "I'll just have one for the road." I had six for the road, or more, got into my car and drove home. There were kids running around all over the house. Before I had the chance to open my mouth, the wife started tearing strips off me in front of all the youngsters. Oh God, but that got my goat. Fuming I was – humiliated – not that I'm saying I was entitled to be. I know now I wasn't. But that's how I felt then.'

He paused, took a handkerchief from his dressing-gown pocket and wiped his eyes.

'It's OK, Seamus. Take your time,' the therapist said.

We were sitting on the edge of our seats, silent, waiting, anticipating, and in my case – dreading.

'Then Angela, my daughter,' he said, 'looked me straight in the eye. "You always spoil everything," she screamed at me. "I hate you." She meant it. I stood there, a dozen kids staring at me in disgust. "Now look what you've done," the wife roared. Well, that was it. I'd had enough. Nobody was going to ridicule me, the man of the house, in front of a bunch of childer. I grabbed my wife, kicked her, thumped her . . .'

His voice was beginning to crack. I could see it all again: my mother, on the floor, my father's boot. I could hear it, whack – scream – thump – groan.

'Angela tried to pull me off her,' he said.

My hands were shaking.

'But she couldn't, so she bit me on the arm. I made a swing for her, but I missed and she withdrew to the corner of the room where her friends were huddled together, crying. "Look at her," I sneered, pointing at

Angela, "fat little bitch. Just like her mother. Arse and tits on her like a heifer." My God, I'll never forget her face—'

'You're a bastard!' I shrieked, unable to control my temper any longer. 'A rotten evil bastard!'

The others sat still, silent, tense.

'I didn't mean it,' he cried. 'It was the drink – the whiskey, it—'

'Oh, stop your stupid slobbering,' I roared. 'You—'

'Teresa,' the therapist said, 'will you please . . .'

That was all I heard. There was no talking to me. I'd lost it.

'You have the cheek to sit there crying, feeling sorry for yourself, you filthy . . .' The therapist was still pleading with me to calm down. The man continued to cry, but I kept roaring. 'You don't deserve to have children, you don't deserve to live—'

'Hey!' another male patient bellowed at me. 'Have a bit of manners and wait your turn to speak.'

'Excuse me,' I said, taken aback, 'but this man here—'

'This man here has a name,' he said, 'and it's Seamus. We're not here to judge him. There isn't one of us in this room in a position to go judging anyone else, otherwise we'd not be here ourselves, right?' he said, looking around at the others for support.

'Aye, that's right,' someone said, the others nodded and murmured their agreement.

'Well, if youse are all as bad as him,' I said, getting up to leave, 'I'm out of here.'

'So *you've* never got drunk and done something you've deeply regretted?' the man continued.

'I've never abused my son. Never.'

'So he hasn't been affected by your alcoholism in any way?'

'I am not an alcoholic,' I told him firmly.

'Then why are you here?'

'If you must know – my sister died tragically and I've had a hard time coping. That's all.'

'I'm sorry for your troubles, missus, but to get back to the point. Can you honestly say that, under the influence, you've never done anything you've regretted or that your drinking hasn't had a negative effect on the other members of your family?'

I had my hand on the doorknob now, ready to leave. This man was annoying me, picking on me just because I'd had a pop at that other bollocks.

'Aside from the past few weeks, with my sister dying, I drink to be sociable,' I said, turning the knob, 'because I like what it does to me. That's all.'

'Fair enough. So do half the population. But do you also *loathe* what it does to you?'

'Only when—'

'No. Don't answer that. Not yet. Hold that thought. When you respect yourself enough to be completely honest with yourself, then tell us.'

'If you already know it all, Mister Perfect, how come *you* ended up here?'

'Because someone loved me enough to sign me in. Again. Otherwise, my friend, I'd be dead.'

A solemn silence followed, broken only when the therapist stood up and said, 'Thanks, everyone. That's it for today. I have no doubt progress has been made.'

I rang Aggie at work and told her not to come to see me that evening. I wasn't ready for visitors yet.

Honesty. It sounded so simple, so straightforward. It wasn't.

I drew the curtains round my bed, lay down, closed my eyes and took deep breaths. I thought about Clint and the last time I'd seen him. It must have been a fortnight earlier. He was staying at Aggie's at the time.

I was barefoot. The dirt from the kitchen floor was sticking to my soles. I didn't know what time it was; the kitchen clock had stopped. I rooted through drawers, presses and coat pockets in search of a cigarette. I hit my toe on the leg of the stool on my way into the sitting room and cursed. I got down on my knees and rummaged through the ashes in the grate for a cigarette butt long enough to re-light, and smiled like I'd struck gold when I found one. I picked it up and blew the ashes from its puckered tip.

'Mam.' It was Clint's voice. Oh God, I thought, I'm hearing things. I'm going crazy. I froze, still on my knees by the fireplace.

'Mam.' I crouched down and covered my ears.

'Are you OK, Mam?' Sweet Jesus! He was there, standing behind me. I scrambled to my feet and turned round. I saw my boy, staring at me, his beautiful face riddled with pain. I felt my heart twist. Then I did what any mother worth her salt would do: I reached out to him, to hold him, comfort him. But as I lunged towards him, he yelped and withdrew like a child spooked by the bogeyman.

'Clint,' I cried out in desperation, but it was too late, he was gone and I was alone. Again. I lay down on the couch and prayed for death to come and take me away, for I was useless and weary; I had lost the will to survive, and the strength it would take to crawl out of my pit of hopelessness.

'I want to talk to you about my life,' I told Julie, my counsellor.

'OK.'

'But I'm scared.'

'I know.'

'But I have to do it, don't I?'

She nodded.

'*You* may be able to listen to what I have to say, but I'm not sure I can.'

'Take all the time you need, Teresa.'

'The day my sister Mary died, I was at home in bed with Jimmy, my lover – her husband.'

I looked Julie in the eye and I knew she wasn't judging me.

I took a deep breath.

Marcella

'Shut up, Marcella. Shut up. You're dreaming,' Bernie whispered, shaking me.

Oh yes, thank you, God. I was awake; I was alive. It was over. For now.

'Ah, fuck you! Amanda's awake now,' Bernie said, as I sat up in the bed speechless, relief sinking in, sweat pouring out.

She was bent over the cot, trying to get Amanda back to sleep, holding the soother in the child's mouth. But Amanda was having none of it as she kicked her legs, opened her mouth and bawled.

With Ma gone, I was glad to have Bernie and Amanda back home. Noel had given Bernie another hiding the day Ma died and had threatened to wallop Amanda too if she didn't stop crying. As Bernie herself said, that was the last straw.

'Ah bollocks on ya, Marcella. She's awake for the rest of the fucking night now,' Bernie moaned, lifting her child from the cot. 'That's the second time this week you've woken her up.'

Amanda roaring, Bernie complaining, it was music to my ears. I was at home, I was back from hell.

'I'll take her downstairs and give her a bottle,' I said. 'You go back to bed.'

'Are you sure?'

'Yeah,' I said, anxious to get out of the bed and downstairs, where I could turn on the lights and make it feel like daytime again.

'Did you have another bad dream?'

'Must have. Can't really remember,' I lied.

I remembered it all too well, but the last thing I wanted was to talk about it. That would make it seem more real, give it a greater presence.

It had been a peaceful dream at first. I was lying alone in a big field, nothing but green grass around me. I could feel the sun on my face. I closed my eyes, still sensing the brightness above me. I felt sleepy, contented. Suddenly the earth rumbled, sending shivers through me. I opened my eyes and saw a black shadow, shaped like a hand, reach across the sky and seize the sun, smothering its brightness, quenching its heat. In the darkness my body began to sink into the soil, its cold grittiness clinging to my skin. I tried to leap up but I couldn't move, every muscle of my body was paralysed with fear. The ground was sucking me up, or down in this case. There was nothing left of me but my face. I was petrified about the bottomless pit beneath me, and the suffocation. I opened my mouth and screamed, the noise filling my head but not the air. I could hear the echo of my pounding heart vibrate in the black sky above me like the death march. As the icy soil began to fill my ears, the sounds began to fade. Whoosh! A sudden drop. I couldn't breathe. Then I heard it – a voice, someone calling me, someone touching me, holding me, shaking me. Bernie. And the beautiful sound of her voice, bringing me back to life, to safety.

I went back to school after the Easter break. It felt strange – everyone around me acting like normal, yakking on about discos, lads they'd shifted, revision they needed to catch up on and the pending Pre-Inter results. Some of the girls and a couple of teachers welcomed me back and said they were sorry for my trouble. And that was it. Subject closed.

'Open your books at page fifty-five.'

All I could see on page fifty-five, or any other page, was a mass of insignificant words. The harder I tried to concentrate, the more I began to hate all the useless information being shoved in my face from all angles. I didn't want it. I turned away from it, like Amanda did with her spoon-feed when her stomach was full. Only she had the mechanism to digest what she'd just swallowed and would soon be ready for more; I, on the other hand, had not.

So I sat back in my chair and thought about Cormac, longing to see him, wishing the time away. My distraction didn't go unnoticed.

'With all you've been through, it's probably best for you to repeat the third year, Marcella,' Sister Goretti, the principal, said. 'But no harm to sit the exams anyway. It will be good practice for you.'

I wasn't capable of thinking about the future. The day ahead was as much as I could contemplate. Getting through it without crying, without remembering, without nightmares. School was no longer somewhere to learn, it was simply a place to go, somewhere to hide from the gloominess of home and Fatima Hill.

Cormac came to my house one afternoon when everyone was out. He put his arms around me and held me to him. I liked being held. I needed to be touched.

We kissed. A peck. Another. Lips brushing over lips. Teasing. Tongues barely touching. A little groan. Two bodies waiting – tick tock, tick tock – hearts beating.

Without saying a word, we undressed each other down to our underwear, both of us groaning, sick with desire. As he ran his fingertips over my breasts, energy poured into my body – a powerful force that had no limits, no fear.

I knew it was going to happen. I couldn't stop it, didn't want to. He removed my underwear, then his. I wrapped myself around him.

'I love you,' he whispered. He did. The love. I saw it in his face like a pain. I felt it in his hands.

His love was inside me, thrusting, giving my body pleasure, pain, comfort.

I slept in his arms afterwards, no fretting – no nightmares.

When I opened my eyes, Cormac was still sleeping. I stroked his cheek, smiling. I loved him, owned him – that's how I felt. He was my strength, my consolation. Da had his drink, Josie and Bernie had their kids. I had Cormac, at least until I heard the back door slam.

It was Da. I could tell by the plod of his footsteps. He let out a rough chesty cough.

'What was that?' Cormac said, waking up.

'Ssh,' I whispered. 'It's Da.'

'Shit! Fuck! I'm a dead man, Marcie.'

'Don't worry. He's not going to walk into the room. He never does. Wouldn't dare. I'll go down and offer to make him a cup of tea. He'll not be able to get out of the seat with the shock. Then you sneak downstairs and out the front door. I'll meet you at the end of the hill in ten minutes.'

'Ah Jesus, what if he—'

'Trust me. He won't. Just be careful on the third step of the stairs. It creaks.'

'Third from the top or third from the bottom?'

'Top,' I whispered, leaving the room and heading downstairs.

I knew from Da's bleary eyes that he'd had a fair few scoops. He was ogling Samantha Fox's tits, which were splashed across page three for the benefit of the hard-ups and perverts. Da fitted both categories.

I started rattling about in the kitchen, making as much noise as possible.

'Do you want a cup of tea?'

'Hah? Who? What?'

'I said, do you want a cup of tea?'

'What are you shouting at me for? I'm not in the next county,' he said, getting up.

'Where are you going?' I asked.

'The bog. Is that all right?'

For a piss or a wank, I wanted to say, but thought better of it.

'Can I go first? I'm bursting.'

'I'm bursting meself,' he said, about to open the sitting-room door.

'Ouch,' I roared and doubled over.

'What's wrong with you?'

'I've a cramp in my stomach. I need the fucking loo, now.' I brushed past him and up the stairs. I checked under the bed and in the wardrobe. No Cormac. I flushed the loo and came back downstairs.

'It's all yours,' I yelled, opening the front door.

'What about me tea?'

'You know where the kettle is,' I shouted, closing the door behind me.

Cormac was due back at Saint Michael's at six that evening. He did not return until after nine. After a long walk, we met up with Gabby and Luke and between us drank two bottles of wine.

'To friendship,' Luke said, holding out the bottle and throwing his arm around Cormac's shoulder.

'And love,' Cormac said, winking at me.

And happily ever afters, I thought, but kept my lips sealed.

Teresa

I had nothing and everything in common with the people I sat beside in group therapy. None of our backgrounds were similar, our personal problems varied, but we had all shared the same crutch, fallen into the same pit, felt the same pain, carried the same guilt and faced the same challenges.

We were all alcoholics. Simple as that, although it took more than a few sessions for me to pluck up the courage to admit it to myself.

The secrets of my life I kept for my counsellor, Julie. Hers was the ear into which I whispered the bad bits, the confessions, the dirt.

'I worked in a bar in Kilburn,' I told her. 'There were a lot of Irish living in the area. They all knew me, the bould Teresa, the cheeky barmaid, the wild one, game for a laugh – and a lot more along with it. "So you're the famous Teresa," a newcomer to the bar would say.'

'All this attention from men – how did it make you feel, Teresa?'

'I remember one particular night. I finished my shift at seven but, as usual, I stayed on in the bar accepting offers of free half-ones from any man who fancied his chances. I was half-cut, flirting with some fella. "You're on to a good thing there," Billy the barman told him.

Nudge nudge. Wink wink. I took it as a compliment. I was sexy, desirable, easy, ready to please. I mattered, for fuck's sake. Isn't that all any of us want – to matter?'

'How do you feel about these men now?'

'I hate them all. Users, the whole lot of them, just like that farmer. The bastard.'

'What farmer?'

'A man I slept with recently. I was drunk. I had just finished with Jimmy. I don't remember much about it. The sex is a complete blank. I know it happened, but I have absolutely no memory of it. Isn't that a good one? I had quit all that screwing around when I came back from England. I had Jimmy to look after me. He was very jealous too. It'd be God help the man he'd find sniffing around me. Jimmy and me – we needed each other.'

'Is he Clint's father?'

'No.' There was a long silence. 'I'll tell you about Clint's father next time.'

'OK, Teresa.'

I was exhausted after each session. I'd lie down and sleep until teatime. They allowed me to eat in the ward, while the others went to the dining room. I would only eat food that was covered – a banana, a triangle of cheese, a bag of crisps or a yoghurt, anything that hadn't been exposed to the dreadful smell.

Then I'd go for a walk round the hospital grounds. Sometimes alone, sometimes with another patient from the ward. I was one of them now, the cooperative bunch, allowed to take a walk, allowed to get dressed.

New patients arrived, hid behind the curtains, cried all night.

Aggie came to visit, bringing me grapes, cigarettes, a prayer book and a lend of her rosary beads. She filled me in on all the gossip and reassured me that Clint was well and getting excited about me coming home soon.

'Remember all those men I told you about, Julie?'

'Yes.'

'Any one of them.'

She looked at me curiously.

'Any one of them could be Clint's father. Poor kid. Not that he's aware of his obscure origins.'

'He hasn't asked?'

'Oh he's asked all right. And I've told him, like I told the rest of my family, that he was the result of a love affair I'd had with a married man, whose wife was ill – an invalid. That's the thing about having a shady past, you can adjust the grey areas, give them a bit of colour – a nice rainbow colour – nothing dark or depressing.'

'I think that the past, whatever colour it might be, is part and parcel of who we are. The grey areas, as you call them, are best brought out into the open, so you can throw some light on them, examine them in greater detail.'

'You really think so?'

'Tough as it may be, I do.'

'Maybe next time.'

'Maybe.'

*

I knew it was coming. We were getting there, me and Julie. She wanted me to get there first, but I was stalling. I wanted her to lead me there, take me by the hand. And in the end, she did.

'Tell me a little bit about your childhood, Teresa.'

'What about it?' I wanted her to be more specific.

'What are your earliest memories?'

It had started.

'Feeling terrified,' I said. 'Down on my hunkers underneath the kitchen table, looking at my mother lying on the floor by the cupboards with her knees up to her chest, and her hands on her head, yelping, while my father kicked the crap out of her. It was desperate. All I could see of him were his two, big black boots, and them swinging and ramming into her legs, sides, stomach, back, anywhere he could get at.'

I shook the last cigarette out of the packet and held it unlit, flicking it like it had a long ash.

'I used to keep my hands over my eyes and look out through the gaps in my fingers. Like this.' I held my splayed hand over my face. 'But I wouldn't move or make a bloody sound either. I was petrified.'

Julie was nodding, holding her chin between her thumb and index finger.

'There were times, I'm not joking ya, I'd hear the oul bastard panting. He'd be out of breath from the pure effort of giving her his best. I'd swear he enjoyed it.

'I remember one time in particular, he got her right in the face and there was blood pumping out of her mouth and he was calling her all the dirty names under the sun. The poor woman was staring over at me . . .'

I pulled my lighter from my pocket, and stroked it several times, but the bloody thing wouldn't ignite.

'Let me try,' Julie said, taking it from me and lighting it on her first attempt.

'Christ, I'll never forget the look in her eyes,' I held the cigarette over the flame and sucked it hard, 'I never saw fear like it. She wanted me to help her, I know she did. And I wanted to crawl out from under the table and go to her, but I couldn't. He was leaning against the table and it was shaking above my head. It was a rickety old thing at the best of times.'

I blew smoke at the ceiling.

'All I did was stare back at her. Some daughter I was, huh?' My chin began to wobble. 'I was useless, totally, fucking useless. I'm sorry, Julie,' I said, starting to cry.

'What for?'

'All this blubbering.'

'Crying is natural, Teresa. It's good for you. It's the unshed tears that do the damage.'

'You know, any time I see a fly stuck in a web, and a big gruesome spider comes and squeezes the life out of it, I panic. The same feelings emerge. I hate spiders. I'm terrified of them. So I stand there, watching until it's all over, until the fly has been crushed. Then I want to throw up.'

'There was nothing you could have done for your mother, Teresa. You were a child.'

'Oh, but that's where you're wrong! There was

something. I didn't know it then – when I was five years old – but I found out at six.'

'Go on.'

'He says I came to him. It was my fault – and maybe he's right.'

She smiled sympathetically at me.

'You know what, Julie? I'm tired. I need to lie down.'

Sometimes exhaustion just hit me, out of the blue, in the middle of telling her something, mid-sentence even. And I'd have to leave there and then. Julie never complained. She was always patient.

'OK. See you Friday. And, Teresa, difficult as all this may seem, you are making progress.'

'You think so?'

'I know so.'

I lay in bed that night, thinking how odd it was that I could make progress only by facing my past. I had to go back in order to be able to move forward.

'It's what might be called a paradox,' Julie told me the next day when I returned to her.

'I couldn't stand the beatings any longer. It made her sad; it made me sad. I don't know about my brothers and sisters. Funny thing is, we never talked about it. I guess we were afraid like I am now.'

'Of course you are. You're human.'

'Yeah? Well there have been times in my life I haven't felt human.'

'When?'

'When I was alone with my father. When he took

my six-year-old hand and made it do things that the six-year-old head didn't understand. When his big, greasy, groping fingers wandered around the six-year-old body, touching parts of it I didn't know existed. And when finally, at seven, having been gradually prepared for it, he gave his daughter a birthday present she'd never forget, no matter how she tried. And to make sure she didn't, he gave it to her again, and again, and again – and in the end, the girl didn't feel the pain, just like her rag-doll, Suzie. You could throw Suzie all around the room, you could lie down on her, squish her, pull her, stretch her, and she never cried. As a matter of fact, she was still smiling – and she was always, always silent.'

'And finally that silence has been broken.'

'Yes. After twenty-five years.' I hadn't yet shed a tear. But I felt freezing cold and numb inside.

'I need a smoke,' I said, shivering.

'You're doing really well, Teresa,' Julie said, looking under papers and folders for the ashtray.

I lit a fag. Julie gave up her search, left the room and returned with an ashtray.

'No chance of a stiff drink, I suppose?'

Julie looked at me. She had a very expressive face. She felt my pain. I know she did.

'How do you do it?' I asked, my teeth chattering.

'Do what?'

'Listen to other people's problems, day in, day out. Does it not get to you?'

'I do exactly what I encourage other people to do:

I listen to them, discuss their problems with them, then leave them where they belong – behind me.'

'Sex with a beast. You reckon I can leave that behind me?'

I started to shake, like I shook underneath the rickety table, like I shook underneath my father. I felt as if he was leaning over me. I could feel his body hair on my skin, his breath on my face, his weight down on top of me. I was screaming. It was the pain that made me scream. The pain he shoved inside me, pain that never went away, pain that spread through me, like cancer. It was smothering me, killing me.

I could hear Julie's voice, but it seemed distant. She was too far away. She couldn't help me. I bolted out of the room. I was running somewhere. Nowhere. Anywhere. There were people around me, holding me. Julie's voice was among the crowd.

'The doctor's going to give you some medication, Teresa. An injection. OK? Is that OK, Teresa? Is that OK?'

I nodded, still overcome by panic. They say that shock can kill a person. Too right it can. Panic almost killed me. My heart had broken its speed limit. It was about to crash, I'm sure it was. I thought it had, until I woke up in the middle of the night in a cold sweat. I lifted my fags and lighter off the locker and tiptoed out to the loo, where I sat in a cubicle crying and smoking until dawn.

Although I hadn't another appointment with Julie until after the weekend, she came to see me the following morning.

'How are you feeling?'

'Like shit on a stick.'

'No relief at all?'

'Maybe a bit. It's like when I had my appendix out. The bad bit has been cut out but the wound is deep.'

'It will heal.'

'You're sure?'

'I'm sure.'

'Thanks for coming in to see me.'

'No thanks required. See you Monday.'

'OK.'

Over the weekend, I felt like my life was hanging in mid-air, stuck between the past and the future. I was scared of both.

'*Dallas* is on,' Rosetta, another patient, told me. 'Are you coming down to watch it?'

'Why not?' I said, following her out of the ward. 'It'll make a change to hear about someone else's problems.'

I was the first one called to see Julie on Monday morning.

'Do you feel ready to carry on?'

'Ready as I'll ever be.'

'The abuse, Teresa. How long did it go on?'

'Last time was the day before my mother died. I was eight.'

'What happened to your mother?'

'Brain haemorrhage. "Just one of those things," they said. The fact that she had had her head kicked in once a week for over twenty years didn't seem to count.'

'And her death put an end to the abuse?'

'Yes.'

'Who stopped it?'

'What?'

'Did he stop coming to you?'

'Yes. He had to. The deal was off. At least, that's what I've always believed to be the reason.'

'The deal?'

'That's what he called it.'

'What did he mean?'

'He meant that *I* had come to him at six years of age and asked him to leave Ma alone, said that I loved her. He said he would but that *he* needed to be loved too. He was stretched out on his bed resting after yet another beating. I lay my head on his chest and I hugged him, to comfort him, so he'd not be angry any more with Ma. I told him that I loved him. He grabbed my wrist, pushed my hand down his trousers, made me – you know – jerk him off. I didn't know it was wrong. I only knew I didn't like it. It made me feel dirty.'

'He didn't stop beating your mother, did he?'

'No, but he said to me once, after he'd finished molesting me, "You've just saved your mother from a hammering." I believed him. I thought I was doing some good. Stupid little idiot that I was.'

'Teresa, you were six years old. You were abused. It wasn't your—'

'My fault? Then why do I feel so guilty? Maybe I could have stopped it, told someone about it – told Ma.'

'You were trying to protect her. Your father took advantage of your love for your mother, your innocence, your fear—'

'But why me? Why not any of the rest of them? I tried to stay out of his way. I tried to be invisible. But he would always find me in the end. I hated it; I hated him. Still do.'

'Teresa, you could spend the rest of your life trying to figure out why your father did what he did, but you'll never find an answer. So don't drive yourself crazy looking for explanations. All you need—'

'He reckoned I was willing. Gamey – that's the word he used.' The tears were flowing again. 'I'm tired of all this weeping, Julie. When will it ever end?'

'It'll get easier in time. I'm not saying you'll ever forget what happened to you, Teresa, because you won't. But what you *can* do and what you're *going* to do here and now is lay the blame in the hands of the culprit: your father. You've been bearing the guilt on your shoulders for far too long.'

'But he's dead now. The bastard.'

'It doesn't matter. It's still his burden to bear. *His* sin. Not yours. Now close your eyes,' she said, holding my hands.

I closed them.

'Now speak to him for the last time. Say what you need to say.'

'He's not listening.'

'Maybe he is. Maybe he isn't. It doesn't matter. *You're* listening.'

'I – I – I – Oh, this is useless. I can't.'

'You can. I'm with you.'

I took a few deep breaths.

'Da – no I can't call him that, he was no da to me. What will I call him? What will I call him, Julie?'

'It's OK, Teresa, take it easy. You don't have to call him anything. Just say what you need to say.'

'OK, OK.' I closed my eyes. 'I never made a deal with you, you bastard. Never. I want you to know that every time you touched me, you really hurt me physically and mentally, and I thought – until now – permanently. But no more.'

Julie squeezed my hands gently.

'Because now I know the truth, you sick fucker. You abused me. You got that? *You* abused *me*. So here you are,' I cried, remembering that stench again, as I stood at his deathbed. 'Take it – all that guilt and shame that's been haunting me for twenty-five years. Take it. It's rightfully yours, and God forgive you, because you can be damned sure I never will.'

I stopped. I heard Julie snivel.

'Go on,' she whispered.

'I do, however, absolve myself from any blame, because now I know it was not my fault, and that, as they say, is the crux of the matter.'

I opened my eyes. I had stopped crying.

'There's only one thing left for you to do now.'

'What's that?'

'Move on.'

*

I could have filled a bath with all the tears I shed over the following couple of weeks. But the fogginess of my life began to clear. I didn't get used to the smell, but I continued to take my medication and I never missed a group therapy session. I learned a lot during these sessions about life, about other people, about alcoholism and about myself.

Jimmy arrived in the ward one evening, wearing a sombre expression, his black leather jacket, black jeans and a black cap.

'You look like the grim reaper,' I said, laughing.

He didn't see the funny side. He was too heavy-hearted.

I hadn't realized until that moment how vulnerable the man could be. He said he missed me. And Mary. He wasn't coping too well in his new situation. He had come, not to give comfort, but to be comforted. I didn't blame him. Why should I have? That was what our entire relationship had been based on – mutual using of each other. Only *I* didn't need to take from him any more. Shaky as I was, for the first time in my life I was beginning to rely on myself, beginning to have faith in myself. I owed him nothing. We were even, and I told him so. He was sitting on the bed next to me. He looked at me like a wounded puppy. I leaned over to give him a kiss on the cheek; I couldn't help it. But he took it the wrong way and tried to kiss me back on the lips.

I drew back. 'No, Jimmy.'

If looks could kill, I'd have been dead.

He charged out of the ward, mad as hell. I knew by the jerking shoulders and the quick step of him that he'd be heading to the nearest bar. A cold pint, a whiskey chaser – oh, I could almost smell it.

'How would you feel about going home, Teresa?' Doctor Kennedy said.

'Home?'

He nodded.

'Nervous, excited, fantastic – and that's just for a start.'

'How about Saturday or Sunday afternoon?'

'Yeah, great. As long as I'm home in time for last orders,' I said, smiling.

'It's been a pleasure,' he said, reaching across the desk, his arm outstretched. It was a warm handshake. A congratulatory one. At least that's what I imagined it to be.

My thoughts over the next couple of days were of Clint and Marcella. I had a lot of ground to make up. I knew that. I tried preparing myself, writing down what I should say. I bought a notepad, filled the pages with sentimental heart-felt words but scrapped the lot in the end. Trust. I needed to earn their trust. Words were not enough. It would take time. Sober time, lots of it. The challenge was enormous and frightening. How could I possibly manage it? Me, of all people.

Stop, I told myself, stop being so bloody negative. You've been sober for several weeks. All you need to do now is to take one day at a time.

Marcella

'Good news,' Bernie said, as I came in through the back door after school one evening. 'I've been talking to Aggie and she says Teresa'll be coming home at the weekend.'

I was surprised to feel upset about the news. I had become used to life without her, had begun to feel less riled. With her back on the scene, I knew there'd be the possibility of crossing her path.

'Aggie's organizing a welcome-home tea for Teresa on Sunday,' Bernie said. 'You'll be there, won't you?'

'No.'

'Why not?'

'I'll be busy revising.'

'Can you not make an appearance for an hour?'

'No.'

'I don't know what to make of you any more, Marcella. Talk about selfish!'

She wasn't even home yet and it had already started. The tension, the defensiveness, the anger. Auntie bloody Teresa – the bane of my life.

I visited Ma's grave on the Wednesday and told her about Teresa's expected homecoming.

'Don't worry, Ma,' I whispered, 'she doesn't fool me. I won't forget what she's done. She can't hurt you now.

No one can. Remember Cormac, Ma?' I said. 'We're in love. I lost my virginity to him and it was wonderful. He was so gentle. And ever since, I have this warm feeling inside, like sunshine in my tummy. You don't have to worry about my heart, Ma. I'll be fine. I think it was fate, me meeting him just before you – you had to go.' I went down on my hunkers and ran my fingers along the cold moist soil. It was as close to her as I could get. 'Remember when I first told you I wanted to go to Loreto and you burst out laughing. You thought I was mad. But now, you see, it was meant to be so I'd meet up with Cormac.' I smiled at the thought of him. 'There's a reason for everything – that's what Aggie says. I'm doing the Inter soon – first of the Buckleys to do it. Don't think I'm going to do too well, though. Haven't been able to concentrate.' The wind blew, spraying my face with the beginnings of rain. 'But I'll try, Ma, because I want to make you proud of me. I'd better go; I think it's going to pour. Miss you, Ma,' I said, standing up and backing away slowly. 'And I'd do anything to have you back.' It was always hard to walk away. She was all alone and cold in her grave and I was deserting her. That's how it felt.

I just made it back to Fatima Hill in time for my five o'clock call from Cormac.

'I have to go home this weekend, Marcie. I won't be able to see you.'

'Why? What's happened?'

'I'm not sure yet. Dad rang and announced he'd be picking me up at four on Friday. When I asked him why, he just barked down the phone at me, "Because I said so," and hung up. So I don't know what it's about.'

'Maybe one of the Brothers has told him you've been arriving back late every Sunday evening.'

'Could be. Although I doubt he'd overreact to something like that. I'll just have to wait and see. Hey, don't worry. I'll ring you on Monday. Usual time.'

'OK. I'll miss you.'

'Not as much as I'll miss you.'

'Love you.'

'Love you too.'

Teresa

'Let me carry that bag for you,' Charlie said.

He picked it up and walked a couple of steps ahead of myself and Aggie as we made our way across the grounds of Saint Andrew's to the car park.

'So how does it feel, love?' Aggie said.

'You mean leaving the hospital?'

She nodded.

'Everything feels new. Different. It's like I'm walking out into the same world but I'm seeing it from another angle.'

'Does it look better?' Aggie asked, putting her arm round my shoulder.

'I think so. Hope so.'

'You look terrific,' Charlie said, as I climbed into the car. 'Your lad will be quare and happy to see you.'

'Thanks. Where is he?'

'He's back at your house,' Aggie said; 'youse can have your little reunion as soon as you get home and then I'll have tea for us all in my house at six. How's that?'

'Yeah, lovely. Thanks, Aggie.'

'You must be bursting to see him after all this time.'

Suddenly the realization hit me that in an hour I would be back with my son again and the thought made my ticker flutter.

'Aggie,' I said, my lips quivering, 'wha— what if . . . eh . . . he doesn't want to see me? I mean he's probably had a better time living with youse over the past couple of months than he's ever had with me.'

'Go way outa that. If ya'd seen the grin on that lad's face over the past couple of days since he heard you were coming home. I'm telling you, I never seen a kid look so happy. Am I right, Charlie?'

'Indeed and you are.'

The whole way home, they did their very best to alleviate my fears and put my mind at rest. But reassurance, even in bucketloads, just didn't have the same immediate effect on me as a shot of liquor would have had. It stopped the fear from growing, but it didn't numb it like a drink would have done. Still, it was enough to get me out of Charlie's car and up to my front door. Aggie had offered to come with me, but I needed to face Clint on my own, nervous as I was.

I rang the bell. I saw his shadow through the frosted glass. He looked taller.

'Hi, Mam,' he said, smiling at me shyly.

'Hi, love,' my voice squeaked through the big emotional lump in my throat. I stepped inside, dropped my bag and closed the door behind me.

'You want some tea?' Clint asked, walking into the kitchen. 'I bought a Swiss roll.'

'Sounds good to me,' I said, following him through.

I sat down at the table, watched him light the cooker and busy himself with mugs and tea bags. Jesus, how I loved that boy.

He mumbled something. I didn't quite hear him. He had his back to me.

'What was that, love?'

'I said, I missed you.' His voice was trembling.

He turned around, tears running down his cheeks. I got up and threw my arms around him. Christ, such emotion. I hugged him, kissed him and cried all over him, just like I had the day he was born. There aren't fancy enough words to describe a love so intense. The second the doctor laid him down on my stomach in the delivery room, I exploded into tears. Four hours of roaring and cursing the wee fecker for causing me such pain, and not a single tear did I shed. Then the minute it was over and I had him in my arms, I bawled.

'What's wrong?' the doctor had asked.

I couldn't get the words out. Probably just as well; he'd have thought I was daft. I was crying because it had hit me that, one day, I would be permanently separated from the tiny ball of perfect love clinging to my breast – by death. Talk about a bloody gloom merchant! I'd had him only a split second when that sad realization overwhelmed me. And it came over me now as I held him in my arms on my first day home from hospital.

Aggie had prepared a wonderful spread of sandwiches, apple tarts, trifles and buns. There was no booze, even for the civilized social drinkers, but there was enough caffeine consumed to have given any one of us a boost. Josie, PJ and Bernie showed up with their kids. There were awkward excuses made for Jimmy's and Marcella's absence.

'Not to worry,' I said. 'I'll catch up with them soon enough.'

Although a little fragile, I was happy to be back and surrounded by family and friends who cared for me and were loyal to me. I didn't feel worthy of such a display of affection, but I was sure glad of it.

'Are you better now, Mam?' Clint asked me when I went into his room to kiss him goodnight.

I sat on the edge of the bed and looked into his dark questioning eyes. Oh, how I wished that I could say, yes, son, it's all over, I'm better now, honest.

I wanted nothing more than for him to trust me, believe in me.

'I'm an alcoholic, son. And alcoholism is a disease. How I'm going to manage the disease, I can't say for sure. But what I can tell you is that I *want* to manage it. I don't want to take another alcoholic drink. I want to be straight with you. And most of all, I don't ever want to hurt you again. I know it's hard for you to under-stand, love, but—'

'I'm scared, Mam – of losing you.'

'I'm going nowhere, pet. I'm not ill, I'm not dying. I just need to find a way to live without alcohol.'

'Why can't you just decide never to drink again?'

'I can. I can make that decision here and now. Sticking to that decision, that's the tricky bit. Look, love, I'm going to a meeting tomorrow night. It's called an AA meeting; it stands for Alcoholics Anonymous. There'll be an Alateen meeting on too and—'

'Ala what?'

'Alateen. For the kids of alcoholic parents. You could go to that and meet other kids in the same situation as yourself.'

'No, it sounds embarrassing.'

'It's up to you. You don't have to decide right now.'

'I don't like meeting new people, 'cos they always ask about my dad and I never know what to tell them. Sometimes, I just say . . .'

'What, love?'

'Ah, nothing.'

'Go on, tell me.'

'Promise you'll not be mad.'

'I promise.'

'I tell them he's dead 'cos I don't want them to think he doesn't love me, or doesn't bother coming to see me. Oh, I'm sorry, Mam. Don't cry.'

'Cry! It's been my favourite pastime this past few weeks,' I sobbed.

'You don't need to cry any more, Mam. You're home now.'

'You're a good boy, Clint,' I said, stroking his cheek. 'What I did to deserve having a son like you, I'll never know.'

'*I* know.'

'Yeah?'

'Yeah. You're the best mam in the world. So you deserve the best son.'

'Thank you.'

'So you're not mad with me?'

'Mad with you? No way.'

'I didn't mean to make you cry.'

'Ssh, ssh. You didn't.' I took his hands in mine. I wanted to tell him the truth about his father. No, not wanted to, but needed to. It was the right thing to do. 'Clint, sometimes people lie, not for the sake of it, but because the truth hurts.'

'Yeah, that's why I say those things about my father being dead.'

'I know, son, I know. And there have been times in my life when I have lied – even to you.'

'You mean, like the times you told me you were going to bingo, when you were really going to the pub?'

'Well . . . yes, I suppose, but—'

'Ah, don't worry about it, Mam. I always knew you were going to the pub anyway.'

'You did?'

'Yeah, 'cos you'd have your nails painted and your perfume on. You never bothered with all that when you were going to bingo.'

'Not much gets past you.'

He was smiling, happy. I was happy, for the first time in a long time. Why spoil it?

'How about that trip to Bundoran?' I said.

'Are you serious?'

I nodded.

'When?'

'Thursday – Friday, maybe. I have a few bits to get sorted first.'

'What about school?'

'Don't worry, I'll send a note in with Hughie saying you're in bed with a dose. What they don't know won't hurt them.'

'Yes!' he shouted, punching the air. 'Amusements, here I come.'

'Just one thing.'

'What?'

'You're not getting me up on that big wheel.'

'Oh yes I am!'

'No way.'

'Yes way.'

'I'm telling you, Clint, no chance.'

'Ah, go on, Mam. You and me on top of the world looking down.'

'Puking down, more like it, on the poor bastards who happen to be standing underneath me.'

He started to laugh. His giggling was contagious. I started too. We were bursting our sides, the pair of us. Not so much over what I'd said, but simply because it was good to laugh. Damn good.

'Hey, you,' I said, when we eventually calmed down. 'Time we got some sleep. It's been a long day.'

'Yeah, but a great one.'

I kissed him on the forehead and left the room. I felt truly blessed.

Marcella

Da arrived home at nine on the Sunday night.

'For fuck's sake,' he shouted, when he saw all my books piled up on his chair, 'can a man not find a place to sit down in his own house any more?'

I said nothing, just gathered them up and took them back up to my room. There was a smell of booze off him, which surprised me. I didn't think Aggie would be passing around the drink at Teresa's home-coming.

I heard Bernie on her way up the stairs with Amanda a few minutes later.

'Have you had a row with Da?' she asked. ''Cos he's stomping about down there like a bulldog chewing wasps.'

'No, he was only in the door before you. I thought maybe something happened down in Aggie's house.'

'What do you mean? He wasn't there.'

'You're joking? Why not?'

She shrugged. 'Youse are as odd as each other, youse two.'

I was gobsmacked. I'd thought he'd be the first one there with a grin on his face and a bulge in his trousers to welcome his little tart home.

'So are you not even going to ask how she is?'

'No.'

'God, but you can be the right hard bitch sometimes. She's been through hell, you know.'

'All her own doing.'

It was always the same with Teresa. She'd have everyone feeling sorry for her. Poor Teresa this, poor Teresa that. Poor Teresa my arse. Had she been Marie Antoinette, she'd have kept her head. She'd have mollified the angry mob with her tales of woe and sent them back to their hovels, weeping, tails between their scrawny legs. That was the kind of her.

I wondered what was eating Da. And what was going on between himself and Teresa? He had gotten very drunk after visiting her in hospital a week earlier. I'd assumed it had annoyed him to see her under such difficult circumstances. Perhaps, I thought, there was more to it. Then I remembered what Ma had said. 'I seen them at it – dirty oul git.' That's when I had wrongly come to the conclusion that she knew about Teresa and Da. So who else was Teresa messing around with? I wondered. Who was Ma referring to? Who had Teresa got her poisonous claws into this time? Whoever it was, maybe Da had found out and had got the hump. I relished the thought.

Gabby was waiting for me by the bicycle shed the following morning at school.

'I heard the bit.'

'What bit?'

'About Cormac's parents. Snobby bastards.'

'What are you on about?'

'Were you not talking to Cormac over the weekend?'

'No. He's ringing me this evening.'

'Oh, sorry, Marcella. I shouldn't have said anything.'

'Ah, come on, Gabby, what have you heard?'

'Shit! Me and my big gob.'

'Just tell me,' I said, a knot tightening in my stomach.

'His parents went spare over him seeing you.'

'But why? They don't even know me.'

'I'm sorry, Marcella, you're not going to like this.'

'Spit it out, will you?' I said, feeling as if I was about to be walloped.

'They know you're from Fatima Hill.'

Now I felt like I had been walloped.

'How do *you* know?'

'From Luke. Cormac told him last night.'

'Damn them! They've no right—'

'Don't worry, he's not finishing with you. But seemingly he had a rip-roaring row with them.'

'He'll probably tell me about it this evening. I can't wait to talk to him.'

'Please don't let on you already know or you'll land me in the shit. Promise.'

'Promise.'

'You were right,' I told Ma at the grave that evening, 'about moneyed people. They don't want anything to do with the likes of us. But Cormac is different. He's no snob. He really loves me. Honest, Ma.'

He rang me that evening and every other evening

that week. He never mentioned his parents. We planned to meet on Sunday.

Teresa and Clint were in the kitchen with Bernie and Josie when I arrived home from school a couple of evenings later. Clint was beaming. He seemed much happier.

'Good to see you again, Marcella,' herself piped up, looking healthier than I'd seen her in a long time.

'Hiya,' I said, before making excuses about having tons of revision to do.

'She's a great lassie; there's no doubt about it,' I heard Teresa say as I hurried up the stairs. I could have split her in two. Sarky bitch.

It was hot on Sunday. I had arranged to call to Gabby's house at two. Luke would collect us there at a quarter past and we'd meet Cormac at the college gates at half past. I was sick with excitement. I wore a khaki-coloured mini-skirt, a white T-shirt and Moses sandals. I'd tied my hair back in a ponytail, leaving two curly strands dangling on either side of my face the way Cormac liked it.

We drove out to Bluebell Forest Park and lazed around there all afternoon. Gabby and Luke spent most of the time halfway down each other's throats. The rest of the time they fought playfully. He was always teasing her about the beautiful girls he would meet in Trinity. It drove her nuts. She'd punch him. He'd defend himself by grabbing her wrists, pinning her down, and they were away again on another kissing session. Passers-by stared at them; children were fascinated by them, ogling them until their parents, shaking their heads disapprovingly, dragged them away.

'So your parents have forbidden you to see me?' I said.

'What? Ah no. Luke and his big fucking gob.'

'Don't say anything to him, please. He'll be mad with Gabby for telling me.'

'I didn't want you to hear about it.'

'I'd rather know. I don't care what *they* think of me, Cormac. It's *you* I love.'

He held my hand and squeezed it gently.

'I told them to back off and mind their own business. Dad can be such a moron sometimes. It's not as if he came from aristocratic stock himself. His parents were working class; his father was a bus driver, for God's sake. And fair enough, Dad worked his butt off to put himself through university, but that doesn't give him the right to look down his dentist's nose on anyone else. He's a hypocrite, and I told him so.'

'What about your mother?'

'She didn't say too much; just got upset when I threatened to boycott the family holiday to Italy if Dad insulted you again.'

'Italy! You're going to Italy on holiday?'

'Probably not now.'

'You mean you'd forfeit a holiday in Italy in my honour?'

'I'd forfeit anything in your honour, Marcie.'

By six o'clock, most people had packed up their

picnic baskets and rugs and were on their way home. Luke and Gabby had gone for a drive. Cormac and I went deep into the woods and did it, lying underneath a sycamore tree. I cried when I felt him inside me. It was lovely. Gentle. Not all rough and brutish like the way I'd seen Da at it with Teresa. It was different for us; we loved each other.

In bed that night, I dreamed about family holidays in Italy: hot days, warm nights, naked bodies. Two children, one of each, they had Cormac's fair hair and blue eyes – like Jeremy and Jemima in *Chitty Chitty Bang Bang*. We spent the days at the beach. In the evenings we ate pizzas and drank fine wine. We were a long way from Fatima Hill.

'Ga ga.'

I opened my eyes and saw Amanda's face in the moonlight. She was beautiful. Bernie was sleeping. I picked Amanda up, cuddled her and brought her into the bed beside us. It was just about a year since I'd heard Bernie crying in the bed beside me when she discovered she was pregnant. A little flutter of panic whirled in my stomach.

'I had sex with him loads of times.' Yes, that was what she'd said, 'loads of times'. I'd only done it twice. I should have been more careful, but it hadn't been planned and by the time we knew what was happening it was too late.

'Ga ga ga ga.' Amanda tickled my cheeks with her soft fingers.

I'd have to go on the pill. Maybe Doctor Gaffney would give it to me. Josie reckoned that she was a real women's libber and that half the young ones of the town were getting the pill off her.

Right, I thought, first thing after school tomorrow I'll call in to see her.

Teresa

Being back home wasn't all plain sailing. I got my first knock when I called to see Mrs Pollock, the woman who'd employed me as her cleaner.

'I'm sorry, Teresa,' she said. 'I've found someone more reliable.'

I was gutted. I'd really liked that job.

There were a few snide remarks thrown at me from the front doors of Fatima Hill too. Not blatant insults, just cutting remarks. Sharp enough to cut right through you, patronizing enough to be passed off as sympathy.

'Good to see you home, Teresa. It must have been awful for you locked up with all them loon— patients.'

'As if things weren't bad enough for you with your Mary dying, but to end up in yon place – I'd rather you than me.'

'I know a woman who spent three months in that hospital with depression. Fuck the bit of good it did her. Ended up hanging herself a month later. Not that I'm saying that'll happen to you or anything . . .'

'I admire you for getting help, I really do. But it must have been fierce hard on your Clint knowing his ma was in the mental.'

Give me the downright brazen full-blown insults any day of the week. I could have handled them by giving back as good as I got, or throwing a punch if warranted. But these sneaky, hurtful digs – they floored me and I didn't know how to handle them. Yet.

When I went to collect my ten weeks' unmarried mother's allowance at the post office and the hicky-looking young female clerk started counting out the money, my hands started to shake.

'. . . five hundred and ninety, six hundred. Six hundred and ten, twenty, thirty, forty, fifty, fifty-five,' she said, loud enough for the long queue of nosy parkers behind me to hear.

'Thanks,' I said, fumbling with the pile of notes on the counter in front of me.

'Next,' she roared before I had the chance to get the money into my handbag and walk away. For someone who looked like a timid mouse, she was as coarse as a bear's backside.

A woman came up beside me, a shopping bag in one hand, a pension book in the other. She started elbowing me out of the way.

'Do you mind?' I said. 'I'm not finished here yet.'

I was stuffing the last few quid into my purse.

She ignored me, her elbow digging into my ribs. The clerk handed her a pen to sign her pension book.

'Thanks, miss,' the woman said. 'You know, in my day, they got nothing. Nowadays, bejaysus, they're rewarding them for their loose morals. I've a good mind to get on to that minister for social welfare and give him a piece of my mind. It's a dis—'

Jesus, I was ripping.

'It's easy be moral,' I snapped, 'when you're ugly as sin and you know rightly that no man would touch you with a bargepole.'

'Do you hear that?' she said to the clerk. 'The cheeky madam.'

'Hey, missus. You're the one who started it, criticizing me for drawing the social welfare, and you collecting your pension. Where do you think *that* money comes from, you silly cow?'

She looked at me aghast. 'I'm not a pensioner,' she said. 'I'm collecting this for my mother, I'll have you know.'

'You could have fooled me,' I said, closing my bag and marching out.

I felt fucking wonderful – triumphant – ready to take on the world and any battleaxe who'd dare to cross my path.

After paying my electricity bill and my rent, I opened a savings account in the Credit Union and deposited three hundred pounds. A fortune. I tried to give Aggie a few pounds for looking after Clint for me, but she wasn't having any of it. So I went to a gift shop and bought her a statue of the Blessed Virgin. I thought it would be a nice touch to have it blessed for her. So off I went to the presbytery to ask one of the priests to do the honours.

Father Carmichael answered the door, looking irritated.

'Howaya, Father?' I said, taking the statue out of the

brown paper bag. 'I was just wondering if you could bless this for me. It's a present for a friend of—'

'Do you realize I'm in the middle of my dinner?' he said, looking down his haughty nose at me.

'Oh yeah, so I see.'

'Pardon?'

'You've cabbage stuck between your teeth. You finish your meal, Father. I'll give this a bit of a blessing myself.'

I turned and walked away. I heard the door slam after me.

'Up your arse, your holiness,' I muttered to myself, as I headed for the church to dip the statue in the holy-water font and do the Father, Son and Holy Ghost bit myself.

Aggie was very grateful.

'Imagine, Charlie,' she said, her eyes welling up, 'she's had it blessed and all.'

I went to an AA meeting the night before we went to Bundoran. Seamus was there, the man I'd turned on that first day at group therapy in Saint Andrew's. I didn't feel the same anger towards him any more. He spoke to me and smiled, obviously not holding any grudge against me either.

Clint gave the Alateen meeting a miss and went off to the cinema with Hughie instead.

The meeting was over by ten o'clock and it was just beginning to get dark. On my way home, I decided to tip into the Well to see if I owed them any money. I knew I'd bought my supplies there before I went into hospital. Whether I had paid them or not, I just couldn't remember. Was I also putting myself to the test? I don't know. But in I walked and headed straight for the busy bar. The place was full of farmers knocking back half-ones after their wheeling and dealing at the weekly mart. The barman couldn't see me behind their thick heads and squared shoulders. I felt a chunky hand squeeze my bum. Bollocks this, I thought, I shouldn't be here. On my way out I spotted Jimmy sitting with his pint over in the corner. A plump, raven-haired woman of about my own age, wearing a low-cut dress, was sitting on his lap. I'd never seen a cleavage like it; it looked more like a bare arse. The pair of them looked well jarred. He didn't even notice me, his gaze fixed upon bigger and better things. I felt a pang of jealousy as I walked out the door and left behind me the man and the life that had been mine. I didn't want it back, but I envied those who could have it, enjoy it and cope with it.

Clint and I arrived in Bundoran with two rucksacks on our backs and plenty of spends. We walked up and down the main street looking for the B&B I'd booked, called Maple Lodge. I'd thought when I was booking it that it sounded posh. I was wrong. After dragging ourselves up and down the street several times, Clint said, 'Here it is, Ma.'

'That's not a B&B,' I said, looking at the drab, dishevelled-looking house in front of us.

'It is. Look,' he said, pointing to the remains of some

adhesive letters that were stuck to the glass on top of the front door. It read, M ple Lo g.

'Jesus!' I said. 'Look at the state of it.'

'You'd never know, it might be nice on the inside,' Clint said, ever the optimist.

'There's only one way to find out,' I said, ringing the doorbell.

A middle-aged woman with peroxide blonde hair and scarlet lipstick on her lips and cheeks answered the door.

'And who might youse be?' she asked.

I glanced at Clint and saw the poor lad was about to explode with laughter. But being the mannerly boy that he was, he'd hold it and choke on it, rather than insult the woman.

'We might be Mickey Mouse and Donald Duck,' I said, 'but we're not. I'm Teresa Reilly and this is my son Clint.'

Clint now had his excuse to laugh, but I had started off on the wrong foot with the not-so-amused land-lady.

She showed us up the steep narrow stairs and down the corridor to our musty-smelling bedroom. The carpet fibres were matted together with filth. I dreaded to hazard a guess as to what the contents of the gunge might be.

'I'll need a deposit now,' she said, her left eye fixed on me while her right eye drifted north like a bubble.

'No problem,' I told her. 'I'll bring it downstairs to you in a minute.'

'Aye, all right so,' she said, suspicion in her voice. 'Breakfast is between eight and nine thirty. Front door closes at eleven,' she announced like a prison warder, before shutting the door behind her.

Clint was sitting on the edge of his bed, trying to look comfortable.

'So what do you think?' I said.

'Yeah, it's fine. It's eh . . .'

'Septic?'

'Totally, Mam,' he said, starting to laugh again.

'Fuck this for a game of soldiers,' I said. 'Put that rucksack back on your shoulders.'

'What?'

'We're out of here. On the count of three, I want you through that door, down the stairs, out the front door and away up the street. Holyrood Hotel, here we come.'

'Mam, you're mad.'

'Son, I know. But I'd be a lot madder if I stayed here. Are you ready?'

'Yeah.' He was in stitches.

'Get up, will you?' I said. And he did. With a struggle.

'One, two, three, go.'

We were in the lobby of the Holyrood before we stopped to take a breath. We got a twin room for three nights, for a hundred and five pounds. Damn it, I could afford it. I was a savings account holder now. Worth every penny it was too. If only Mary could have seen me, sauntering about the hotel like some big-shot, ordering coffee with cream and scones, relaxing like a lady of leisure in the sun lounge. I'd have loved it if she'd been with me. I missed her something rotten.

Clint couldn't wait to get to the amusements. He was two steps ahead of me the whole way down the street. A couple of attractive young girls passed us by. Clint gave them a nod, then eyed them up and down. One giggled, the other blushed. My kid – a teenager already. He was growing up so fast. It was still very much on my mind to tell him the truth about his father. He was too old to be left in the dark, too young for the crudeness of the truth. I thought long and hard about striking the right balance.

I loved the amusements, the warm night, the neon lights and upbeat music. It made me feel like a teenager again, flying through the air on the chairoplanes, the cool sea breeze blowing in my face.

'Come on, we'll go on the big wheel,' Clint said, before I had a chance to recover from the chairoplanes.

'Hang on, I'm still dizzy.'

'Hurry up, they're about to start.'

Before I had time to think twice about it, I was sitting beside Clint in a seat on the big wheel, a fella buckling us in and pushing the bar down over our knees. The next thing I knew the ground was far beneath us. Screams filled the air as we continued on our upward journey. I was in a state of shock. I didn't make a sound. Clint hung onto me, laughing with a mixture of excitement and fear. I closed my eyes tight and left them that way until the movement stopped. My head was spinning. The chair was swinging.

'Clint, are we down?'

'Yeah. You can open your eyes now.'

I did just that. Unfortunately. We were suspended in mid-air at the very top of the wheel with the seat rocking and creaking. I let a scream out of me that I'm sure made its way out across the Atlantic Ocean and rung in the ears of New Yorkers. I continued screaming all the way back down and up again – and again. I let go of all the screams that had been bottled up inside me for over thirty years. I didn't stop until I felt the ground beneath my feet.

'That was great crack, wasn't it, Mam?'

'Clint,' I gasped, 'I've done some mad things in my time, but that – that – that was . . .'

'Great?'

'No.'

'Awful?'

'No. The best damn bit of therapy I've ever had.'

After a fish and chip supper, we went back to our hotel room, made ourselves tea and stretched out on our beds.

'Remember what I told you about your father, Clint?'

'Yeah.'

'And remember how I told you last weekend that sometimes people lie to avoid the truth?'

'Yeah.'

'I have a confession to make.'

'Go on.' He sighed and looked away.

'Look at me, son, please.'

'I hate this. You're going to tell me something bad, aren't you?'

'I'm going to tell you the truth, love.'

I took two cigarettes from my pack, lit them and passed one over to him. 'Here you are. I know you have the odd ciggy behind my back, and I can't say I'm gone on the idea of you smoking at thirteen, but—'

'Nearly fourteen.'

'You're still too young, love. But what I'm trying to say is, I'd rather we were both upfront with each other. OK?'

'OK.' He took a few drags, his head hung low waiting for the disappointment.

'It wasn't a long love affair. And he wasn't a married man with an ill wife. It happened—'

'I don't understand you, Mam. I really don't,' he said, hurt in his voice.

'Of course you don't, Clint, because I've lied to you. I had no right to. But I want to change. I'm trying to do the right thing here.'

'Go on.'

'You know about sex, don't you, love?'

'I'm not stupid,' he snapped.

'I know. Your father and I had a brief encounter,' I said. I thought that was a nice way of putting it. Kind of Mills and Boon.

'You mean a one-night stand. He shagged you and left you. Was that it?'

'Clint!'

'What?'

'I – I . . .'

'I'm right, amn't I?'

'Where did you hear stuff like that?'

'Like what? Fellas getting sex off a girl, then dumping her? Happens all the time, doesn't it?'

'Not all the time. No.' I felt so sad. So taken aback by his response. Disappointed at his lack of innocence, his hostility.

'But it happened to you, right?'

'Something like that,' I said. I felt ashamed and embarrassed.

'Who was he?'

'What?'

'Who was he?'

'I . . . eh . . . I – I don't know. I mean—'

'You didn't even know him? Oh, Mam!' He burst into tears and ran out of the room. I lay on the bed sobbing.

I began to feel concerned and panicky when he hadn't returned after an hour. I put on my cardigan and went downstairs and into the lobby. The porter was sitting reading a newspaper.

'You didn't happen to see a young fella—'

'A black-haired kid, about fourteen?'

'Yeah, that's him.'

'He went outside.'

'Which way did he go?'

'I'm sorry, missus, I didn't notice.'

'Right. If he comes back in, give him this key and tell him not to leave the room.'

It was half past twelve. The town was still buzzing. I walked up the main street, putting my head into each amusement arcade as I passed it. I went down to the fairground. It was closed. There was no point in trying the pubs, he wouldn't have been let in. I walked along the seafront, tearful, stopping everyone I met. 'Have you seen a young fella on his own? Black hair. Thirteen.'

'No, sorry,' some said. Others were too drunk to answer.

I went down onto the beach and checked in all the shelters. There was a drunk man lying across a bench in one of them, nursing a bottle in a brown paper bag. I could have done with a slug. I could hear the waves crashing against the rocks; their harshness sent a shiver down my spine. The drunk let a grunt out of him. I turned and saw his arm outstretched, offering me the bottle. My hands were shaking. I reached out and took it from him. Whiskey. I loved that smell. So familiar, so comforting. I sat down on the bench. I could see the man's bare toes gaping through the holes in his shoes. He smelled of human excrement. I couldn't see his face for all the pocks, scabs and facial hair. I wondered what he looked like underneath it all, what sort of child he'd been, where his family were. I felt sorry for him. I got up and stood over him. He had his eyes closed. I tightened the cap on the bottle and tucked it in under his arm.

'Thanks,' I said, 'but I won't have a drink. Not today. Look after yourself, whatever your name is.'

'Johnny. My name is Johnny.'

'Do you want me to ring somebody for you? To take you home?'

'I am home,' he muttered, his eyes still shut, 'and this here,' he said, tapping the bottle, 'is my best friend. But thanks for the offer.'

I wanted to help him, but I didn't know how. So, instead, I prayed for him. I got down on my hunkers beside him and started to recite the serenity prayer. 'God grant me the serenity to accept the things I cannot change . . .'

'. . . the courage to change the things I can,' he mumbled, 'and the wisdom to know the difference.'

'I have to go,' I said. 'I need to find my son. You take care of yourself.'

'And you,' he said, pointing at me, still not opening his eyes, 'don't end up like me.'

As I walked back to the hotel, I cried for Johnny, then thanked God for giving me the strength to resist the whiskey.

'He's back,' the porter told me at the front door. 'About fifteen minutes ago.'

He was in bed when I went back into the room, pretending to be asleep. I knew by his shallow breathing that he wasn't.

'I'm sorry, Clint,' I said, sitting on the edge of his bed. 'I understand that you feel let down by me. I had no right to lie to you.'

'Sorry. How many times have I heard you say that word in thirteen years? What does it mean anyway?' he said, sitting up in the bed. 'Nothing. It means nothing, Mam, not any more.'

He didn't look at me. It was as if he was thinking aloud, trying to figure it all out in his own mind. He wasn't angry. I almost wished he was, because anger usually blows over. He looked disillusioned, resigned to disappointment, like an old man who'd had more than his fair share of hard times and had given up on hope. And I was the cause of it.

'It's the same thing year in, year out – row in, row out. You say you're sorry, I forgive you – and then what? It happens all over again.'

'I know. I've been an awful mother. I—'

'Shut up. Don't start that feeling sorry for yourself crap. I'm sick of it. I'm sick of you. Come to think of it, I'm sick of me too, or of being me. Clint Reilly, the fella with the weird name and the even weirder mother.'

'You think I'm weird?' I said, my lips quivering.

'That's what the fellas in my class say about you. Did you know that? So what does that make me? Will I tell you?'

'I'll kill the little—'

'That makes me the loony's son – spa's son.'

'The bastards,' I said, seething with rage. 'Who are they, the little shites?'

'Why? What are you going to do? Knock the living daylights out of them and show me up even more? No, Mam,' he said, raising his voice. 'It's not them I need protecting from. It's *you*. The only problem is you're all I've got. And you know it, don't you?'

'Oh, Clint, please. Don't—'

'You know that all you have to do is buy me something or turn on your tears and I'll come running back, because if I don't forgive you, I'm all alone. I've no father or brothers or sisters to turn to. It's just you and me.'

I had always been realistic enough to accept that my behaviour had hurt Clint over the years, and, thankfully, in hospital, I'd been given the opportunity to deal with that hard fact. I wasn't, however, until that night, either strong or insightful enough to have understood the depth of his pain.

There in front of me, sitting with his knees drawn up to his chin, sat a boy who'd done no wrong to anyone in his life. A boy so beautiful even in sadness that he made me want to cry. A boy I needed to reach, but couldn't, even though he was physically by my side. He was like a sad song, full of minor notes and melancholy words.

'So,' he said, in a serious tone, 'if you want me to forgive you, fine. I do.'

'No, Clint. I don't,' I said, taking his pale, limp hand in mine. 'I don't want you to forgive me. Not yet. Not ever, if you don't want to. And yes, unfortunately for you, you're stuck with living with me for now. But I'm not going to nag you or bribe you into being my friend. If the time comes when you feel you can trust me again, fine. OK?' I said, squeezing his hand gently.

He raised his eyelids at last, and looked me in the eye.

'OK,' he said. 'I can't switch my feelings on and off like a light bulb – hot one second, cold the next. And I don't want to talk about a whole lot of heavy stuff any more. I'm tired of it. If you want to help me, Mam, just be normal like other mothers. That's all.'

I wanted to tell him that I was a normal mam, that I had the exact same instincts as any other mother, that I loved him more than life itself, that I'd lay down my life for him, that I'd rip the head off anyone who'd dare to hurt him the way I had hurt him. But he wouldn't believe me. And he had every reason not to.

Maybe one day I wouldn't need to tell him I was a normal mother, 'cos he'd already know. Maybe.

Marcella

The night before my first exam, the doorbell rang. As soon as I opened the door, Gabby dashed past me and scurried up the stairs as though there was a Rottweiler at her heels. By the time I got back to my room she was sitting on the bed, hands over her face, bawling.

'It's not the exams, is it? Because they're not worth getting yourself into—'

'I don't give a shite about the exams. It's Luke. He's finished with me.'

'You're joking?'

'Does this face look like it's fucking joking?' she wailed, exposing it briefly.

'No, I suppose not.'

'Oh, Marcella, I wish I was dead.'

'Don't be daft.'

'No really, I do. Give me a dozen aspirin and I swear I'll swallow them.'

'And what would I do for a best friend then?'

The hands came down. She gave me a slight smile.

'OK, maybe not suicide, but attempted suicide – that would show him, the bastard.'

'Show him what?'

'How much I love him. How cut up I am.'

'He's not worth it,' I said, foolishly.

'You wouldn't say that if Cormac broke it off with you, would you?' she snapped.

'Sorry. What did he say anyway?'

'That we're too young to be getting serious. He doesn't want to be tied down – he'd be going away in September anyway, so what was the point in prolonging the inevitable – stuff like that. That he may die roaring. Arsehole.'

I was glad to see her getting angry. I could cope better with her rage than I could with her desperation.

'I need a stiff drink. Go down and nick a bottle from the drinks cabinet.'

'Drinks cabinet! Is that what youse call it out on the Dublin road?'

I went down and made two coffees, lacing one with Da's whiskey.

'Try that,' I told her.

'Fucking lovely. Cheers. You know, you could be for the chop next.' I saw a flicker of hope in her face when she said it.

'That's not going to happen, Gabby. We love each other.'

'Yeah, so I hear.'

'You mean Cormac told Luke that he loved me?'

'No. He told him ye were doing it – going all the way – riding each other. I wasn't supposed to let on that I knew, but feck it—'

'He told him *that*?' My heart was banging so hard in my chest, I could hardly hear myself speak.

'Yeah. Luke reckons Cormac's a lucky bastard. Hey,

maybe that's why he's finished with me. He thinks I'm too frigid. I should—'

'Shut up for a minute. When did Luke tell you?'

'The Sunday we went to yon forest park in the back of his daddy's car, when he was trying to get the knickers off me. Oh, I should have let him, Marcella.'

'How do you know he wasn't just saying that about me and Cormac to try to persuade you—'

'You mean ye didn't do it at all? That's the lying – oh Jesus, I can't think of a bad enough name for him.'

I didn't enlighten her one way or the other. What if Luke really was just chancing his arm. It was unbearable to think of Cormac bragging about what we'd done.

Gabby continued ranting and knocking back her drink.

'I swear,' she spat, 'if I ever get my hands on Luke Lynch again, I'll pluck every pubic hair out of his big fat ugly dick. Any chance of another drink?'

'No way. You've had enough. It's ten o'clock, Gabby, and the Inter starts tomorrow, remember?'

I wanted to get rid of her so badly. I needed to be alone. To panic. To think.

'Will you walk me down the hill?'

'Yeah, OK.'

'Cos I'm not joking you, the looks I got on my way up this hill, anyone would think I was a fucking alien.'

'Shut up and come on.'

'I'll never stop loving him, you know? Never.'

'You will.'

'No, I won't.'

'Yes, you will.'

'I fucking won't. Right?'

'Right.'

Cathy Sheridan and two of her sidekicks accosted me on my way back up the hill. Cathy was in the middle, a girl on either side, linking her.

'Don't you go bringing your big-shot boyfriend or your snobby-arsed friends up our way again, Miss Loreto. Dey're not welcome. Right, girls?'

'Too right,' the other pair said in unison.

'Get out of my way,' I retorted.

'Say please.'

'Piss off,' I said, stepping off the footpath and passing them.

'A posh prick like tat could only be after de likes of you for one ting. Slut,' Cathy jeered, then spat on the ground beside me.

'The lads up here not good enough for you?' one of the others shouted after me.

'Traitor, traitor, traitor, traitor, traitor, traitor . . .' they chanted at me until I closed the front door behind me.

Bernie had just got home from Josie's.

'Here,' she said, handing me a card. 'I've had this in my pocket for the past few days. I forgot all about it. It's from Teresa. She told me to give it to you before your exams started, seeing as she'd be away.'

I snatched it off her and went up to the bedroom.

It was a good luck in your exams card. It read, 'Hope you do well. Will say a wee prayer for you. Love Teresa and Clint.'

I tore it up and pegged it in the bin.

Sleep was impossible. It was away out there in the distance. Beyond Cormac, beyond the annoyance of what he'd done, beyond the humiliation, beyond the dozens of invented excuses for such a betrayal.

We sat in the examination hall the following morning in alphabetical order. I was in the front row, next to the window, with Mary E. Brady to my left. E as in Elizabeth, Gabby had informed me on my first morning. It seemed a long time ago now.

'You may begin,' the supervisor said.

It was English. Paper 1: comprehension and an essay.

I was tired and distracted.

Mary E. was clicking her Parker pen on and off continuously with one hand, twisting a strand of her greasy hair with the other, and wobbling her right leg like a lump of jelly. She was driving me nuts. I tried to get her attention so I could make a signal to her to quit fidgeting. I dropped my pen on the ground. She didn't look around. I coughed. No joy. I sneezed. Nothing. I sighed. Still no response. Fuck you, I thought, let's see how you like it. I started to wobble my left leg and glared at her. The silly cow was in some sort of trance, staring straight ahead of her, like she'd been shot by a stun gun. That fucking Parker pen. Click on, click off, click on, click off, click on, click off – he loves me, he loves me not, he loves me, he loves me not, he loves me, he loves me not, he—'

She started to write. No, I thought, don't stop.

Click it again. Click it again, you stupid bitch, just one more time.

I walked down to the telephone kiosk on the hill that evening at five. The phone rang and rang. I waited until it stopped, then walked out to the graveyard to visit Ma.

On my way home through the town I met Luke. He was with another lad from school. I didn't stop to talk. They both smiled at me, knowingly I thought, but I wasn't sure. Maybe it was me. I was paranoid.

In bed that night I imagined Cormac in his dormitory telling all the other boarders about him and me. Marcella Buckley, great ride – pass it on. Marcella Buckley, easy lay – pass it on. Hey, Cormac, can I have her when you've finished with her? You jammy git, McCairn, good on you. Although no tears fell, I was crying inside.

'Cormac rang me last night,' Gabby told me, just before our exam started the following morning. 'Says he tried ringing you yesterday evening but there was no reply. He'll ring you on Friday at five.'

Friday, I thought, why not tonight? Or tomorrow night?

I had cramps in my stomach all through the exam. The onset of my period or nerves, I wasn't sure which. I was carrying the contraceptive pill around in my uniform pocket, just in case. The doctor had told me to start the course on the first day of my period, which was just about due.

*

Friday was a long time coming. I'd had three days of tough exams and even tougher dilemmas. I would have to confront Cormac. On Tuesday night I had been determined to find out exactly what had happened, to know the truth. By the time Friday came, love had made me feel so desperate, all I needed was an explanation – a good one, a middling one, even a lame one. Anything that would allow me to let him off the hook.

The phone rang at five.

'Hi, Marcie.'

'Hi.' I was shaking.

'How did they go?'

'What?'

'The exams. What else?'

'Oh yeah. So so.'

'Is there something wrong, pet?'

I took a deep breath. 'Why did you tell Luke about us having sex?'

'That's the idiot! Shit!'

'Why, Cormac? Luke of all people. He can't hold his piss. You said so yourself.'

'What the hell did he say to you?'

'Nothing. Gabby told me.'

'It's not what you think. I wasn't bragging. I swear, Marcie. I wouldn't—'

'Just tell me why.'

'I – I asked him to get some condoms for me from across the border. He goes up there for cheap petrol every week. I didn't want us taking any more chances if we were—'

'So what did he say?'

'Nothing much.'

'Luke say nothing much!'

'All right, all right. He asked if you were hot, but I told him to mind his own business.'

'Swear! Swear that's all you said.'

'I swear.'

'OK.'

'So am I forgiven?'

'This time you are, but please don't talk to that eejit about us again.'

'I won't. I promise, Marcie.' He let out a big sigh of relief. 'So I'll see you tomorrow then?'

'Suppose so.'

'Our last date for nearly a month. It's going to—'

'Nearly a month! Why?'

'I'm heading home on Thursday after my last exam. We're away to Italy on Saturday.'

'You're going?'

'Yeah.'

'So you've made it up with your dad? Has he decided to accept me?'

'To be honest, he didn't say any more about it one way or another. Mum rang and said it would spoil her holiday if I didn't go. What else could I do, Marcie?'

'Nothing, I suppose.'

'Hey, we still have tomorrow. I can't wait to see you.'

There was a long silence. I wasn't sure what to say. I was feeling downhearted, unsure of myself, frightened.

'Marcie,' he said in his Donald Duck voice. 'Earth calling Marcie.'

'Yeah, I'll see you tomorrow. What time?'

'Three o'clock. I'll call for you.'

'OK.'

'Bye.'

'Bye.'

'Still love you,' he said.

'Do you?'

'You know I do.'

'Yeah. Me too.'

I could hear the tick of my watch on the bedside locker that night. I'd never noticed it before. Time was passing me by. I couldn't hold on to it.

We went to a jazz session in the Forge the following day. Cormac had a few pints and became very sentimental.

'Me and you, Marcie,' he said, holding on tight to me, 'we're perfect together. Aren't we?'

'Yeah.' I started to cry. I didn't want to say goodbye. I didn't want him to leave.

'Ssh,' he said, burying my face in his chest. 'Don't cry. I love you.'

'Then stay. Don't go to Italy. *Please.*'

'I have to, Marcie. I can't let my mum down. Anyway, it's only for three weeks. And I'm going to bring you back something really special.'

We kissed and caressed each other until I felt like I was going to burst out of my skin.

'I'm going to miss you,' he whispered.

'Me too. Now go. It's late.'

'Ah, fuck it.'

'Go, before you get yourself into any more trouble.'

He walked away, staggered a little, then turned around and smiled. There was a tightness across my chest fencing in my heart.

'See you on the tenth. Watch out for the postcard,' he shouted back to me.

I blew him a kiss and walked away.

I worked full-time in Katie's Coffee Shop as soon as my exams were over. I ran home every day on my lunch break to check the post and walked back empty-handed. I blessed myself every time I needed to go to the toilet and sighed when I didn't see what I wanted to see. Most evenings after work I visited Ma. She was the only one I could talk to about my fears, the only one sure to keep my secret. Every night, before getting into bed, I marked the calendar hidden in my drawer. Days without Cormac – one less. Days overdue – one more. Sometimes I'd feel dizzy and I'd convince myself it was just panic. When I wasn't convinced, I'd have a hot bath and hope for the best. I felt lonely when I found myself on my own in the house, lonelier when I found myself alone with my father. It was hard hating some-one for so long.

Teresa called into the coffee shop several times. Sometimes alone, sometimes with Clint.

'So it's all off between the lovebirds, is it?' I asked her one day as I lifted an empty coffee mug from under her nose. I was referring to herself and Da.

'I don't know, Marcella. You tell me.'

'What?'

'You and that Cormac fella. Are you still seeing him?'

'Of course I am – not that it's any of your business.'

'Oh good. I'm happy for you.'

'Ah, give over. You know you're wasting your sweet-talk on me, Teresa. My opinion of you will never change. So do me a favour and stay out of my face.'

'Fair enough, Marcella, but you know where I am if you need me,' she said, getting up to leave.

'Me need you! Don't make me laugh.'

Gabby called in to see me regularly. She'd spend hours over a Coke while moaning about her life without Luke.

'Any word from Cormac?' She asked the same question every time she walked through the door.

'No. Not yet.'

I called to the post office to check how long it took for a postcard to get from Italy to Ireland. 'A week or two,' they said.

The card arrived the day before he was due to fly home.

It read: 'Weather beautiful. Having a ball. Spent two nights in Venice. See you soon, Cormac xxx.'

I read it over and over. About a dozen words. Meaningless words. No mention of missing me, or loving me. Still, there were three kisses. That *had* to mean something. Of course it did. I would be seeing him the following Saturday and I wouldn't have to suffer alone any longer. Cormac would comfort me, just as he had done when Ma died.

Bernie and I were sitting in watching TV on the Thursday night. I sensed she was keeping a close eye on me.

'Is there something wrong with you?' I asked.

'No,' she said, blushing.

Josie arrived shortly afterwards. She wouldn't sit down. She was pacing the floor. There was something up.

'What's happened now?' I asked, breaking the silence.

'Me and Bernie are wild worried about you, Marcella.'

'Why? There's nothing wrong with me,' I said, trying to sound calm.

'You're not eating. You've lost weight. And you—'

'I'm just on a bit of a diet.'

'A diet! You, on a diet? Are you sure that's all it is?'

'Yeah. It's no big deal. Half the girls I know are on diets.'

'But why? You've a lovely figure.'

'Go away. I've a huge arse.'

'No you haven't. Has she, Bernie?'

'No way,' Bernie said.

'It can be fierce dangerous, that dieting. I know a woman whose daughter had that anna . . . anna . . . What do you call it?'

'Anorexia,' I said.

'Aye, that's it.'

'I'm not anorexic.'

'Are you sure?'

'Look, I'll quit the diet if it makes you feel any better. I'll eat chips and chocolate till the cows come home. Anything just to shut you up and get you off my back.'

'It's not the diet we were worried about. Teresa had me and Bernie convinced you were pregnant.' She laughed.

'Teresa said that?'

'She just thought you were looking very peaky. She cares about—'

'Ah, don't give me that crap. Yon one's a fucking eejit. Me pregnant! Have a bit of manners,' I sneered, feeling a bout of nausea come over me.

'You're absolutely sure?' Bernie said.

'Two hundred per cent. I have my period, for fuck's sake. How the hell could I be pregnant?'

'Right,' Josie said, clapping her hands. 'I need a bloody drink after that. Who's coming down to the Well for one?'

'You go on with her,' I told Bernie. 'I'll mind Amanda.'

As soon as they left, I opened a pack of tampons, left them on the bathroom windowsill and flushed one down the loo. Then to be doubly sure, I spilled a drop of beetroot juice on the sheet before climbing into bed to pray for a miracle.

An acidy stomach had me awake early the following morning. I tried some Andrews Liver Salts and then threw it up. The panic came in waves, as did the nausea. I wondered what it was like, the little thing inside me, playing havoc with my stomach and my head.

On my way home from lunch that day, I turned into the doctor's office. I was in the door before I had time to think too long about it.

'I don't have an appointment,' I said to the receptionist, hoping she'd tell me to come back another time.

'She's not busy. Take a seat. There's only one ahead of you.'

I sat there, pregnancy and baby posters staring down at me from all angles. If I'd had the strength in my legs, I would have scarpered.

'Marcella Buckley,' the doctor called.

'I think I need the loo,' I said, before I sat down.

'Here,' she said, handing me a small plastic cup. 'Just in case I need a sample.'

I burst into tears before she had even done the test.

'When was your last period?'

'Eight weeks – maybe nine,' I sobbed.

'Any sickness?' she asked, dipping a stick into my urine sample.

I nodded.

'Lie down over here,' she said, indicating the examination bed.

She pressed my stomach gently, the expression in her eyes confirming my fears.

She removed the test stick from my sample and examined it.

'It's positive, Marcella,' she said, helping me to my feet. 'I know.'

She got me to stand on the scales. 'Have you someone at home to talk to about this?'

'I don't want to. Not yet.'

'It's a tough burden to carry alone.'

'I'm not alone. I have my boyfriend.'

'That's good. Sit down again and I'll check your blood pressure. Just roll up your right sleeve.'

My heart felt like it was throbbing in my ears.

'So he knows you're here today then, this lad?'

'No. He's on his holidays, but he'll be back tomorrow. Everything will be all right then.'

'I hope so, Marcella. But, if it doesn't go too well for you, there are support groups for—'

'No, no. It's all right. I'll be fine.'

'OK. I'll need to see you again in a fortnight. Make an appointment with the receptionist on your way out. And the best of luck tomorrow.'

I hung around the house the following day, waiting for Cormac. It was the tenth. He'd said he'd see me on the tenth. It rained all day.

Bernie was down in the dumps.

'Fuck that rain. There's nothing worse than being stuck inside all day with a baby,' she moaned. 'I suppose there's no chance of you minding—'

'No, Bernie.'

'Ah, go on. It's not as if you're doing anything else.'

'I'll be going out in a while. Sorry.'

'It's all right.' She sighed. 'Oh, by the way, them sheets upstairs need changing.'

'Right. I'll do it now.'

I was relieved to be alone in the room. I lay on the

bed wondering how I should tell Cormac about my pregnancy, but I knew that there was no easy way to drop a bombshell and no gracious way to receive it.

Still, nothing could alter the fact that we loved each other. Cormac was a decent fella, well brought up, responsible. He'd do the right thing and stand by me – marry me even. I didn't feel ready for marriage or motherhood, but anything seemed possible so long as Cormac was with me.

Josie had arrived with her kids by the time I'd finished upstairs. We'd been seeing a lot more of her since Ma's death. She was standing at the stove in Ma's apron, cooking a fry for lunch. The smell was turning my stomach.

'Do you want an egg with yours, Marcella?'

'No thanks.'

Sammy and little Jimmy were fighting in the sitting room. Josie could see them carrying on through the open door, but was passing no remarks. She just raised her voice so she'd be heard above their screaming. They were giving me a headache. I turned on the TV, hoping to find a cartoon, anything to shut the pair of them up. No cartoons. Just Wimbledon and more Wimbledon.

'Oh, leave that on, Marcella,' Josie shouted, coming through to the sitting room. 'I love watching that Jimmy Connors fella. Would you just look at the arse on that?' she said, gazing at the screen. 'Come on, Jimmy boy. Give it socks – yes! Yes!' she roared. 'Great shot. Poetry in motion, that's what he is.' She sniffed the air. 'Ah, fuck, me sausages!'

The doorbell rang. My heart missed a beat. It was only Aggie.

As the day dragged on, I began to feel uneasy. Several times I felt like bursting into tears, but I couldn't. I had to act normal. I didn't want to raise their suspicions again. Not after Teresa opening her big trap!

It didn't stop raining until eight o'clock that night. The house was empty again, except for Bernie and Amanda. I sat out on the front windowsill, scrambling for answers to the constant flow of questions that trickled into my head. Then I thought of Luke. I went back inside, got twenty pence and headed down to the telephone kiosk.

'Luke, it's Marcella.'

'Oh, hiya.'

'Just wondering if you've heard from Cormac? He was supposed to come and see me today.'

'Really?'

'So have you been talking to him?'

'Yeah. I spoke to him last night. He never mentioned coming up here today.'

'Maybe he got the days mixed up.'

'Look, Marcella, I'm sure if he wants to get in touch with you, he will.'

'This was arranged before he left. He—'

'Yeah, well a lot can change in three weeks.' I wondered what he was getting at. He sounded unfriendly and condescending.

'Can you give me his home number? I'll talk to him myself.'

'If he wanted you to have his number, he'd have given it to you.'

'I didn't need it when he was at school, did I?'

'I'm just saying—'

'You know what you can do, Luke? Stick it up your fat arse. I'll ring directory enquiries.'

'No point. The number is ex-directory. They won't give it to you.'

'You're enjoying this, aren't you? Some bloody friend you are.'

'Hey, don't turn on me. I wasn't the one who stood you up. If you want some friendly advice, Marcella, I'd say forget him. He's left town, for fuck's sake. He's away to college in September to start a new life and—'

'I know all that.'

'No, just let me finish. He's only eighteen years old. He's going to want to play the field, not get tied down with—'

'So he's told you all this, has he?'

'As good as.'

'What's that supposed to mean?'

'Just think about it for a minute. A fella like Cormac McCairn on his holidays in Italy for three weeks – ah, look, I'll say no more. It's up to him to tell you.'

'So he met someone when he was away?' I said, feeling I was about to throw up.

'Hey, lighten up, will you? I don't know why you girls have to take everything so seriously. I mean, look at Gabby—'

'Just shut up and give me his number.'

'Ring me back in five minutes. I'll phone and ask him if he has any message for you. That's the best I can do, Marcella. Sorry.'

'No! Just tell him to ring me straight away at the usual number.'

'OK.'

I hung up and waited, trying hard not to crack under the cloud of humiliation that was hanging over me. Within a couple of minutes, the phone rang.

'Hello?'

'Marcie.'

Tears rolled down my cheeks. 'I waited in all day for you, Cormac.'

'Sorry.'

'Luke said that—'

'Oh, never mind him. I was going to call to see you tomorrow. We need—'

'You mean, he was lying? You don't want to finish with me?'

'That's what I was going to talk to you about tomorrow, but there's no point in dragging it out, Marcie. It's not fair on you. I think we should—'

'Don't,' I cried out in desperation. 'Please.'

'I'm sorry, Marcie. I really am. Look, we've had a great time together. The best. But being away – it made me realize . . . please don't cry, Marcie. You're beautiful. You'll meet someone else. I—'

'I don't want anyone else. I love you,' I sobbed.

A few seconds' silence followed. He didn't say what I so badly needed to hear.

'It just got too heavy between us.'

'This is all because of your father, isn't it? So much for standing up to him.'

'It's nothing to do with him. It's my decision. I'm sorry I've hurt you, but in a couple of months' time you'll have forgotten all about me. I promise.'

'I won't.'

'Of course you will.'

'No, Cormac,' I roared, 'I won't. Because in a couple of months' time, I'll be four months pregnant with our baby. So don't dare tell me I'll have forgotten all about you. I wish to fuck I could, you bollocks.'

I squeezed my eyes shut and held my breath waiting for his reaction. There wasn't a sound.

'Are you still there?'

'I'm here.' He sounded like a different person. A younger person. More like Clint.

'I've been cracking up over the past three weeks, Cormac. I've been scared fucking shitless.'

'Jesus Christ, you're bloody well serious, aren't you?' His voice was trembling.

'You think I'd joke about something like that? What the hell do you take me for?'

'I'm sorry, Marcie. I'm sorry. Shit! Fuck it.'

'I know.'

'But we only did it a couple of times.'

'Yeah, and as far as I can tell, it was the second time that did the damage.'

'Christ! What are you going to do?'

'What am *I* going to do? You mean, what are *we*

going to do? It wasn't all my doing. We're in this mess together.'

'I didn't mean it like that, it's just—'

'What?'

'I can't take it in. It's a disaster.'

I hated him saying that.

'I know, but it's happened now. We'll just have to deal with it.'

'You could always – you know.'

'What?'

Don't say it, Cormac, don't say it.

'Go to England.'

'For an abortion?'

'It'd be best for everyone. You're only sixteen, Marcie. Can you imagine being stuck with a kid for the rest of your life?'

'Not exactly, but—'

'If you have this baby, you can kiss goodbye to having any sort of decent future.'

'And if I don't – what? You think I'll be able to forget all about it?'

I knew by the clicking sound, he was biting his nails.

'Just like that,' I said, 'like it never existed. Abracadabra! Baby disappears.'

'It's not a baby yet, Marcie. I mean, do you really think it's fair to bring a baby that neither of us wants into the world.'

His words were killing me.

'And what if I had it, would you stand by me?'

He let out a long sigh. 'I don't want a baby, Marcella.'

'Marcella!'

'Marcie. I'm sorry.'

'Well, fuck you too, Cormac McCairn. I don't want this baby any more than you do. The sooner it's gone, the better.'

The hurt I felt was unbearable. The humiliation even worse.

'Stop crying, will you? Calm down. Getting yourself into a state isn't going to help.'

'Come and see me.'

'I don't know, Marcie. That'll only make things harder for both of us.'

'Please.'

He didn't answer.

'Please, Cormac, I'm begging you. Just one more time.' I could have cut my tongue out for saying it. I hated begging. It made me feel pathetic.

'OK, OK.'

'That way, we can sort things out face to face. It's awful talking about it over the phone. I need a hug. I'm scared.'

'You must be. Look, meet me off the bus tomorrow. Is that OK?' His voice was calmer now.

'Yeah, thanks. What time?'

'There's one due in at two. I'll be on it.'

'Cormac, just one more thing.'

'What?'

'I need an honest answer.'

'OK.'

'All those times you said that you loved me. Did you mean it or were you . . . ?'

284

'I did love you.'

'Did? As in past tense?'

Another sigh. 'I still have very strong feelings for you but—'

'Don't,' I sobbed. 'Don't say any more. I have to go now. I'll see you tomorrow. Two o'clock, right?'

'Right.'

I hung up.

The next day came. I stood at the bus stop in the rain. I saw the bus coming round the corner. My heart leapt. Two old women and a young lad with a rucksack stepped off. A mother and child climbed on. The bus drove off. My heart sank. My stomach tightened. I was alone. Nine weeks pregnant and petrified.

Over the following week, I tried to go on as normal, hanging on to the foolish notion that, given time, Cormac would have second thoughts and realize he still loved me.

I thought about him every hour of every day. I saw him get on a bus in Ashbourne – northbound. I saw him on his way up the hill. I heard his voice – Marcie, Marcie, Marcie. I saw myself on a bus – southbound. I heard him tell his father he loved me. I wondered what he was thinking, what he was doing. My heart made excuses for him. My head cursed my heart. I wanted to hate him; I tried hard to. But I couldn't, because I longed for him to come back to me, and still believed that he would.

I met Luke in town one evening on my way home from work. He offered me a lift.

'No thanks,' I said.

He was wearing a suit.

'Just on my way home from the debs. It was on last night in Navan,' he said.

'Oh,' I said, as if not interested, but dying to know if Cormac had gone.

'It was a wild night. McCairn was plastered.'

'Did he say anything about me?' I couldn't help myself.

He hesitated before he spoke. 'Look, I may as well tell you, 'cos you'll hear it from some of the others who were there – he invited a girl from Dublin.'

'Goodbye,' I said, walking away.

'Marcella! I'm sorry. At least let me give you a lift.'

I didn't turn around. I didn't want him to see me cry.

I walked on. My head was heavy, my eyes clogged with bitter tears. The thought of another girl with Cormac, her hand in his, his lips on hers. I wanted to scream, just open my mouth and let the pain out. I felt dizzy, but hurried on.

A horn blasted. I covered my ears and froze, waiting for the thump. The thump that had knocked Ma to the ground – to her death. Someone grabbed me roughly and pushed me forward, making me trip on the edge of the footpath and fall to my knees.

'Sweet Jesus, Marcella, what the hell are you doing?' It was Teresa. She was on her hunkers beside me. I heard a car door slam and steps coming towards us.

'Is she all right?' a man's voice asked. 'I'm really sorry, but she walked straight out in front of me, honest—'

'It's OK. I saw what happened. You did well not to hit her. It wasn't your fault,' Teresa said.

I was still on my knees, weeping.

'Do you know her?' the man asked.

'She's my niece.'

'If you want to take her home, I'll give youse a lift.'

'Good man. Come on, Marcella,' Teresa said, stroking my head gently. 'I'll take you back to my house and clean up those cuts.'

My hands and knees were burning with the pain. Blood was trickling down my shins, as Teresa and the man struggled to get me to my feet. I couldn't straighten my right leg.

'Throw your arms around our shoulders there, Marcella. We'll carry you over to the car,' Teresa said.

I hated leaning on her, but I had no choice. She sat into the back of the car beside me, pulled tissues from her bag and started mopping up the blood.

I shrugged her off and turned away.

'You saved that lassie's life, missus,' the man said. 'Only for you getting her off the street, I'm not sure I'd have been able to stop in time.'

'You were on the ball yourself, fair play to you.'

'It's a terra too what can happen. Sure it's only a lock of months since some poor woman lost her life on that very same spot.'

Neither Teresa nor I made any comment, but for a

moment I wished she had not been there to save me.

'I believe the poor driver of that van has been in a bad way since,' the man said. 'Killing someone is a hard cross to bear, accident or no accident.'

I sat staring out the window as we drove up Fatima Hill. There were men sitting on their doorsteps in the sun; women, in twos and threes, chatting, arms folded, heads wagging. Children were playing on the footpath – little chips on little shoulders. There were people on the move, some sluggish, some brisk, up the hill, down the hill, turning corners. I watched them thinking that it didn't matter how quickly they moved or how many corners they turned, they would never get away, not from Fatima Hill. It would follow them wherever they would go. Away was not an option. Not for them. Not for me.

'If you pull up here, mister, that'll do grand,' Teresa said.

As I hobbled out onto the footpath, a sudden wave of hatred overcame me. Hatred of the very ground I was standing on. Hatred for the fucking bitch who was my aunt. Hatred of myself, being pregnant, being nothing but a stupid tramp from the Hill. The throbbing in my grazed hands and bleeding legs was nothing in comparison to the pain inside me.

'Come on, Marcella,' Teresa said, helping me to the front door. 'You've had an awful nasty shock, you poor divil, but—'

'Fuck off. Who do you think you are? Mother Teresa? I just want to use your loo and then I'm out of here.'

'Right,' she roared. 'Go to the bloody toilet and fuck away off with yourself, you stubborn wee bitch.'

I sat on the loo, crying, rocking, frightened. No Cormac to look after me or comfort me. Bastard. I couldn't get him out of my head. He filled it with turmoil, with grief, with hatred, with his baby. Part of him, growing inside me, making me sick, making me desperate, damning me to failure, to Fatima Hill, to a life I so passionately wanted to escape. Hatred and anger. Two forces raging through me, driving me berserk. I felt crazy – violent even.

'To hell with you, Cormac McCairn,' I screeched. 'To hell with your fucking baby.' I had my fists clenched now and was punching my stomach furiously.

'Marcella. Marcella. Open that door, love. It'll be all right. Come on—'

'Fuck off, Teresa. Just leave me alone.'

'I'm going nowhere.' Her voice was gentle.

My arms were tired from the thumping, my stomach was sore.

'Look,' Teresa said, 'I'll help you any way I can. If you want me to tell your da—'

'Tell my da! You'll do no such fucking thing.'

'OK whatever *you* want.'

I could just see his face when he'd heard the news: disgust and contempt written all over it. Yet, he'd fucking love it, me getting my comeuppance. Nasty bastard. No way was I going to give that man the satisfaction of watching me grovel to him for forgiveness and a roof over my head. To hell with him. To hell with

Cormac. And his goddamn baby. If I couldn't have him, I didn't want it. It had to go. An abortion. The sooner, the better. Yes. That's what I'd do.

'Marcella, please come out,' Teresa said. 'If you don't want to talk, fine. But at least let me—'

'OK.'

I got up, limped to the door and opened it. I was in a different mood. I was a different me, a tougher me.

'You said you'd help me, right?' I said, the calmer tone of my voice obviously surprising her.

'Yes – yes, of course I will,' she said, warily.

'So where's the bandages?'

'Oh, right,' she said, sounding relieved. 'I'll help you down to the kitchen.'

I sat on one chair and rested my legs on another. Teresa gently cleaned the cuts with a warm sponge before dabbing them with TCP.

'This might sting a bit,' she said.

I didn't flinch. 'Where's Clint?'

'Hughie's.'

'What time will he be home?'

'He'll be ages yet. Why?'

'Just wondering.'

I could see she was happy to have the opportunity to do something for me. It was easing her guilty conscience.

'You weren't . . . I mean, you didn't—' she said.

'Didn't what?'

'Walk out in front of that car on purpose?'

'What do you mean?'

'I saw you crying. I was only a few steps behind you on the footpath. You were chatting to some lad in a car. Then you walked off, in tears.'

'So?'

'Were you trying to . . . you know.'

'Get myself killed?'

She nodded.

'Yes,' I lied. 'So fucking what?'

'Oh, Marcella,' she cried, throwing her arms around me, 'you poor thing. Thank God I was there.' I sat still, letting her slobber all over me. I didn't shed a tear.

'The baby – it's that Cormac fella's, isn't it?'

'Yeah – worse luck.'

'So you're not seeing him any more, then?'

'Shut up, Teresa. I don't want to talk about him. I just want rid of it.'

'Rid of it?'

'Yeah.'

'No,' she sobbed, pulling a handful of tissues from a box and handing me one.

'I don't need that,' I said, giving it back to her. 'I'm going to have an abortion and I want *you* to help me arrange it. You've lived in London. You know the score.'

'There are other options, love.'

'Oh yeah, right. Other options being have it or – what? Oh yes, have it. Great fucking options, they are.'

'But abortion – it's not right.'

'Teresa, I'm not here for a fucking lecture on morality, especially not from you. I kept your sordid secret. You help me out now and then we're even.'

'It's not that simple.'

'Yes it is.'

'I'll help you out any other way, but this—'

'Teresa,' I said, raising my voice, 'if you don't help me, next time I'll make sure the car is going fast enough. You want that on your conscience?'

She got up, lit a fag and started pacing the kitchen floor. She was still crying. I could see she was under pressure, but at least she was considering helping me out. I said nothing, waiting for her to speak, to make her decision. Then I saw her shaking her head as if to say no.

'Forget it,' I said, getting off the chair. I limped through the hall to the front door. 'But do me a favour and keep your gob shut. You owe me that much, at least.'

'What are you going to do?' she asked, anxiously.

'What do you care?' I said, turning the latch.

'Are you going to tell Josie and Bernie?'

'Don't be stupid. As far as they're concerned, women who have abortions are murderers. But don't you bother your arse worrying about me. I'll manage, with or without you.'

'With me.'

'What?'

'You heard me. Now close the door.'

Teresa

She was a woeful sight. Frightening to look at. It wasn't so much her physical state that bothered me, though she was pale and drawn, it was her steely eyes and the hurt that lay beneath them. I couldn't let her walk out that door. She was full to the brim with hatred for me, her father and Cormac, the only boy who'd ever been close to her, the first boy she'd ever loved and trusted. He had softened her heart, comforted her when her mother died, given her hope and, when she most needed him, he had deserted her. She had nothing left to lose.

'Give me one of those,' she said, snatching the pack of cigarettes out of my hand.

She coughed and spluttered at first, but didn't give up. Every drag was inhaled with spite and determination. Even the retching in her stomach didn't make her stop.

'How far gone are you?'

'Ten weeks,' she said, coldly.

'Ten weeks!' The thought of an abortion at ten, eleven, or maybe even twelve weeks by the time she'd get an appointment, made me feel nauseous.

'So the sooner you stop asking me questions and get

on with it, the better,' she said, staring straight ahead.

She was right. If it was going to happen, I had no time to waste.

'OK,' I said, pulling up my chair next to hers. 'I'll make the arrangements. It's not that I agree with what you're doing, because I don't, love, but—'

'I'm not your love, so quit calling me that.'

'OK. I can see how hurt you are by what's happened to you this past year, Marcella. And I'm sorry for contributing to that pain, but having an abortion isn't going to solve all your problems. Believe you me.'

'Believe you me, she says! You're the last person on this earth I'd believe, Teresa Reilly. You think I'm going to have Cormac McCairn's little bastard and end up like you, an unmarried no-hoper from Fatima Hill? No fucking way. So don't you tell me that abortion isn't the answer because, as far as I'm concerned, it's the only answer.'

'Fair enough,' I said quietly. 'It's your decision. You can go on home now. I'll make a few calls for you tomorrow and let you know. OK?'

'How long do you think it will take?' she asked, her tone a little more mellow.

'Dunno. A week maybe.'

'Will you help me pay for it? I'll pay you back as soon as I have it. I wouldn't ask, only—'

'Yeah, I'll lend you the money.'

'Will it be hard for me to find my way around London?' she asked, forcing back tears.

'I'll go with you.'

'There's no need.'

'Yes there is.'

'Suit yourself,' she snapped, determined not to show any gratitude or relief.

'Tell Bernie and Josie that you're thinking of going away to Galway with that Cormac fella for a couple of days. Then, when the time comes, you'll have your excuse to go.'

'What about Clint?'

'I'll be going to an AA conference in Dublin. Aggie'll keep him for a couple of nights.'

'Lies just roll off your tongue, don't they?' she said, getting up to leave.

'Not this one, Marcella,' I said.

The little bitch. She was hell bent on keeping up the barrier between us. Not even in her most desperate hour of need was she going to soften towards me. I wanted to shake her until that bloody wall she'd built around herself crumbled, so I could get to her, talk to her and have her listen to me. But most of all I wanted to hug her and have her hug me back, and mean it. Instead, I let her walk out the door, knowing that at least she wouldn't throw herself in front of the next passing car.

I had the arrangements made within a couple of days. We were to get the boat from Dun Laoghaire the following Wednesday afternoon. I booked us into a B&B in Holyhead for that night, then we'd travel to London by train the next day and stay in a hotel on the Thursday and Friday nights before and after the abortion. There was a check-up arranged in the clinic for nine a.m. on Friday morning and, all going well, the abortion would be performed at three that afternoon.

I called to see her at work on Monday. She asked her boss if she could take a five-minute break and sat down beside me at a corner table.

'Fine,' she said, when I'd put her in the picture. She displayed no emotion whatsoever. 'I'll see you on the bus Wednesday morning.'

'No second thoughts?'

'My break is over,' she said, getting up off her seat.

On my way home, I met Bernie coming down the hill with Amanda in a new buggy.

'What do you think?' she asked. 'Amanda loves it. Don't you, pet? She can sit up and see out now.'

'Yeah, it's a great yoke. What did you do with the old pram?'

'Traded it in for this. It only cost me twenty quid.'

'You got a good deal, no doubt about it.'

'Could you do me a favour, Teresa?'

'Well, I'll try. What is it, love?'

'I'm going to the pictures on Friday night. Could you babysit for me?'

'Sorry, Bernie. I'd love to, only I'm away to Dublin myself. An AA conference.'

'God, you're doing great, Teresa, fair dues to you. Ma would be very proud of you.'

'So, who's taking you to the pictures?'

'Have you seen the new postman?'

'Indeed I have. Him?'

'Yeah. Gorgeous, isn't he?'

'I must admit, I wouldn't throw him out of the bed for eating crisps. You're over Noel then?'

'I think so. Anyway, I hear he's shifting Cathy Sheridan now.'

'Cathy – which of the Sheridans is that?'

'She was in Marcella's class in the tech. A right little bitch.'

'Oh, I know the one you're talking about. Well matched, the pair of them. Speaking of Marcella, how is she?' I asked, just to see if she suspected anything.

'You know our Marcella. Moody as ever. She's talking about going away for a couple of nights with that Cormac – lucky thing. I'd do anything to get out of this town for a couple of days. It's the middle of August and I haven't had as much as a day out.'

'Has she quit that dieting lark?'

'Dunno, to tell you the truth. She's up and away to work before I get out of the bed and doesn't come home for her lunch any more. So I don't know what she's up to. She looks all right though, doesn't she?'

'Aye, she does – the last time I saw her anyway.'

Once I had confirmed her lack of suspicion, I said goodbye.

Aggie was more than willing to keep Clint for a couple of nights.

'You know, Teresa,' she said, 'there was many's the day before you went into hospital, I was convinced you were going to drink yourself into an early grave. And look at you now doing so well. It's a credit to you. God is good.'

Tell that to Marcella, I thought. As for me doing well, yes, so far so good. But it was far from easy. I often longed for a drink; I missed the comfort of it. Some days were fine, almost easy, but there were times when one day at a time was too big a challenge. It seemed impossible, so I broke it down and tried to survive the hour rather than the day, the minute rather than the hour. Those days went on for ever.

I tried not to dwell on the abortion. In my heart and soul I felt it was wrong. But then, who was I to judge? I kept wondering if I'd agreed to help her out just to get back into her good books and have her forgive me. But no. I'd had no choice. She was suicidal, for Jesus' sake. What else could I have done? Her life had spiralled out of control since Mary's death. She was looking for a way back. This baby would throw her life into even greater disarray. I knew Marcella; she could not live her life like that. It just wasn't her. I had myself convinced that the abortion was, in this instance, the lesser of two evils – until Tuesday night.

I couldn't sleep. I kept looking at my watch. The baby's life was ticking away. It was freaking me out. I took a sleeping tablet. No joy. Every time I closed my eyes, I saw it. Tiny fingers, tiny toes – helpless. I prayed for guidance, not the Hail Mary full of Grace stuff, no. I looked up at the ceiling and said, 'If You want to save this baby's life, show me how.'

I stayed awake waiting for inspiration. None came.

'Right,' I said, feeling sleep drag me away from my thoughts, 'don't say I didn't ask for Your help. I want none of this guilt crap when it's all over.'

She was already on the bus when I got to the bus station on Wednesday morning. Our eyes met through the window as I queued up to get on. She looked away immediately, but I saw the relief in her face at my arrival. I put my bag in the overhead compartment above her seat and was about to sit down beside her when she told me to clear off down the back, there were plenty of empty seats there. I told her I didn't like the back of the bus, it was too bumpy, so she would just have to put up with me. She was not impressed, just narrowed her eyes, tightened her lips, then turned and stared out the window until we were well on our way to Dublin.

'Would you like a Silvermint?' I asked.

She took one from the pack. Her hands were white and shaking. I had so much sympathy stored up inside me bursting to escape, I couldn't help but reach over and take her hand in mine.

'You're cold,' I said. She pulled her hand away like she had touched hot coal.

She bit her bottom lip. 'I'm all right,' she said, her voice trembling, 'or at least I would be if you'd leave me alone.'

'You don't have to put on an act in front of me, Marcella,' I said quietly. 'No one knows better than I do how it feels to be frightened.'

'Stop trying to compare us, Teresa. I'm nothing like you.'

'No, you're not. Doesn't mean we don't share the same fear though, does it?'

She didn't answer. We spent the rest of the journey to Dublin in silence.

It was still drizzling when we got off the bus at Dun Laoghaire.

'The last time I walked down this road the sun was shining,' I said. 'I was on my way to London. Seems like yesterday. I thought going to London would solve all my problems. It didn't.'

'Obviously not' came the reply, in a deadpan voice.

'Thought I might meet someone famous in a big city like that,' I said, not so much talking to Marcella as thinking out loud. 'I wanted to be rich and famous, once upon a time.'

'One out of two isn't so bad, is it?'

'How do you mean?'

'Well you're not rich, are you?'

'No, but I'm not famous either.'

'Ah now, I wouldn't say that, Teresa. Your reputation is known far and wide, I'd say.' She let a sniggery little grunt out of her. The clever wee whore had an answer for everything.

'We don't need to sit together,' she said, as we walked onto the ferry.

'Suits me fine,' I snapped, sick of her razor-blade tongue. I was bursting for a drink. My blood needed it, to cool it down, to stabilize it. In my head I said the serenity prayer over and over. I made my way to the top deck and sat outside. It was almost empty. I pulled up my windcheater zip and hood.

I was sixteen years old again. Alone, broken-hearted, leaving behind me the man I loved, the sister I'd betrayed. I was riddled with guilt, sick with jealousy. I loved and loathed her. I loathed the thing Mary was carrying inside of her – her baby, his baby, their fucking baby. Damn it. I cursed it. I wished it dead. It was driving me away from my family, my lover, my home. It was a she. They called her Marcella. A right fancy name for a kid from Fatima Hill. They said she looked like him. I didn't set eyes on her until she was five years old. They were right about the resemblance.

I don't remember the boat setting sail. I didn't notice the rain become heavier, until a man in an oilskin jacket tapped me on the shoulder and asked if I was OK.

'Yeah,' I said automatically.

'You're drenched. You'd be more comfortable inside.'

My feet squelched as I walked along the wooden deck. Cold raindrops and hot tears zigzagged down my cheeks. Inside the boat, passengers roamed around aimlessly, trying to find their sea legs. Other people lay horizontally across several chairs, their weary heads resting on their luggage. Then there were the groups of noisy drinkers, in holiday mood, cheering, swilling beer, oblivious to the vibrations underneath them.

I started to shiver with the cold. I made my way to the loo to dry myself off and change my socks. Some poor unfortunate in another cubicle was puking her guts up. There was an odious stink. She was still at it as I was washing my hands at the sink.

'Are you all right in there? Do you want me to get you a glass of water?' I said.

'Teresa,' she cried. 'Help me.'

'Marcella, oh you poor thing. Open the door, love.'

'I can't – I can't get up,' she managed to say before another bout of vomiting started.

I had to get to her. I'd have kicked the door in only I guessed she was lying behind it. I went into the cubicle next to hers, climbed up onto the toilet seat and peeped over the partition. She was on her knees, her head hanging over the toilet bowl, her red hair matted with vomit.

'Hold on, pet. I'm coming to get you.'

I stepped onto the cistern and threw my left leg over the partition.

'You're gonna fall on top of me,' she cried.

I had a firm grip on the top of the partition and was lifting my right leg across when I lost my balance and landed arse first onto the toilet seat, knocking my head on the back wall on the way down.

'Jesus, Mary and Joseph,' I heard someone say and a door closed.

Marcella was sitting on the floor, her head forward, resting on her knees.

'Come on, love,' I said, getting to my feet, my head throbbing. 'I'll look after you now.'

'Oh no, there's more coming,' she wailed, reaching

out to grab the toilet bowl. Green liquid spewed out of her with such force, it made her whole body jerk. I held her firmly in my arms. Both of us were crying.

Someone came and stood outside the cubicle. 'This is Lucy. I'm a member of the cabin crew. Is there something wrong in there?'

'Yes,' I cried. 'We need help. My niece is feeling very ill.'

'Open the door. We'll get her down to the sick bay.'

Marcella got a bed to lie on and some pills for what Lucy said was a severe case of seasickness.

She slept for an hour. I sat by her side, stroking her head. She was peaceful. So much so that I almost dreaded her waking up and feeling well again. No longer needing me, she would probably cast me aside, reject my love.

But she didn't and when I heard her voice whisper, 'Thanks, Teresa,' I hung my head and wept.

Marcella

I thought I would die, hanging over that toilet bowl, sickness squeezing the last ounce of strength from my weary body. My head felt like a punctured ball. My heart was pounding farther and farther up my throat, as if it was trying to escape a sinking ship. Keeping up the tough act was out the window now. I wanted rid of my misery by any means whatsoever, be it death or Teresa, it didn't matter. Teresa came first.

When I woke up afterwards in the sick bay, she was still by my side. She was sitting on a hard chair, leaning forward, her bony elbows piercing her lap, her head drooped and resting on the palms of her hands. She had her eyes shut.

'Thanks, Teresa,' I said. My voice was weak, barely audible.

She sat up straight and looked at me in disbelief. My lips felt like they would crack if I spread them, so I smiled at her with my eyes.

She lowered her head again and cried.

Part of me wanted to reach out and touch her, tell her how sorry I was for treating her so badly, but I was reluctant to close the gap between us. I felt compelled to keep a distance from her. I knew how double-crossing she was and how easy she found it to be that way. I just couldn't trust her. She had let me down once too often.

'Why are you crying? All I said was thanks.'

She looked at me, her cheeks smeared with tears and mascara, her eyes heavy with emotion. 'You don't know how much it means to me, you thanking me,' she said, still sniffling. 'I'm so tired of all the bad feeling between us. I just want us to be friends. How about it?'

'Teresa, I'm grateful for all your help this past while, I really am. And if it makes you feel any better, I'll forgive you for all that carry-on with Da, but don't expect me to be all palsy-walsy with you, because I can't.'

'OK,' she whimpered.

'I loved Ma – still do. I need to honour her memory. I can't do that and be your friend at the same time, Teresa.'

'I understand.'

'So when this is all over, we're quits. Right?'

'Right.'

My lips stung with soreness. My tongue felt shrivelled.

'Will you get me a drink of water?'

'Sure,' she said, and went out the door, drying her eyes with a crumpled tissue.

Speaking to her again was one thing – she deserved that much after all she'd done for me – but friendship was a step too far.

I looked round the cabin. The date on the wall calendar caught my eye. The tenth of August: Bernie's wedding anniversary. Her wedding day was when it had all started: the trouble.

I remembered the sing-song that had started up that night and had gone on until the wee hours of the morning. Their blood laced with booze, the wedding guests belted out song after song, arms flung around each other's necks, swaying in unison. Someone called on Josie to sing. She didn't need to be asked twice. Before she got an 'Ah, go on', a 'Let's hear it for Josie' or a dig in the ribs, she was standing on the table brainwashing her audience with Johnny Logan's song 'What's another year?' By the time she got to the chorus, everyone had joined in. A couple of women became very emotional as they sang along. I watched them as tears fell from their bleary eyes and rolled down their hardened faces.

I was sitting in the corner unmoved. I didn't shed a tear until I was lying alone in the cabin considering what another year had meant to me and all *I* had lost.

'Just one thing, Marcella,' Teresa said, coming back in with the glass of water. 'You told your da that your ma knew about me and him. How did she find out?'

'Why do you want to drag all that up again? Why can't you just forget about it? She knew and that's all there is to it.'

'Did you tell her?'

'Shut up.'

'I wouldn't blame you if you did. Honest to God. I just need to know.'

'You'd have no right to blame me,' I snapped. 'I did nothing wrong.'

'So you did tell her.'

'Leave it, will you?' I said, closing my eyes. 'I'm tired.'

'OK,' she said, sitting down. 'You sleep.'

The truth – what harm could it do? I thought. If she realized Ma hadn't known about her betrayal all along, it might ease her conscience. Would that be such a bad thing? I lay there mulling it over. I kept my eyes shut. She sat beside me all the while. Sometimes she'd sigh.

'She was in a bad state that day,' I said eventually, opening my eyes and focusing on the ceiling. 'She was upset . . . nervy. When I got home that evening, she was tearing the place apart looking for an old childhood photograph of you and her. I didn't like the look in her eyes. It frightened me. The room was a right tip. There was stuff scattered around the place, photographs all over the floor. Then she found it, the photo she'd been looking for: you were just a baby, she was ten.'

'Oh yeah, I know the one.' There was a quiver in her voice.

'She went on about how much she'd loved you back then, how she'd wanted to protect you. Reckoned she used to take you out in your pram when the rows would start. The noise, she said, would have frightened you.'

'Oh, my poor Mary.'

'I held her hands. They were shaking. "There's things I know about. Bad stuff," she said, staring at me with wild eyes. "What things, Ma?" I asked. "About Teresa. She doesn't think I know, but I do. Seen them at it," she said, "dirty old git." What was I supposed to think, Teresa? I thought she was referring to you and Da.

How was I supposed to know you were screwing some other fella as well. Someone else's husband, no doubt.'

I waited for her to contradict me, but she didn't.

'Then I told her that I knew about youse, too. That I'd seen youse at it twice. It was only when I saw the confusion in her face, I realized I'd got it wrong. She hadn't known at all.'

I felt a tear trickle over my earlobe and into my ear.

'So now you know,' I said.

Teresa remained eerily silent. I looked at her. Her two hands were cupped over her mouth and nose. Her eyes were wide open, but deadly still.

'Say something, will you?'

'Someone else's husband, you say, you presumptuous little cow. Hah!'

'If I got it wrong, I'm sorry. I'm only saying—'

'Oh no, Marcella,' she said, a hiss in her voice, 'you're absolutely fucking dead on, as usual. He was, in fact, someone else's husband. Yes, indeed he was.'

'What are you getting all narky with me for?' I said, surprised by her hostile reaction.

'Ah, shut your face, before I shut it for you.'

I needed to burst into tears, but I didn't want to give the bitch the satisfaction. She had no right turning on me like that.

'I think I'll go have myself a fucking drink,' she spat, and bolted out of the chair.

'No, Teresa, don't! Please,' I cried after her. But she was gone.

I had to follow her, stop her, somehow. If she went on a bender, I'd never make it to London. That was the thing with Teresa, she was so unreliable, so fucking weak. As soon as the going got tough, Teresa caved in.

I stood up. My legs felt shaky. Black blobs floated before my eyes. I held on to the chair and tried to steady myself.

Here goes, I thought, taking a step forward. But it was no use. I was still woozy. I lay back down on the bed again and lost hope.

After a while the door opened. It was Lucy, from the cabin crew.

'Are you feeling any better?' she asked.

'A bit,' I said, 'but I can't walk. I'm still dizzy.'

'Drink plenty of water, love. You're bound to be weak after all that vomiting.'

'I need my aunt. Can you get her for me? I think she went to the bar.'

'Sure,' she said. 'Don't worry, we're over halfway there. It'll soon be over.'

It'll never be over, I thought. The pain. It will always be with me. How could I possibly ever forget this hurt? This abandonment? I wouldn't. Couldn't. And maybe shouldn't. Who wants to make the same mistakes twice?

Twenty minutes passed. There was no sign of Teresa.

With a bladder full of water, I needed the loo. It was just next door. Although still wobbly, I was able to make my way there and back.

When I opened the cabin door on my return, I was surprised but relieved to see Teresa sitting by the bed.

Her eyes were bloodshot and hung drearily on what looked like two sagging pillows.

'I thought you were going to run out on me,' I said.

'No.'

'I take it you've had a drink.'

'No.'

'How come?'

'God knows,' she said, shrugging.

'I'm glad you didn't.'

'Are you?'

'Yes, of course I am. I really didn't mean to tell her, you know,' I said, sitting on the edge of the mattress.

'I believe you.'

'It's just the way she was going on about—'

'I said, I believe you. OK?'

'OK.'

She picked up a magazine and flicked absent-mindedly through the pages. It was a British Rail sailing brochure. She settled on one page and pretended to read.

I sat there wondering what had sparked off such a dramatic change in her mood. It didn't make sense. All I had done was confirm her already well-founded suspicion that I was the one to blab to Ma about her and my da, albeit by accident.

She took a deep breath and threw the brochure to one side.

'So go on, ask me,' she said tetchily.

'Ask you what?'

'About who your ma was referring to that day.'

'You already said. He was some married man. Any-way, you don't have to tell me. It's none of my business.'

'My father.'

'What about him?'

'He was the other man. I was just a kid.' Her voice was monotone, her teeth clenched.

'What are you getting at, Teresa?' I didn't want to think what I was thinking.

'Oh, I think you know,' she said, gazing blankly at the wall in front of her.

'No!'

I didn't believe her. She was talking shite. She had to be.

'You're having me on,' I said half laughing, but her expression didn't change. Maybe she *had* downed a couple of half-ones after all. Yes, that would explain it. I sniffed the air. Nothing. Oh God!

'If this is your way of getting your revenge on me, Teresa, I'll tell you right now, it's bloody well working.'

All the times I'd cursed her for lying to me and now I wanted nothing more.

'Teresa.'

'What?' she said, turning to me.

I looked into her eyes, searching for the lie, but I couldn't find even the slightest hint of deception. It was all beginning to make sense, to fit horribly into place.

'Big, grubby hands,' she said, looking right through me, 'the smell of porter.'

'Stop, Teresa.'

'His chapped lips . . .'

'Don't.'

'Beads of sweat raining down on me . . .'

'No!'

'Fingers poking at me . . .'

'That's enough,' I shouted, squeezing my eyes shut.

'His tongue slithering along my skin like a poisonous snake . . .'

'Stop it. Now. Why are you doing this to me?'

'All the times I asked that same question.'

'You shouldn't have told me.'

'Why not?' she shrieked, grabbing me by the face. 'If you're so fond of the fucking truth, why the hell not?' Her fingers were digging into my cheeks. They were strong for skinny fingers.

'You're hurting me,' I cried.

She held me still. Through my tears, her face was a blur.

'I'm sorry,' she whimpered, loosening her grip.

'So am I, Teresa,' I cried. 'I'm really, really sorry.'

'It's not your fault,' she said, her slack fingers sliding down my cheeks and flopping onto the bed. 'It's all making sense now.'

'What is?'

'The carry-on of your mother.'

'What about it?'

'All those times I tried to tell her about it, but the oul bitch wouldn't let me. As soon as I'd get anywhere near the truth, she'd change the subject and start whingeing about her own life or leave the room –

anything that would prevent me from telling her what she already knew, and had known for years.'

'Maybe you've got it wrong, Teresa,' I said, hoping there was another explanation. 'She might have been thinking of someone else she'd seen you with.'

'No. She knew. And what did she do about it? Sweet Fanny Adams. Because, Marcella, let's face it, your ma was a fucking coward.'

'No!' I shook my head. 'Don't say that about her. She loved you.'

'Love! Get out of here! She was at least your age when it was going on. She should have known better. She *did* know better. And there was you thinking that *I* was the rotten apple.'

I didn't know what to say. I was still trying to take it in. It hurt. It made shite of all the feelings I had for Ma.

'Yeah,' Teresa said, 'a fucking wimp, that's what she was. She couldn't even be a full-blown, up-front failure like me, no, she had to hide under the covers, her and her Valium, and cease to exist. How pathetic is that?'

'Exactly.'

'What?'

'How pathetic *is* that?'

She looked at me. She was calmer now, but totally wretched.

'Please don't hate her,' I sobbed. 'She hated herself, Teresa. I think she suffered enough. Don't you?'

'Oh God!' she groaned, standing up and pacing.

She pressed her hands firmly on her head, as if she

were holding down the lid on something explosive. She sighed and puffed and drew rasping breaths, her face contorted with pain.

What she'd been through was unimaginable to me, so dark, so sickening that I hadn't the stomach to think about it. I didn't want the images in my head. The rotten, evil, sick bastard! Oh Ma, you loved her, I know you did. Why couldn't you have done something? Anything? Stuck a bloody knife in him, if necessary. If anyone tried anything like that with our Sammy or Amanda, I'd kill them stone dead.

How did Teresa live with it? Why didn't she scream out, tell someone? How could anyone carry that burden around with them all their lives?

'Oh Teresa! What can I do, only hate him for you?'

'You mean with me?'

'Yeah, with you.'

She shook her head.

Brazen bitch that I was, I'd always maintained she was her own worst enemy. Little did I know that he had died many years ago and left her to survive his abuse. The miracle was that she had.

I couldn't stand what I'd done to her, the things I'd said, the times I'd sneered. And despite my bitchiness she'd never given up on me, not once. I felt so ashamed.

'Your father was a perverted bastard, Teresa, but Ma was wrong too,' I said, standing in front of her.

'What?' she said, sounding confused.

'Ma, Teresa. She was wrong. She should have done something.'

She nodded pensively.

'But you know that underneath it all, she loved you, don't you?' I said. 'Don't let him take that away from you too.'

She raised her head slowly. 'Yes,' she said, her voice beginning to crack, 'and I loved her. Still do, Marcella. Despite him.'

'Thanks, Teresa,' I said, hugging her. We were both crying.

I was thanking her for forgiving my mother, for forgiving me. After the way we'd treated her, I don't know how she found it in her heart but, at that moment, I was sure glad she did.

She drew back and stroked my cheek with the tips of her fingers.

'Does anyone else know about what happened to you?'

'Julie, my counsellor, and you. That's it and that's how I want it to stay.'

'You can count on me.'

'I know.'

'And thanks.'

'What for?'

'Confiding in me.'

She smiled, not a big beaming happy one but a contented one.

'I think I'm dehydrated from all the crying,' she said. 'I could murder a cup of tea. Want one?'

'Yeah, I'd love one. Thanks.'

I watched her as she walked out the door. She was the same Teresa who'd stepped onto the bus that morning, but not in my eyes. Before she had just been Teresa – the wild one, the alco, the tarty bit of stuff – all legs and lipstick. A bit of an eejit, really. I'd had no respect for her. I didn't trust her. She was weak, fickle.

Now I saw Teresa – the child, the mother, the fighter and the survivor. She was still wild, still tarty and still an alcoholic, although a recovering one. The difference was that now I knew she could succeed. She had what it took: a kind heart, a passion for life, whatever it threw at her, and the guts to live it.

'Open up, Marcella. My hands are full,' she shouted from behind the door.

When I got to my feet, something fluttered in my stomach. It felt strange.

I let her in. As she placed the two polystyrene cups down on the shelf, it happened again.

'Shite,' I said, feeling a bit nervous.

'What's wrong?'

'I don't know. It feels like there's something twitch-ing in my stomach. I thought maybe I was going to get sick again, but I don't feel sick. I'm not sure. Damn, there it is again,' I said, sitting down.

'Show me where,' Teresa said.

I took her hand in mine and laid it on my stomach. And as I did, it happened again – a little ripple.

'It's the baby,' she whispered.

'What? It can't be,' I said, wishing she wouldn't refer to it as a baby.

'It is. You're almost twelve weeks pregnant. It has all its—'

'Don't,' I said. 'I don't want to know. There's no point in thinking about it. It's too late for that.'

'It's never too late, love.'

'It is for me.'

'Fair enough.'

I lifted my tea off the shelf and took a sip.

'Four o'clock,' Teresa said, looking at her watch. 'This time tomorrow, it'll be all over.'

'Can't wait,' I said, trying to sound cheerful about it. In fact, any time I let myself think about it, I was terrified.

'Does Cormac know?'

'About what? The baby or the abortion?'

'Either.'

'He knows I'm pregnant. He found out just after he dumped me. He said I should get rid of it. Bastard. He was supposed to . . . to . . . eh, come and see me, but . . .'

Talking about him brought it all back to me, those desolating feelings of rejection and loss.

'It hurts so much, Teresa,' I said, my chin wobbling uncontrollably.

'Oh, you poor kid.'

'I really thought he loved me,' I blubbed, unable to hold back any longer. 'He told me so.'

'I know.'

'I'm such a stupid fool.'

'No, you're not. You fell in love. That's all.'

'This wasn't meant to happen, not to me.'

'I know.'

'I swore I'd never get myself pregnant unless I was married. I didn't want this. I wanted to be decent, to get an education, a good job, a respectable husband, a life I could be proud of. And now I've blown it.'

'No you haven't. When all this is over, you'll get back on track.'

'No, I won't.'

'Of course you will. Once you're back at school—'

'It makes no difference what I do now, Teresa. I'm never going to feel decent again. And there was I thinking I was better than the rest of the girls from up the Hill.'

She said nothing, just wiped my eyes and nose with a tissue, and stroked my hair.

'Look at me now – the biggest fool of the lot.'

'It's not about who's better than who. It's—'

'Ah, but it is, you see. Only *I* didn't know my place. I got carried away with my *high notions*, as Ma used to call them. I thought she was a bit of a fool and all, but she warned me about Cormac. I remember her exact words. "The likes of them moneyed people," she said, "would never settle for the likes of you." Oh God, Ma,' I cried, 'I wish you were here to tell me, I told you so.'

'You always have been and will always be a decent lassie, Marcella Buckley,' Teresa said, grabbing me by the two arms and shaking me. 'It's him who hasn't an ounce of decency – that Cormac – to leave you on your own at a time like this.'

'I still love him, Teresa. I can't help it. I try not to, but the feelings just won't go away.'

'I know it hurts. And nothing I say will take away that pain. But time will. You'll see.'

'Were *you* ever in love?'

'I was.'

'With Clint's father?'

'No.'

'Da?'

'Yeah, once upon a time. I idolized him, even as a little girl. He was the one who rescued Mary from my father – the ogre. It sounds silly now, but I wanted him to come and rescue me too.'

'And did he?'

'I liked to think so, at the time. But no, in the end, the only one who could save me was me.'

We sat in silence for a couple of minutes. I could still feel the sway of the boat beneath me. Over and back, over and back. Just like my thoughts.

There was a gentle knock on the door. It was Lucy.

'Just wondering how you're feeling now, Marcella?'

'Middling.'

'Are you travelling on from Holyhead this evening?' she asked, sitting on the edge of the bed.

'No,' Teresa said, 'not until tomorrow.'

'That's good. Would you like to try some toast, Marcella?'

'Yeah, I'll have a slice, if you don't mind.'

'It's been some journey,' Teresa said when Lucy had left.

'Sure has, and it's not over yet.'

'The train journey in the morning will be a lot easier. Don't worry, once you're off this boat, you'll be fine.'

'Tell me this,' I said. 'When you found out you were expecting Clint, did you ever consider—'

'I did. Even went as far as making an appointment at the clinic.'

'So what changed your mind?'

'Something someone said to me.'

'Who?'

'The landlady in the pub where I worked.'

'What did she say?'

'She said if I travelled the length and breadth of the earth, I wouldn't find a single mother who regretted being a mother.'

'Oh. So would you say she was right?'

'I would.'

She didn't elaborate. She didn't need to. I knew how she felt about being a mother.

Lucy arrived back with a tray.

'Will you be around for a few minutes to keep an eye on her?' Teresa asked her. 'I just want to go up on deck for a smoke. I'm gasping for one.'

'Yeah, sure. Fire away,' Lucy said.

I lifted a piece of toast from the plate and took a small bite.

'Here,' Lucy said, unscrewing the cap of a Lucozade bottle. 'Try this, it should give you a bit of a boost.'

'Thanks.'

'Are you visiting relatives in London?'

'Yeah.'

'What part?'

'Oh – dunno, I forget.'

'How long are you staying?'

'Just a couple of nights.'

'You're travelling back on Saturday?'

I nodded. I thought about the journey home: the abortion would be over, my problem solved. I was frightened at the thought of the operation, how they would do it, how painful it would be for the foetus, or baby, as Teresa called it.

We'd had a priest and a female anti-abortion activist visit the school once to lecture us on the moral implications of abortion. They had documented evidence, they said, to prove that aborted babies had been heard to cry from rubbish bins where they'd been discarded and left to die, that their tiny bodies had been sucked from their mothers' wombs, dismembering body parts in the process.

When the talk was over, the priest had asked if we had any questions. There was silence but for the rustling sounds of the woman gathering up her papers and charts, and placing them in a folder. All heads turned at the grating sound of iron chair legs scraping across the polished wooden floor. The school punk, a fifth-year known as Roxy, was standing in front of the vacated chair with her hand up.

'Yes, young lady,' the priest said.

'When an abortion takes place, who is responsible? The doctor performing it? The nurse assisting him? The girl having it? The boyfriend who abandoned her? The parents who rejected her? The neighbour who gossiped about her? Society for labelling her? Or the priest who stood in the pulpit and told her that using contraceptives was wrong?' She paused for a couple of seconds.

There was a collective intake of breath. 'Whose sin is it, Father? That's what I'd like to know.'

'God, the balls of her!' Gabby whispered and both of us started sniggering. I didn't for one moment consider that any of the issues being discussed would one day be relevant to me. I thought I knew myself better. I didn't know myself at all.

I was about to cry again, but I held back and took control of myself, allowing only one tear to escape and run down the side of my nose.

Lucy smiled at me gently. 'You'll be fine,' she said. 'You're not the first girl to make this trip in your condition, and you won't be the last.'

'How did you know?'

'I've been working on this route for almost ten years, love. I've seen it all. I know the signs.'

'These other girls – do you think they get over it?'

'Yeah, I think they do.'

'That's all I want – to be over it, to put it behind me. I want to get back to the way things were before—'

'I don't think you can ever get back to the way things were, but you can move on. You just need to be sure you're doing the right thing for *you*. It is *your* choice I take it. You're not being forced to—'

'Oh, God, no. If my family had their way, I'd be having this baby.'

'You're luckier than most. I've met lots of young girls who've had no choice in the matter, not that they've actually told me so but I could tell by the sadness in their eyes and the cold expressions on their mothers' faces.'

'I'd hate that, someone telling me what to do.'

'What about the baby's father?'

'He doesn't want to know,' I said, feeling a little ashamed.

'Would your choice have been any different if he had stood by you?'

The question perturbed me. I didn't know what to say. She had caught me on the hop. Upon what exactly had I based my decision? I wondered. Cormac's rejection? The humiliation I would feel when Da, or Leona O'Brien, or Ricky Doyle found out? The thought of pushing a pram up and down the hill and everywhere else I'd go, at sixteen? Fear of letting go of my dream of a better life? Or all of the above?

I knew by the probing look in Lucy's eyes that she was waiting for my answer, but I didn't have one. I hadn't sorted it out in my head yet. So I shrugged and passed it off as if it didn't really matter.

In truth, it was all that mattered.

'Will we be there soon?'

'Twenty minutes.'

'I'd like to go up on deck.'

'OK. Come on. The fresh air will do you good.'

It was a bit of a struggle getting up the steps, but with Lucy's help, I made it.

It was warm and windy outside. It had stopped raining.

'Is that Holyhead out there ahead of us?'

323

'That's it,' she said, sitting me down on a bench. 'You stay there. I'll go find your aunt.'

I sat looking out at the choppy water. Holyhead was getting closer. I'm not sure what I was expecting, but I thought it looked grey and drab. It could have been any town in Ireland. I wondered what London would be like.

'Ah, there you are,' Teresa said, edging in beside me, a half-smoked cigarette dangling from her mouth. 'Sorry I was so long, but I had to queue up to use the loo first.'

'You're all right.' I swept the hair back off my face.

She put her arms round me. 'I'll always be here for you. You know that, don't you?'

I nodded. We'd come a long way in a year.

'How do you think Da would react if he knew I was pregnant?'

'Why do you ask that?'

'Just curious.'

'He'd get the quare gunk, I'll tell you that. But he'd not turn his back on you.'

'He turned his back on me a long time ago.'

'You don't mean that.'

'Don't I?'

'It's all down to me, the trouble between you two.'

'No, it's not. We've never got on, me and Da. We just rub each other up the wrong way.'

'You know your da, Marcella. His bark is worse than his bite. But he cares about you, about all his family. He's protective of youse.'

324

'Go way outa that. He treated Ma like a doormat, made her life a bloody misery.'

'No, you're wrong there. He was never abusive towards her. OK, they didn't have the kind of relationship that you're hoping for whenever you get married. And fair enough, you're entitled to have greater expectations of life than your ma had, but despite what you think, she loved your da and depended on him. So don't go blaming him for her unhappiness. The seeds of her misery were sown long before she ever met him.'

'He still did the dirty on her.'

'Yeah and he shouldn't have. But life has been no picnic for him either. An unhappy mother makes a very unhappy home. I should know. So, he had his kicks whenever he could. But he's guilty of no more than that.'

She looked at me pleadingly, willing me to forgive him, I suppose. I didn't speak, had nothing to say. It was too soon.

'To get back to answering your question,' she said, after a minute or so, 'as to how your da would react if he—'

'Ah, never mind. It doesn't make any difference; it's not as if I'm going to be telling him.'

'Let me just say, Marcella, that he'd give you more support than the wee bollocks who got you pregnant in the first place.'

As much as it hurt to hear it, she was right. I meant more to the father I hated than I did to the boy I loved – whatever kind of fool that made me.

This thing growing inside me, I thought, will never know the upheaval it has caused in my life. It was a sad thought. I did my damnedest to ignore my feelings, blaming them on the emotional day I'd had. But doubt lingered, in the same way as love did – long after the act.

An announcement was made for all passengers to make their way to their designated exit areas. Teresa and I shuffled along with the crowd.

'I can see you're having doubts, Marcella,' she said, touching my shoulder, 'but don't worry about it for this evening. You're far too tired to make a decision like that. Wait till morning and the answer will come. You'll see.'

As we walked off the boat and over the ramp, the crowd began to disperse. Teresa broke away from me to go and ask one of the dockers for directions to the guest house. I stood leaning against the railings and watched them talk. She had his undivided attention. They were both smiling as they chatted. After about a minute, I wondered what was keeping her, what they were blabbing on about. I watched her lips move, imagining her words: 'My father abused me when I was six years old. And my sister was killed just a few months back. Oh, by the way, I'm an alcoholic. See that girl over there? She's my niece, on her way to have an abortion . . .'

'It's too far a walk, he says. There's a taxi rank around the corner,' she said, approaching me with a smile.

'Let's go then,' I said, putting my rucksack on my

back. As we walked away, I looked over my shoulder. The man still had his eye on Teresa, but he didn't see her pain. As far as the eye can see, I thought, isn't very far at all.

'Twenty-two Croyton Place,' Teresa told the taxi driver. She turned to me. 'How do you feel now?'

'Funny. Not funny ha ha. Not funny peculiar either. Funny calm, you know, considering.'

'Ah well, that's good.'

The car pulled out into the stream of traffic.

'Do you know what frightens me most, Teresa?'

'What, love?'

'Having regrets.'

'We all have them.'

'Yeah, I suppose.'

'Nobody goes through life without making mistakes and having regrets. Look at me: I've had more regrets than I've had – men, and there's been more than a handful of them, let me tell ya.'

Her bluntness made me smirk.

'I'll never be a teacher if I have this baby.'

'Jaysus! You don't want to be a teacher, do ya?'

'Yeah, why?'

'They're all a shower of bollocks as far as I can remember. Except for this one little nun, Mother Christina. Ah, she was a pet.'

'Well, I could be a nice teacher like her.'

'Yeah, you could, even if you have that baby.'

'Huh! I doubt it.'

We came to a junction. The street ahead was blocked

327

by workmen drilling and there was a sign saying ROAD CLOSED. Attached to a telegraph pole, another sign read DETOUR, with an arrow pointing to the left. The taxi driver turned on his indicator.

'There you are, you see,' Teresa said, 'there's always another way to get to where you want to go.'

I put my head down on the rucksack on my knee and shut my eyes.

The taxi driver started to fiddle with the radio tuner.

'Oh no!' I said into the canvas fabric, putting my hands over my head. 'Not that gobshite!'

'What are you on about?'

'Rod,' I said, looking up at her drearily.

'Oh, lovely stuff. Hey, boss,' she tapped the taxi driver's shoulder, 'will you turn the radio up a bit?'

She started singing along and bobbing about in the seat.

'Do you think I'm sexy?' I nudged her. 'The bloody cheek of him to even ask.'

'Oh you wee . . .' she held her hand over my knee like she was going to give me a slap '. . . gem,' she said, slipping her fingers through mine.

Acknowledgements

Thanks to Eileen from Kilroy's College whom I've never met, but whose unsparing praise and consistent encouragement made me believe in myself.

To my agent Jonathan Williams for that first letter dated 8 January (my birthday) which said, *I would be glad to see more of what you have written*. Phew! For taking a chance on me and for all your time and gentle advice, cheers!

To my editor Patricia Deevy, it is both an inspiration and a pleasure to work with you. Thanks.

To all the early readers, Mum, Dad, Vera, Michael, Nuala, Annette and Eamonn, thanks for the feedback and for taking the time.

To Martin Markey, for all the technical support when my ageing computer had one too many senior moments.

To my sister Vera, who is my sounding board and whose advice is always spot on. Thank God it's free.

And finally to my husband Eamonn for taking great care of our children every Sunday in order to give me the time and space to write.